## SHOWDOWN!

In the full light of the fire Dunmore paused, gun in hand. The outlaw gasped and spun like a frightened cat, stooping low and bringing out his gun as he swung about.

No man beneath the sky could have moved faster. His quick side-leap made the first bullet fly wide of the mark; but Dunmore's second shot roared as the outlaw's own weapon spoke for the first time.

A whiplash mark of crimson sprang out on the naked side of Dunmore; but he saw the outlaw stagger, and held his fire.

The gun dropped from the outlaw's hand. He made a few staggering steps forward with an oddly blank face, then sank to one knee. He coughed, and red bubbled on his lips. . . .

**Books by Max Brand**

Published by POCKET BOOKS

# Max Brand

## KING OF
## THE RANGE

PUBLISHED BY POCKET BOOKS NEW YORK

POCKET BOOKS, a Simon & Schuster division of
GULF & WESTERN CORPORATION
1230 Avenue of the Americas, New York, N.Y. 10020

ISBN: 0-671-83374-X

First Pocket Books printing May, 1949

15   14   13   12   11   10   9   8   7

POCKET and colophon are trademarks of Simon & Schuster.

Printed in the U.S.A.

# • CONTENTS •

# I

## • EXCUSE ME •

UNDOUBTEDLY, Colonel Clisson was angry. All through
the first day of the rodeo his anger grew, and on the second day it waxed mightily. He represented the whole of
Texas and all of Texas ways, and it cut him to the very
heart when he saw dally-men from California and Nevada
come into his territory, and at his own pet rodeo, at which
he had himself offered most of the prizes, carry away the
glory and the hard cash.

The invaders had won at the shooting contest on the
morning of the first day, distinguishing themselves with
both rifle and revolver; and on foot, kneeling, prone, or in
the saddle on a moving horse, they had excelled the tie-
men in every respect.

Some said that his half dozen of center-fire riders were
professionals, and not real cowpunchers at all. That is to
say, they were a group who went from rodeo to rodeo
throughout the country, splitting between them the prizes
that they won. Such men, with none of the dull and aim-
less hours on the range to burden them, were able to de-
vote all their attention to the fine points which were most
likely to count in a contest. They could bulldog, for instance, for a month at a time, and work up their skill close
to perfection. Some of these men went into circuses, in the
end, and traveled East and amazed the thousands.

But, professionals or not, Colonel Clisson was enraged
by the successes of the invaders. After their victory in the
shooting, they had been victorious in bulldogging, in riding wild steers, in roping, fancy and for time, in all the
contests; and when it came to the riding of the horses,
which was the concluding portion of the entertainment,
they stood well together at the top.

"They are professionals," said the colonel's foreman.

1

"In that there grama country, they don't learn to scratch their hosses none when they're pitchin' around. But look at that buckaroo now—look how tight he's settin' and swingin' his spurs mighty fine. I wouldn't hate to lay my bet that he ain't drawed a pay check off a ranch inside of five year'. Look at the color of him. He's as pale as a dude gambler!"

The colonel snorted.

"There was a time," said he, "when this country of mine was filled with punchers who would climb up the side of anything that called itself a hoss. But that time is gone, and I'm glad, sir, yes, I'm glad to see strangers come in and put our people in their place. Not one man, Pete, has dared to so much as ask to have a look at my mare, here."

Pete Logan, the foreman, felt that there was a cut intended in this speech and he scratched his chin for an instant, and with thoughtful eyes watched the contest progressing between the center-fire buckaroo and the wrong-headed roan.

It was a prize bucking horse, that roan. It fought like a pair of wild cats thrown over the shoulder of Old Nick. But, nevertheless, the stranger was flapping his hat and working his cruel, scraping spurs, and taking the heart out of the roan rapidly and surely.

Pete turned his head and looked at the mare in the pen. The walls of that pen were nine feet high, because it was said that over a smaller barrier she would either leap or scramble, and up and down behind the bars she swung back and forth, like a panther walking at its cage screen.

She was a fury, a thorough and educated bad one. When she felt the eye of the foreman resting upon her, she paused in her pacing to and fro and looked back at him, flattening her ears.

Pete Logan was upset and turned his head hastily away from her. He knew horses from beginning to end, but this was a very different matter. To enter a contest with her would be like entering the cage of a tiger. Even her beauty made her more terrible. For she was clad in chestnut silk, dappled over with leopardlike markings of shadow, and the gloss of her flank was as bright as burnished metal. She had had five years of glorious freedom on the range. Three times she had been caught up by roving horse thieves, whose eyes were taken by her glory.

The first one left a small scar on her back and a confirmed hatred of the human race in her proud heart. The second was pitched into a dreadful nest of Spanish bayonet, where even Excuse Me would not follow, and where he would have died like a tortured wild cat, with the mare prowling on guard about him, had not a range rider found him the next day and cut him free, and carried him off to the ranch house to wait for a doctor, and jail. The third would-be horse thief must have been a magnificent rider, for he had stuck to Excuse Me until his spurs had deeply scored her sides. But his fate was the worst of all, for they had found him where he fell and where the demoniac mare had pounced on him. He was battered to a rag, literally beyond recognition.

When the colonel heard of that he went out with a rifle to shoot her. But when he looked down the sights, and the round of them held the perfect beauty of her head, he relented. Instead, he ordered her to be caught up and gentled with the utmost care.

She was accordingly brought in. They said that she fought like a beast of prey, rather than a horse, rushing at the punchers instead of away from them, and biting at the ropes which restrained her. Then, for six months, the colonel himself supervised her training. There was nothing in the shape of a horse that could not be gentled and trained, he said. And he knew how to do it! But at the end of six months he was wearing a plaster on his right temple, and he walked with a limp. She was like fluid fire, said the colonel, and no precautions could make the handling of her safe. So he brought her to his rodeo to be given to the man who rode her!

That man never would come over the horizon, he was sure, but nevertheless, it would be a beautiful and terrible thing to see Excuse Me perform!

However, he had brought her in vain. The punchers, when they asked for horses in the contest, paused only for one glance through the bars at lovely Excuse Me. Then they went hastily on, some with a visible shudder. For, in fact, as has been said, her beauty made her only more grim to behold.

"Not even asked to try a saddle on her!" exclaimed the colonel with increasing savagery. "They ain't a man of 'em that wouldn't rather get on top of a tank of nitroglycerine."

"Why, sir," said Pete, with a rather lopsided grin, "I feel the same way about it."

"You do? And ain't you got no shame, Pete, to stand here, a strappin' young feller like you, and confess that to my face?"

"The fact is," said Pete, "that the nitroglycerine might not go off, but Excuse Me you doggone know would bust every time!"

The colonel snorted, which was his habit when he was cornered past the rescue of words.

"Young man, young man," said he, "I've seen the day that no hoss in this country would go unchallenged. I've seen men that have walked fifty mile, for the sake of tryin' their hands at a man-killin' hoss. What you got that fool smile on your face for?"

"I was recollectin' of the day," said Pete Logan, "when we ties the sack of crushed barley onto the back of Excuse Me and turns her loose. Maybe you disremember that day, sir?"

"Bah!" said the colonel.

"I was smilin'," said Pete Logan, "to think that she bucked so hard that she split open the side of that sack and sent the barley squirtin' out like water!"

"I remember," said the colonel dreamily, "that on that day she then spent a long time smashin' that good barley into the mud of her corral!"

"Yeah," drawled Pete, "she's a lamb, I reckon!"

He raised his hat. "How d'ye, Miss Furneaux?"

The colonel hastily followed the example of his foreman and removed his hat to a woman of middle age who now rode up to them. She had a handsome, sun-browned face, lean and clean-looking, and the most honest gray eyes in the world. She smiled at them both.

"Our boys are not having much luck," said she.

"I would rather have us represented by the women, Elizabeth!" said the colonel. "I would rather have the girls of this country represent us than the spineless, weak-hearted, chicken-livered rascals who are out here now, lettin' themselves be bucked off like so many sacks of wheat—half-filled sacks, at that!"

He ended by pointing with a stiff arm.

"Look!" said he.

And, at that moment, aptly to illustrate what the colonel had been saying, one of the Texas contenders was seen to leave the bowed back of his pony and fly upward without wings from his saddle, then drop like a plummet to the ground. The impact was audible!

"I hope he's broken his neck!" said the colonel.

Miss Furneaux looked at Clisson without a smile, but also without malice, for she understood thoroughly the bigness of his heart.

"Why, that's Archie Hunter!" said she.

"Archie Hunter?" repeated the colonel. "Why, then, I must say that he sticks in my mind, in some way connected with your name, Elizabeth. What is it?"

"He was the dearest friend of Rod," said she.

"Ah?" said the colonel.

He began to add other words, but checked himself, seemed half choking, and turned a violent crimson.

Elizabeth Furneaux looked at him with the same faint smile of understanding.

"You want to ask me what the latest news is about Rod, I suppose?" said she.

"Why, Elizabeth, my dear child," said the colonel, putting out a hand toward her, "I never want you to speak a word that will hurt you! I never want that!"

"I don't mind telling you," said she. "I had a letter from him not long ago, but, as usual, he says nothing about what he's really doing. Except that he's found a girl in the mountains. Something too exquisite to be human, I gather! Also—you probably know that they've attributed another shooting scrape to Rod?"

"The man near Denver, do you mean?"

"Yes. The man is dead, I've just heard. That's all the recent news. Good-by, colonel. I'll see you again before the rodeo breaks up."

She rode off, and the colonel looked at his foreman with bared teeth, and Pete Logan looked back at him in the same fashion.

"I wish," said the colonel, after a moment of sustaining

this vicious grimace, "I wish that Rodman Furneaux were thrown into the pen with Excuse Me. Confound him, I wish no better than that!"

"They might get on fine," said Pete Logan. "They'd be birds of a feather, after all!"

## II

### • CARRICK DUNMORE •

SAID the colonel: "Everything lost—everything ruined—everything gone to a lot of single-cinch——"

The rest of his language defied reproduction.

"Here's Sam Parker," said Logan. "I been wonderin' where Sam was. There's a he-man when it comes to ridin' a hoss!"

"Bah!" snorted the colonel. "That Parker is drunk. He can't keep in the saddle hardly. You, Sam Parker, come here, sir!"

Sam Parker came.

He was a brown-faced youth with not much forehead and a vast smile over a lantern jaw. He looked at the colonel with the indistinctness of crossed eyes and a clouded brain.

"Sam," said the colonel, "are you gunna ride?"

"I reckon I am, sir."

"Are you gunna stick on like a man?"

"I reckon I ain't, sir."

"Sam, you're drunk."

"Yes, sir," said Sam, "I been collectin' and collectin' and collectin' this here bun for three days, and now I guess I'm pretty well ripe. This here is about the best I ever been; I had an ol' master to help to put on the finishin' touches!"

"Some of those center-fire sneaks have got Sam drunk," suggested the colonel. "Otherwise——"

"Who you been with?" asked Pete Logan.

"I jus' lef' ol' Carrie Dunmore over to Chaffey's Crossroads Place. We been lettin' the redeye percolate until it's got into our bones and made 'em jus' so sof' that fallin' off of a hoss wouldn't hurt."

"Hold on!" exclaimed the colonel. "Did you say Carrie Dunmore? *The* Carrie Dunmore?"

"Yes, sir. Ol' single-shot Carrie. He's over there. He's jus' warmin' up strong."

"Why didn't the underbred coyote come on to the rodeo?" asked the colonel savagely.

"Because he said that the sun was shinin' warmer and the sittin' was softer and easier there in Chaffey's Place."

"The lazy scoundrel!" cried the colonel.

"Yes, sir," answered Sam with a vaster smile than ever. "I've heard of the gent that was so lazy he starved to death because he wouldn't go to the smokehouse to get him a side of bacon. But I reckon that Carrie Dunmore is the most outlazyingest gent in the whole world!"

"That's an honorable distinction," said the colonel. "Is the fellow as drunk as you are, Sam?"

"Him, sir?" asked Sam Parker. "Is you referrin' by any chance to my frien' Carrie Dunmore? I gotta tell you, sir, that they ain't enough liquor and time in the world to percolate into the insides of Carrie. He jus' gets the outside a little pickled, but inside, he's fine as could be!"

The colonel grew absent of eye and mind.

Suddenly he said: "Pete, take Charlie and Joe. Take an extra set of hosses along, too. Ride like fury. It's only two miles to Chaffey's Place, and if you can't get there in five minutes, you lose your jobs with me! Get that wo'thless, no-account, set-in-the-sun Carrie Dunmore, and bring him here!"

The foreman looked anxious.

"That's only three of us, sir," said he.

"Suppose there are only three?" roared the colonel. "Is he a grizzly bear or a mountain lion? Besides, ain't he drunk, by the report of that wo'thless Sam Parker? Go get that man. Rope him, tie him up, and bring him here! I'll make him ride, confound him!"

Pete Logan departed at once. Along the fence he picked up Charlie and Joe, seasoned cow hands, and told them what was wanted. They listened with long faces.

"Why don't you ask me to go an' pull the teeth of a live buzz saw?" asked Charlie plaintively.

"It ain't a question of wantin' or askin'," said the foreman. "It's a question of gettin' and doin'. The old man is nutty, he's so mad. He wants Carrie Dunmore."

"For a watch charm, maybe," said Joe with delicate sarcasm.

But they rounded up an extra horse and started at once on a dead run. And in the specified five minutes their puffing, dripping horses halted at the roadside place of Chaffey.

Sounds of mirth issued from within, and the foreman risked a spy-glance through the window before entering. He returned, cursing. "There's four of the best doggone cowpunchers in Texas in there," said he, "and they're all hangin' around watchin' Carrie juggle knives. It depends on how lubricated those gents are, what luck we have. Joe, you're a neat hand with a rope. I'll go in and get his attention—if I can. When I get in, you daub a rope onto him. Charlie, you stand by to help in any direction you might be needed."

So, determined, grim-faced, they advanced through the door into the place, and there they found five cowboys stamping on the floor and singing a thundering herd song, while Chaffey himself, behind the bar, smote the varnished surface with the flat of his pudgy white hand in time with the music.

All this accompaniment was for the benefit of a large young man who was dancing a jig with uncertain and fumbling feet, laughing at his own clumsiness; but while he danced, his hands were seriously occupied.

On the bar were laid nine or ten knives—hunting knives and big bowie knives. Of these he had taken three and was juggling them into the air as he danced. As the newcomers entered, he greeted them with an Indian yell and added a fourth knife to the three which were in the air.

This complicated his performance. What with the stumbling feet, and the flight of four knives, it seemed that at any moment he might blunder under the heavy, descending point of one of the weapons. Indeed, he seemed to be drawing his head from side to side to escape their fall.

"We'd better stop this!" said Charlie. "He'll be carving with one of those bowies, before long."

"They're gunna stop you, Carrie!" yelled one of the audience.

Carrie answered with wild laughter, and actually turned his handsome head for a fraction of an instant toward the trio.

Yet he managed to keep the knives flowing upward without an interruption, yelling: "You there, Pete Logan —you line up agin' the wall, ol' hoss, line up there with your hands over your head, or I'll split you right in two!"

Pete Logan hesitated, but he did not hesitate long. The wild light in the juggler's eyes convinced him that there was a real danger, and back he went to the wall and stretched his arms above his head, only growling as he did so:

"I knew that we'd land in the mud, Joe!"

In the meantime, the chorus of five liquor-ridden cowpunchers grew louder, until it thundered, while Carrick Dunmore, still laughing, still reeling, flung a knife that stuck humming in the wood half an inch from Logan's right ear.

"Hey!" yelled Logan. "Look out, you'll murder me!"

"If you budge ag'in, old hoss, I will!" shouted Carrick Dunmore, and suddenly the knives flowed brightly from the flat of his hands—the four he had in the air, and the others from the edge of the bar behind him. With them, he outlined the head of the foreman, who remained rigid with horror as, with shock after shock, the murderous steel flew home into the wall and hedged his head about in a close circle.

And all the time the song of the cowpunchers thundered, and the knives flowed in beat with the song!

When the last knife was thrown, however, enormous laughter swallowed all other sound.

Then: "Step out, Pete, and look at your picture drawed on the wall, there!" ordered Carrie.

Pete stepped out and nodded to Charlie, and that worthy instantly had his rope over the shoulders of Carrick Dunmore.

It happened with wonderful speed and unison of effort. While the five inebriated punchers were still helpless with excess of mirth, three pairs of hands were applied to the neck of the lariat, and Carrick Dunmore was yanked from his feet, dragged over the floor, and out the door, which was slammed and locked behind them.

"Hey!" shouted Dunmore. "You poor, puddinghead-ed——"

Then laughter seized him again and shook him helpless; and similar roars still bellowed from the saloon, to tell of the hysterically weak men within. The trio, still grim enough and frightened enough, grappled Dunmore. His body was utterly relaxed, but it was not soft. It was loose, with the looseness of supple steel cables, as they heaved him into a saddle, and then lashed his feet together beneath the belly of the horse.

And still he laughed as they started down the road. He reeled heavily from side to side. Only the lashing that gripped his feet seemed able to keep him in place, but still with inexhaustible laughter he roared and wept for joy of his own jest, as they thundered along, four men now, and three of them as proud of this exploit as though they had seized a robber chief from the midst of his band and carried him off to the power of the law.

So it was that they galloped onto the field of the rodeo, where the bucking contest still was in progress, though drawing toward a close, for the sun was sloping far to the west, and the dust which whirled up from the riding field floated golden in the air.

As they came, they could hear the bawling of an angry cow pony, and the whooping of an exultant and equally fierce rider.

"One of them center-fire Californians ag'in," said the foreman, "but maybe we can do something agin' 'em, now! Where's something to sober up this here Carrie Dunmore?"

They found a bucket of water and dashed it over him, and as he emerged from it, spluttering, but still laughing with inextinguishable good nature, they led him to the judges and demanded his right to ride.

The judges regarded the unsteady newcomer with interest.

"They's only two hosses left to ride," said they. "One of

them is for Tom Bizbee. The other is the colonel's mare. Would you like to try her, Dunmore?"

"I al'ays loved the ladies," said Carrick Dunmore. "Lemme see this pretty girl?"

And they led him eagerly across the field to visit Excuse Me, for the first time.

## III

### • A MIGHTY GOOD RIDER •

MISS FURNEAUX went straight to the judges. There she looked them calmly in the eye and said: "That big young man is going to try to ride the colonel's pet roan, and she'll kill him. Do you realize that?"

"He's a mighty good rider, ma'am," was the first answer.

"Good? He's a drunken rider, just now."

"Miss Furneaux, a man with too much liquor in him is rarely hurt, except with a bullet! Let him alone. Carrie will come out all right. There goes Bizbee, by the way, and he's caught a hummer!"

Tom Bizbee was a serious young man who would not have been afraid of climbing the side of a thunderbolt and sitting on its back, stirrups or no stirrups. He rode the gray mustang that had fallen to his lot bravely and well to the very center of the bucking grounds, but there the gray rose, as it were, and dissolved like a skyrocket into a tangle of head, tail, legs, and Tom Bizbee.

From this explosion the mustang dropped lightly down, and Tom Bizbee fell in another place, and fell not to rise again. He lay stretched flat on his back, with his arms thrown wide.

And, spinning like a top, the gray horse whirled to savage him!

It was too sudden for thought; too horrible for expectation. And the time for succor was some fifth part of a sec-

ond before those steel-clad hoofs would smash in the
breatbone or shatter the face and skull of poor Bizbee. But
with the yell of distress that arose mingled the sharp,
hoarse bark of a revolver.

The gray mustang lurched up on his hind legs, wavered
in the air, as though about to drop on the fallen man, and
then crashed backward dead.

"What a wonderful shot!" said Elizabeth Furneaux.

"Him that fired it was the same drunk cowpuncher!"
said the judge.

She stared. The crowd was flooding onto the field and
examining the wound—a bullet hole through the head of
the gray! But Carrick Dunmore was gripping the bars and
looking through them at the mare within.

"Who is he? What's his name?" asked Elizabeth.

"Him? That's Carrick Dunmore, that——"

"Carrick Dunmore? Great heavens!" she exclaimed,
and changed color.

Her horse moved off, and she seemed too stunned to
handle the reins and check him in place.

"What's the matter with her? What's Carrick Dunmore
in her life?" muttered one of the judges.

"Why, I never thought of it before now. But wasn't her
ma's name Dunmore?"

"Hey! Then maybe they're related in some way?"

"Why, maybe! What'll Carrie do? Ride the dappled
chestnut?"

"Oh, he might try. But no man's son's gunna ride that
mare, my boy!"

Carrick Dunmore was still at the bars, considering Excuse Me.

"What's the breeding of this here mare, colonel?" he
asked.

"Well, what'd you guess, Carrie?"

"I'd guess she was sired by a streak of lightnin' out of a
black nor'west blizzard, colonel!"

The colonel laughed.

"She's nobody's pet lamb," he admitted.

"Don't look like a man would be none at home with
her," remarked the thoughtful Carrie Dunmore.

"Who'd you expect to be easy with her, Carrie?" went
on the colonel, enjoying this conversation.

"Why, a couple of well-growed grizzly bears might handle her; or a pack of mountain lions might have some chance, if she didn't kick out their hind sights."

"Dunmore," said one of the judges, coming up, "she's the last horse that hasn't been ridden, or tried. Do you want her, or do you stay out of this?"

"If they was fifty hosses here in these here pens," said Carrick Dunmore, "and if I was to have the first choice, I wouldn't pick nothin' but her. Where's all these cowboys? Ain't they got an eye in their heads? Payin' all that attention to common muts when they's a thoroughbred queen of Spain standin' here to take 'em in one jump all the way to glory? Lead out beautiful. I wanta be interduced!"

Six men, busily, cautiously laboring, snubbed her head short against a post, then worked the blanket and saddle onto her velvet back.

She did not struggle greatly. Now and again there would be a ripple through the shoulder muscles, or a bending of the back upward. But like one that knows that the time has not yet come to strike, she waited.

"She's pretty quiet, ain't she?" said the colonel.

"Aw, she's quiet," said Dunmore. "She's about as quiet, it seems to me, as a blast of powder, before the fire gets to it. I bet that she's got wings!"

They led her out, blindfolded, and Carrick Dunmore mounted.

He was still far from recovered from the fumes of drink. His foot twice missed the stirrup, and he seemed to need the help of many hands to heave into the saddle. But once he was fitted into it, he squeezed the mare with his knees, and she grunted at the enormous pressure.

Elizabeth Furneaux, lingering near, watched this performance with a pale face and with eyes that burned with a peculiar interest. Then she turned her horse and deliberately rode away from the grounds, only stopping to speak for a moment to the colonel.

Behind her arose a wild whoop from the crowd, and looking back, she could see Excuse Me black against the sun, with the hat of her rider batting her ears, and the swinging legs of him scratching her fore and aft.

She waited to see no more, but with a shudder put her horse into a canter and hastened home.

In the meantime, Excuse Me showed her worth.

Her exhibitions had been limited affairs in every sense, before this. It was like putting a heavyweight champion against an amateur feather, to see her entertaining the best of cowpunchers who had come her way, but now she had met a master of the craft, and she did all that horse could do.

She fished for the sun, and, landing, strove to jam her forefeet to the heart of the earth. But the earth was furnished with springs, as it were, and cast her up again into the air.

She was like a hawk which, missing its prey as it stoops, leaps with the bracing of its wings almost to the same vantage point and so shoots down again and again as rook or dove hurries for the shelter of the woods.

So Excuse Me went across the field.

Her rider lost his right stirrup at the second jump; got it at the third; lost both stirrups at the fourth; found them again at the next. He circled the field, sometimes with the sun showing between him and the saddle, but still in his place.

It was dreadful work. For Excuse Me threw in sudden variations, here and there, sometimes spinning in a circle, with wonderful speed, the most deadly of all the tricks of a bucking horse. And sometimes she fence-rowed for a bit, her feet flickering in a jigsaw frame upon the ground.

As that first slow circle was completed, men saw that blood was streaming from the nose of Carrick Dunmore.

"But he's got her licked!" they told one another.

Fiercely they said it, whispering, gripping the rails of the barrier, while they set their teeth hard, and hoped.

The six strangers, who had done so well, were gathered in one group, watching very thoughtfully, not with malicious eyes, but with a profound appreciation, such as one consummate artist yields to the work of another, even when it is entered in competition with his own.

Twice around the pair worked.

And then, as the mare was covered with flecks and streaks of foam, and markings of blood where the cruel spurs had rasped her skin, men could see, also, that the face of Dunmore was deadly pale; his mouth opened; his eyes empty.

"By gravy!" cried the colonel, "has she got him?"

"Nobody never rode no better," said Pete Logan, at his side. "Good ol' Carrie! Ride her, boy! Bust her! Hey there——"

Excuse Me had flicked over backward to the earth, her rider swerving sideways from the saddle. She rolled and pitched her feet, reaching her head about viciously to tear the leg of Dunmore.

But a fist of leaden weight smote Excuse Me upon the muzzle and as Dunmore settled into the saddle, she skyrocketed, twisting over in mid-air, and so went crashing down upon her back!

Dunmore, cast from the saddle, slowly crawled to his knees, and the mare lay for an instant still, also, then twisted over, and pawed her way up to her feet.

Dunmore would have risen, but he could not. His legs seemed paralyzed, but he was seen to drag himself upon his strong hands toward the mare, and as she lurched up, he reached for a stirrup leather and raised himself by it, grappled the saddle horn, and so, as she lurched to her feet, she swayed him up with her.

Men saw him reach back with is right hand and drag his right leg over the cantle. It flopped down helplessly and dangled, regardless of the stirrup, and a groan of sympathy and disappointment came from the watching crowd.

The very next fling of the mare would surely throw him. But Excuse Me flung no more.

She stood for a while, with hanging head and with legs spread far apart. The reins hung idly down.

"Beat!" said a single voice from all that crowd.

And though so many sounds were in it, it was not a loud voice; but as though each man and woman were announcing to himself a miracle.

Then Dunmore slipped still farther forward. His arms hung over the neck of the mare, and with him in that position, loosly sagging toward the ground, Excuse Me walked quietly back to her pen and entered it veritably like one returned after an arduous and trying journey.

They took Dunmore from her and stretched him along the ground. A doctor kneeled by him, and listened to his heart, to his breathing. Then he touched him here and there with a needle, and watched the reaction of the nerves and the muscles.

Then he stood up.

"I'm very glad to say that there's nothing serious," said he. "Only a temporary paralysis of the legs after the fall. And one other remarkable fact, my friends. This man is unconscious now from that fall. And—he must have been unconscious when he crawled back to the mare and mounted her with his hands alone!"

The doctor went away.

He said to his wife as they climbed into their buggy: "And rather a pity that he wasn't killed. It would have been a fine ending for a perfectly worthless life!"

# IV

## • DUNMORE HISTORY •

FROM his long trance Carrick Dunmore wakened in a large, sunny room. His stunned brain had slipped into a deep sleep, and so he had spent a round of the clock and more. It was the prime of the day, and the sun flowed brilliantly through the lofty windows. It was an old-fashioned house. By the big, square room, and the time-thinned carpet on the floor, he could guess the face of the house on the outside. It would be of wood, with a romantic wooden lantern built up from the center, and a good deal of gingerbread work about the eaves. It was one of those places made to look a little like a castle on the outside and a little like a palace within.

Nevertheless, Carrick was impressed, and wondered how he had got here. But his brain refused to work hard on any subject. He lay back on his pillow and contentedly, lazily, watched the quiver of the shadows of the lace curtain falling upon the opposite wall. He noticed that the wallpaper was ragged, and there were water stains which proved that the roof had not been kept in very good repair.

But chiefly he occupied himself with a painting which was on the wall facing his bed. It showed a town of twisted streets and red-tiled roofs swarming up the side of a hill; terraced olive orchards lay on either side like puffs of dissolving smoke; and in the sky was eternal sunshine and eternal peace.

"Hello!" said a voice at the window.

It was a handsome woman of middle age, with a brown look of the outdoors.

She was leading Excuse Me, and the window sill came so close to the ground that the mare was easily able to put her head in. She snorted in the direction of her master, and then looked half fiercely about the room.

"She knows you," said the woman, "the beautiful rascal!"

"And I know her," said Carrick Dunmore, "but I'm afraid that I never met you, ma'am."

"No, you haven't," said she. "But I'm Elizabeth Furneaux. When you were hurt, of course you were brought to my house."

He looked puzzled, and she went on: "Partly because I'm close, and partly, of course, because I had to do what I could for the head of my family. Well, I wanted you to see Excuse Me, and now I'll go bring you some breakfast."

She disappeared, and Carrick Dunmore pondered with a startled brain a phrase she had used. He—the head of her family!

However, he grew drowsy almost at once, and very nearly had to waken from deep sleep when the door opened and Miss Furneaux came in carrying a tray of food. She put it on a bed tray that straddled him, and uncovered to him the fume of oatmeal porridge, with a yellow jug of cream beside it, two broad slabs of ham fried to a crinkle at the edges, and four eggs mounted richly on the field of that ham. Then there was another covered dish which contained wedges of hot corn bread, three inches thick, and a dish of butter.

She stood without smiling at the foot of the bed and surveyed him with a mild and direct gaze such as he never had received before except from a man—and very few men indeed looked at Carrick Dunmore so straight.

He, looking back at her, decided that she not only had brought in the tray, but that she had cooked the food that was on it. By her hands, somehow, he could tell it; and the flush of heat about the lower part of her face. In one stroke, he wrote her down as a woman who was a lady by birth and a man by necessity. Her work ranged from the kitchen to the herd, and he was sure of it.

"I'll go out, if you'll eat more comfortably when you're not watched," said she.

Dunmore smiled at her. He had one of those surprisingly bright smiles that light up a face as though a veil had been brushed aside before it.

"Crowds never bothered me, Miss Furneaux," said he. "I could sleep through all the noise of a boiler factory, and I could sit down and eat with a thousand ladies and gents walkin' by and lettin' fall their monocles at the looks of me."

With this, he poured the contents of the cream jug upon the oatmeal and heaped a white island of sugar in the center of the cream. This he then entered with a table-spoon, vigorously.

"It makes me hungry to watch you," said Elizabeth Furneaux, laughing a little in a very pleasant voice.

"You," said he, "are what I'd call a good provider! This would be somethin' to dream about, if hotels could frame up such chuck!"

"My dear Cousin Carrick," said she, "of course I'm delighted to have you—as long as you'll stay!"

He paused, halfway through the ham and eggs.

"Am I your cousin?"

"Not a shadow of a doubt of it. My mother was a Dunmore of Virginia, you know."

"Dunmore—Virginia," he repeated. "Why, that's a funny thing, isn't it? And that's what you meant by callin' me the head of the house, I suppose?"

"Exactly."

"No more men left in Virginia?"

"No. Except Alf Dunmore's pair of twins. Their picture came last week and they're cute little fellows. But only five years old!"

"That's old enough to make a steer mean," said Dunmore, "but I suppose that it ain't old enough to make a boy into a man. But I've gotta say that if the house has me for a head, it's not goin' to use its brain, much. It'll be more apt to crawl along on hands and feet!"

She nodded and smiled a little.

"Life hasn't bothered you a great deal, Carrick, I suppose."

"Not a rip," said he. "Never bothered me a bit. As soon as I was big enough to know the difference between sunshine and shade, I liked the sunshine and loved to lie in it. The sun is never dangerous except to them that work in it, Cousin Elizabeth. You sure that I got a right to call you that?"

"Of course I'm sure. You have the look of the whole family, besides."

"Have I?"

"Certainly you have."

"Look here," said he, "suppose there might be other branches of Dunmores back there in Virginia?"

"It's not a common name, and the blood isn't common, either, thank Heaven," she answered with a frank pride. "Which makes me all the happier to have the king out here. Let me bring you some hot corn bread, Cousin Carrick?"

"No, thanks. King?" he echoed.

She laughed.

"Of course, you remember the story about the first Carrick Dunmore?" said she.

"Never heard of him before."

"Dear me! Never?"

"Not a word before."

"But that doesn't seem possible! Never heard any of the jolly old tales about Carrick Dunmore?"

"I must've missed something," said he, smilingly.

"You bet you did," said she heartily. "That about the king, for instance. One of the Dunmores had been arrested —not one of the people in the castle, but some poor relation on the outskirts of the village had had too much ale and had cracked a man's head with his staff. He was arrested. Carrick Dunmore came ramping to the jail and took the man out. He threatened to tear down the jail if such a thing happened again.

" 'But the king's law?' they said to him.

" 'Robert Bruce is King of Scotland,' said he, 'but I am king of the Dunmores!' "

She laughed at the end, and he joined her.

"Well, well," said he, "a fellow like that would have had a pretty excitin' life in the days of Robert Bruce, I suppose, what with whangin' each other around in armor, and all that sort of thing! But I reckon that it would be kind of apt to rust a gent's constitution, wouldn't it? I don't suppose he lasted long?"

"For those days, he did. He lived to be almost fifty, which was a ripe old age in the thirteenth century, you know."

"I didn't know," said Carrick, "but I would've guessed that they was scared of fresh air; and ironclad shoes must've raised pretty good crops of chilblains and rheumatism. What did the King of Scotland do when he heard what Carrick Dunmore had said?"

"That was a story, too," she said. "The king was cross, of course, and he asked who Carrick Dunmore was, because he never had heard of him before. They told him that the Earl of Carrick lived in Carrick Castle in the town of the same name, and among his serfs were a number of people called Dunmore. One day as the earl was out riding he found a crowd in the village street watching a ragged fellow juggling. The earl was pleased by the juggling, and when he found out that the man was one of his own Dunmores, he ordered him to come to the castle to entertain the guests at supper.

"This ragged man looked the earl in the face and told him that he had made a vow never to enter the castle except as its master. Naturally, the earl was very angry. When he got back to his castle, he ordered one of his knights to arrest the serf. The knight tried it, but came back minus his horse and armor, and with this as a starting point, young Dunmore gathered a gang of border riders and became a raider. A year or so later, he came back and popped into the castle of the earl one night; and in the morning, he was the master of the place. He gave the earl and his wife and son a horse apiece, and sent them away; but he took the name of Carrick to put in front of Dunmore. That's how the name came into the family, you see."

"What did the king think of that story?"

"He was amused. Then he sent word that he wanted to have Carrick Dunmore come to his court in order to be made a knight. The Dunmore sent answer that no man would ever lay a sword on his shoulders without getting paid back with an ax; besides, he never knelt except in prayer, and that only on Whitsuntide and Christmas Morning, because it was a family habit!"

Dunmore laughed heartily.

"I would've liked to meet him," said he.

"He would have liked to meet you, Cousin Carrick."

"And what did the king do then?"

"It makes another story," said Elizabeth. "And I have to make bread this morning. Is there anything you need?"

"Not a thing. Except a new pair of legs."

"You'll have to wait for time and the doctor, for those," said she, and left the room.

# V

# • ELIZABETH ENTERTAINS HER GUEST •

ALL the excitement that ordinarily will come to an idle and a drifting life had come to Carrick Dunmore, but he felt that this was his strangest adventure, in a way. This calm acceptance of him into a family of which he never had heard the day before seemed to Dunmore a dreamlike thing. And, above all, there was about Elizabeth Furneaux an air almost of reverence, of covert reverence, as she waited upon him.

It made Carrie Dunmore smile a little, as he considered it—and then he went to sleep again, deeply in sleep, and into a profoundly vivid dream of himself, ax in hand, battering down the wall of the jail and taking from it an unlucky fellow of his own name.

"Robert Bruce is King of Scotland, but I am the king of the Dunmores!" he was saying, when he wakened, and found that it was late afternoon, the room filled with soft blue shadow, and at the foot of his bed was Elizabeth Furneaux.

"You're a grand sleeper," said she. "The doctor has been here and thumbed you over like a schoolboy's textbook, and you didn't open an eye."

"What does he say?"

"He says that you can get up in the morning."

"That's a good thing," said Dunmore. "Sit down, Cousin Elizabeth. I'm mighty glad to see you ag'in."

"You're hungry," said she. "I can see that you're ravenous."

She smiled, as though the idea pleased her.

He pointed toward the picture on the wall.

"I've been walkin' up the streets of that town," said he, "ever since I fell asleep. I was so far inside of that picture that it seems queer to lie here clean outside of it ag'in."

"Do you like it?" asked she.

"I like it pretty fine," said Dunmore.

"Thank you," said she, "because I painted it. That's a little town between Monte Carlo and Nice. It looks as though it will slip off the shoulder of the mountain every minute. The castle is up here. A mighty good castle that a whole army could bump its head against. From the walls all these roofs go winding and tangling down beneath you. One of the old owners of that castle used to heave a rock from the battlements whenever he was angry with one of the families, and the rock would go smashing through the house from attic to basement."

Dunmore grinned.

"Those were the good old days," said he.

"Oh, yes," said she, "the good days for people like Carrick Dunmore."

She interrupted herself with a laugh.

"I mean the Carrick who was the friend of Robert Bruce," said she.

"Did those two get to be friends?" asked Dunmore.

"Yes, they did. Robert Bruce was very angry, of course, when he had such a saucy answer made to him by a man who was simply a partisan leader—not a noble, not even a knight. So the king summoned his army and went rushing across to pull down Carrick Castle. The Earl of Carrick went along to enjoy the fun. But when the earl's own men tried their hands at the outworks they got such an unlucky reception that they ran away without stopping for their dead and wounded.

"The king considered the castle as a hungry dog considers a bone, but finally he felt that the bone was too thick and also that there were more wasps than marrow inside. So he sent for Carrick Dunmore under a flag of truce, and the Dunmore went down to see him. He sat at meat with the king, and Robert Bruce gave the great Carrick a good many compliments. Among other things, he said he was sure that such a man must have great ancestors, and Carrick said that he had.

"'This is the reason that I have attained to some honor,'" said Carrick Dunmore. "'This is my great-great-grandfather,' said he, and laid hold on a heavy lance, 'and this is my great-grandfather, my grandfather and my father!'

"As he said this, he took hold successively of his shield, his sword, and his heavy battle-ax."

"The king would've liked that, I guess," suggested Carrick Dunmore.

"Of course he did, but he said: 'All these ancestors will be of no avail to you unless you also carry with you the blessing of Heaven!'"

"'I have that, too,' said Carrick Dunmore, and he took out a poniard as sharp and thin as an icicle that had almost been worn away in the sun."

"So he and the king were friends after that?" asked the young man.

"They were friends ever after, but Carrick Dunmore never would take a title. The king used to ask him why he would not become a noble, and Carrick would answer: 'You have in your country a good handful of dukes, a bushel of earls, and more lords, baronets, barons, and knights than would make ten acres of standing wheat, if every helmet were turned into an ear of corn. But in all Scotland, there is only one Dunmore!' That was a good answer, don't you think?" finished Elizabeth.

"A mighty good answer," said her guest, and they laughed together. "I suppose he died rich and happy?"

"He was rich enough, I suppose, though he never had

broad lands, as the word went in those days. He was a lazy fellow, you see, and it took a rude earl, or a king with an army, or some such thing, to stir him up."

"Ah," said Carrick Dunmore, rising himself on his elbows, "was he really lazy?"

"They say that he would sit all day with the sun in his face and never stir a hand."

The youth was greatly impressed, and listened with an inward look in his eye.

"Well, well," murmured he, "how did he get rich, if he didn't work a great deal?"

"That's what the king asked him. He wanted to know where were the estates that enabled him to live so richly, because there was hardly a patch of land beyond the castle and the village that he could call his own. Carrick took Bruce up to the top of his keep and pointed at the horizon.

" 'Look all around,' said he. 'There to the south, my cattle are grazing.'

" 'On what lands?' asked the king.

" 'On the lands of the horizon,' said Carrick, 'and they're getting fat on the blue of the sky.'

" 'How far south do you pasture your cattle?' asked the king, who still did not understand. 'As far south as Oxenford,' said Carrick. That was as much as to say, as far south as Oxford. You see, this rascal of a Carrick Dunmore actually had raided as far south as Oxford in England.

"Then he pointed to the west.

" 'There are some of my richest meadow lands and my best crops, growing,' said he.

" 'Man,' said the king, 'I see there nothing but the naked blue ocean!'

" 'You are right,' said Carrick Dunmore, 'and on it graze the fattest cattle in the world. I have there round-sided galleys from Ireland, and now and again I go out there and catch a good rich bull from Spain, fat with the sweet Spanish wines; I find bluff-browed English bulls there too, and the joy of my blue meadows is that my cattle are so wild that they give me beef and hunting at the same time.'

"The king understood and laughed.

" 'Your cattle,' said he, 'always graze on the blue?'

"'Yes,' said Carrick. 'Always!'

"That was how he came to be called 'Dunmore of the Blue.'"

"Blue being a polite way of saying: 'Dunmore of the Highway?'" asked young Carrick.

"Well, highways run into the blue edge of the sky somewhere," answered she. "I'll go off and get your dinner ready."

So Carrick Dunmore dined mightily, and he slept again until the room was warm with the sun of the next morning.

Then he rose and tried himself. He stretched each limb. He flexed and unflexed the muscles of his arms and legs. And he found that he was fit again. So he shaved and dressed and went out of the house. He found Elizabeth Furneaux raking up some alfalfa hay which grew among the fig trees of the front yard and was irrigated by water from the windmill.

From the outside, the house was exactly as he had imagined it. It was a big, white, square-shouldered place, with the paint peeled off, here and there, leaving a dull bluish look to the walls. It had a baronial air as it lifted its head above the old surrounding trees, but plainly the house had come to its dotage.

And everything looked pleasant, and homelike, and poverty-stricken.

Elizabeth Furneaux seemed very surprised to see him.

"You shouldn't be up," she said, "until the doctor permits you to! You'd better go back to bed!"

"I wouldn't have any use for doctors," said Carrick Dunmore, "if they were gold set with diamonds and small enough to be worn on a watch chain. Gimme the rake, Elizabeth, and I'll finish this bit of alfalfa."

She held him off, with an air of horror.

"Let an invalid come out to work in a hayfield? I should say not! You go back and rest, Carrick!"

He went back, willingly enough, and sat in the sun under the fig trees until she had finished the raking and hurried into the house to get his breakfast ready.

The last of the dew was evaporating, though the dust of the back yard was still darkened by it; and a sweet smell of hay floated to Carrick Dunmore; and out of the distance he heard the lowing of cattle. Somewhere, too, on the edge of the sky, a dog or a wolf was baying loudly.

He smiled to himself, as if it were a voice speaking to him from the country of Dunmore of the Blue! He liked the idea of this man. It was doubly soothing to him to know of an ancestor so important, wearing his name, and also, above all, lazy like him! For he detested every physical effort except play. He reclined dreamily beneath the fig tree, until Cousin Elizabeth came out bearing to him a huge breakfast tray with twice as much on it as on the preceding morning.

"Convalescents are always mighty hungry!" said she, and stood by with an encouraging smile to see him eat.

But a touch of shadowy thought came into the eyes of Carrick.

"Tell me," he said suddenly, "how many men you keep to run your place?"

"I can't afford hired men," said she.

"What! None at all?"

"There isn't so much to do. I only run a few head of cows; then I have a few more for milk; a few chickens; I can sell milk and eggs in town for a very good price; and it's only now and then that I have to get in hired help for plowing and harvesting the river bottom land."

# VI
## • THE FACE IN THE PORTRAIT •

Now Carrick Dunmore looked at her in bewilderment.

And across his mind flashed the picture of himself, at an early time of boyhood, idling about his father's ranch, refusing to work, drifting off into the wild fields in the morning with his horse, hunting birds, or coyotes, or deer, and returning in the evening to meet the bitter words of his tired father, and the silent, worn face of his mother.

He had hated himself, at times, for the pain which he

allowed them to endure without effort upon his part; but always his indolence was greater than his shame.

Now he felt a great impulse to do something for this woman. But what could he do, except physical labor spread over weary months and months of monotony? No sooner did the great impulse soar in him than it faded dim again.

These were not the days when a man could pasture his cattle on the horizon blue, or hunt the fat-sided ships on the blue of old ocean. These were not the days of the first Carrick Dunmore!

So he sighed as he looked at Elizabeth Furneaux.

"Have you always carried on like this?" he asked.

"Oh, no," said she. "Things were a lot easier when my nephew was here with me."

"What became of him?"

She hesitated.

"You've never heard of Rodman Furneaux?" she asked him.

"No. I guess not."

"Well, Rod has a dash of the true Dunmore blood in him, of course. He wants happiness, but he expects to get it by short cuts."

"What do you mean by that?"

"I mean this, in short. He worked here, well enough, but work was not really what he wanted. Work brings in dollars, but I don't suppose any true Dunmore ever cared a lot for a bank account. And—at last he went off into the blue!"

"On the highway, you mean?" asked Carrick bluntly.

"Well, to be frank, I'm afraid that's it. He's joined Tankerton and his gang, they say!"

"He's joined 'The Bull'?" said Carrick Dunmore.

"I suppose he has."

"That sort of beats me," said he. "You take a brute of a man like Tankerton, why, what would keep your nephew up there with him?"

"The fun of the thing, Carrick. Just the fun of it."

"It ain't so much fun to get your neck stretched!"

She shivered.

"Boys don't think very far ahead," said she.

He fell to musing, and when he looked up again, she had gone back with the emptied tray.

Carrick Dunmore stood up suddenly and rolled himself a cigarette.

"I'd better drift!" said he.

He went out of the corral and found the mare, there. She was now his, for had not Colonel Clisson vowed that the man who rode her should have her? She lifted her fine head and watched him curiously, but without fear.

He wanted to see her in action, and to study the flowing lines of her gallop, so he waved his hands, but Excuse Me stood fast and merely backed into a corner, at last.

When he went up to her, that tigerish beauty did not so much as flatten her ears, but she cringed a bit when he extended his hand, and the very heart of Carrick Dunmore winced within him. He could see on her velvet skin the marks of his quirt and the long lines of the scratching spurs which had raked her fore and aft and he knew that she had been injured in more than flesh.

He gentled her with his hand and spoke softly, and Excuse Me turned dreamy and wondering eyes upon him. So swiftly had she been tamed—if only her spirit were not utterly broken. He thought of various mysteries as he stood beside her, stroking her, and of how women, and men, also, may be made or broken by the right or the wrong touch.

Carrick Dunmore, for instance—suppose the earl had not blundered upon him as he juggled in the street of the village, and made a rudely overbearing demand—why, then, in that case the boy would have remained a clod, a cowherd or some such thing, to the end of his days! From the deeps of his heart, Carrick Dunmore the First must have thanked his lordship in after days for the whipstroke of discourtesy which had roused his heart!

Such a stroke, mused the new Carrick Dunmore, might fall upon him, also, one of these days.

He looked back to the big, looming shoulders of the house above the trees, and then scowled as he thought of his cousin washing dishes inside. His impulse was to go and help her; his second thought was that it was no use to make one pleasant gesture!

He spent two hours with the mare.

From the grain bin, he fed her crushed barley out of the palm of his hand. With shining eyes she would nibble at it, and then toss her head wildly, and back away; but she would come again, until at last she seemed to lose her fear that the flattened hand might be a steel trap about to spring shut on her tender muzzle!

The moment she began to trust Dunmore, his heart suddenly enlarged and embraced her with love. He wondered how it could be that in one day she had been subdued; in one day she had learned to forget her tigerish manners; but then it occurred to him that she never had failed of her own way since the day she was foaled. That made the great difference!

He strolled back to the house to see his cousin for the last time and to thank her for what she had done for him; and he found her already through the dishes and hanging out a few scraps of laundry on the wire line that ran from the edge of the creamery to the corner post of the rear porch.

"I suppose I'll have to start on," said he.

"Before the doctor gives you marching orders?"

"Yes. I'd better drift."

"Well, wait a moment, then."

Somehow, he had thought that she would make it difficult for him to leave. It rather surprised him and hurt him that she let him go so readily. But now she came out again with a thick envelope.

"That's the prize for the riding contest," she told him. "Colonel Clisson raised the prize two hundred dollars! Wasn't that fine of him?"

He reached for the paper and then checked his hand; he looked at her face and colored a little.

"Cousin Elizabeth," he said at last, "I've been wondering how I could pay you back for the way you've taken me in. Now, look here. You keep that envelope, will you?"

She lowered her hand; he saw that she was smiling gently at him, and his heart bounded.

"Why should I take your money, Carrick?" said she. "Do you want to pay me because I've had the pleasure of taking care of the head of our house for a day or two?"

Her smile persisted; she seemed waiting for him to argue. But Carrick felt oddly out of place and ill at ease. It

was not the first time that she had called him the head of
the house, and the idea troubled him. It was a position of
importance; it dragged in its train certain responsibilities
which he did not at all wish to shoulder, and Carrick Dunmore blundered out:

"All that fencin' around the corral ain't so strong, and
maybe you'd use this to put up a new fence, Elizabeth. I
want to do something!"

"Of course you do. I know that you've got a heart of
gold, Carrick. But you see that I can't take it. Oh, if I were
desperate, of course I wouldn't hesitate an instant. I know
that you'd feel a bit of responsibility about us all; but that
time hasn't come, Carrick. I still get along very well. Do
take your money!"

He took it, beginning to feel hot and wishing that this
farewell ceremony were over, but now she suggested that
he might want to see the rest of the house, and he had to
consent. She took him up to the very top, where there was
a sort of captain's walk that her father used to walk up
and down on and from it overlook the country. She led
him through the bedrooms, and named the big, faded, enlarged photographs which hung upon the walls. Carrick
Dunmore began to feel that he was walking through a
house of death until, in a rear bedroom, she showed him a
new photograph of a handsome youngster.

"That's poor Rod," said she. "Such a dear boy, Carrick.
But I suppose I'll never see his face again!"

"And why not?"

"Ah, well, he's the kind to take great chances, and perhaps he's grown callous; Heaven knows what his end will
be, but I think it will surely come inside the next six
months. And then I'll——"

She led the way hastily out of the room, and Carrick
Dunmore followed with a gloomy face. And then—she
would be left utterly alone in the world, with the failing
house and the failing farm upon her hands.

He sighed, and then followed her down the stairs to the
first floor, over the hushed carpet of the parlor, with its
pattern of roses bright at the edges and fading toward the
center, and so to the library, a room of real dignity.

There, also, were several portraits, and pointing to a
corner Elizabeth remarked:

"That's said to be the picture of the first Carrick Dunmore."

He looked at it in amazement. He had heard so much about this first of his line that now he walked closer to the portrait curiously. He saw at first only a blur of brown and black shadows, with the paint peeled off to the wood, in spots. It had been painted, apparently, in imitation of the effigies which appear of the good knights in parish churches. The mailshod feet pointed down, with tapering toes, and the long hands were pressed together. A cowl of mail covered the head, but the face itself was quite distinct, and when he had seen it, Carrick Dunmore suddenly shaded his eyes and stared again.

Then he looked wildly around at Elizabeth Dunmore.

"Can you make it out?" she said. "It's a dim old thing, isn't it? And I don't suppose it looks a whit like him!"

"Great guns!" said he. "Look at it again, and then look at me, will you, Elizabeth?"

She looked a bit askance at him, and then obediently came nearer. But when she was quite close, she cried out in her turn and caught at his arm.

"Carrick!" she cried. "It's your face over again!"


# VII

## • HIGH RESOLVES, AND— •


It seemed to Carrick Dunmore like the appearance of a ghost—as though it were not paint but spirit that looked out at him from the old warped wood of the image. For, beyond a doubt, there was his face reproduced!

It was not an exact thing. One could not have expected that, but it was very clear that there was a great resemblance. Some of the paint was peeled or crumbled off; the left eye was streaked across by a great crack, and the right cheek was falling to bits, but it was as though he looked at his own image in muddy, rippling water. The features

were dim, but all that could be seen were his own. It was a
similarity that overrode all chance, or possibility of doubt;
it was not likeness, or kinship; it was the actual reproduction of the same man, the same flesh, the same spirit! And
as he stared, vague and vast thoughts arose in the mind of
Carrick Dunmore and flooded dimly forward upon his
consciousness. He had heard of such things as reincarna-
tion!

But his mind was set against the acceptance of any such
nonsense. Of all men, none was more earthly-minded,
more concerned with the affairs of the moment only, than
Carrick Dunmore. And, for that reason, he was shocked
and upset to the core of his being. Indeed, he had to grip
the back of his chair and look at the portrait again and
again.

He turned toward Elizabeth Furneaux, at last, and saw
that she was looking first at the picture and then at him in
fully as great amazement as he suffered.

"It's the same! It's the very same!" she said. She rubbed
her knuckles across her eyes. "Good heavens, Carrick,"
she exclaimed, "I must be losing my wits! Such things
can't be!"

She went hastily to the window and threw it open, and
he followed her, very glad of that air.

"We'll have a look at it in the sun," said he firmly.

He brought the picture, therefore, straight to the window and held it where the sun flooded across it.

There was, at first, an effect of making the whole thing
vanish in confusion, which was perhaps caused by the
gleam of the broken surface of the paint, and of the var-
nish which someone had applied some century or so before to preserve the original, apparently. But, when Carrick Dunmore's eye grew accustomed to the thing, he
could see all that he had seen before, and even more.
There was the effect of standing before a mirror with a
very poor backing of rust instead of quicksilver, but as
much as could be seen was perfect, in his eye.

Elizabeth Furneaux, her eyes staring rather wildly, held
the picture beside him and looked at him and then at it,
studying with a frown that grew more dark and lips that
were more and more compressed. At length she went silently to the wall and hung the picture in its place. When

she turned to Carrick Dunmore, she looked plainly fright-ened.

"Carrick," she said. "I don't know— What are you? A ghost?"

"Ghosts don't eat four pounds of beefsteak," said he.

She smiled faintly.

"This is something like algebra and advanced chemis-try," said she. "I can't get my hand upon it. I can't begin to understand it. But the thing's there! You are Carrick Dunmore!"

At this, Carrick answered grimly: "He slapped the face of the King of Scotland, took an earl's castle, and put a whole herd of cattle in each vest pocket when he went out for a walk. Will you say that I'm Carrick Dunmore?"

Her glance steadied on him.

"You speak perfectly well, Carrick," she said, "when you forget yourself. You're only ungrammatical because you're careless! Well, about the similarity between you and the picture—it isn't just the features that matter to me. It's the expression. That's the amazing thing. The ex-pression is just the same!"

"It is!" admitted he finally, and he drew in a quick breath; he still had need of air!

She concluded briefly: "People don't have the same ex-pression without having the same sort of mind and nature —I—but I don't want to talk about it. It's too spooky!"

He agreed with her. It fairly made his flesh crawl, and he was glad to go outdoors with her a moment later. She pulled on a pair of old gloves and tied a leather apron around her.

"What are you going to do, Elizabeth?" he asked.

"I'm going out to the blacksmith shop. There's a broken brake rod that I have to weld."

He stared as he answered: "You? Weld it?"

"I can do all sorts of odd jobs," said she, and smiled at him.

He went with her without a word, and found the black-smith shop quite a spacious shed on the edge of the corral. Around it was the usual junk heap which accumulates on an old ranch—broken wheels, ribs of iron, a rake with a sagging back, a decrepit mowing machine, tangles of wire and barrel hoops of iron, and some fifty more items. Inside, the place seemed thoroughly gone to pieces. The roof was partly gone, and a sheathing of tin insufficiently replaced the shingles in two places. There were few tools and much junk; everything was very old; and the iron curled back from the much-battered faces of the hammers.

However, she went to work at once on the brake rod. It was a clumsy job because of its length, but Dunmore helped her by handling the weight of the rod while she worked the bellows and attended to the fire. She, too, did the hammering when the glowing iron was brought from the fire—he saw her set her teeth and apply the strokes quickly and with skill; the sparks showered; and it seemed to him that he never before had been so little a man as he was now!

The welding was finished in an amazingly short time, the tempering and cooling accomplished, and then he carried out the rod and helped her refasten it beneath the wagon. It was an old, two-ton, wooden affair, with the wheels sagging in and out in perilous attitudes.

"Is that your best?" he asked her.

"That's our best!" she assured him. "Carrick, I know you want to be riding on. Don't you bother about these odd jobs now. I know you'd like to stay and help, but you have your own life to lead."

He took a long breath. Then he said: "Elizabeth, there's not a shadow of doubt that I'm a Dunmore of the old line. That picture was enough to wipe out any such idea. I've got to stay here and do my share."

"It's no use, Carrick," she assured him, without bitterness. "The family fortunes have been skidding for so long that it would take ten men digging their heels in to stop them going downhill. Tie yourself to something that's going up, not down. There's no use in that, you know!"

He looked vaguely around him.

Everything that he saw was sagging. The fence posts stood at odd angles, showing plainly that they were rotted away at the bottom; the barbed wire drooped or hung in festoons; the back of the barn had fallen in, and the eastern end of it, on the nearest side, was quite broken through.

"Elizabeth, is that pile of shakes intended for the roof?" said he.

"Yes, for the roof of the barn. When I have a chance to put in a couple of days, before the rains?"

"You'd climb up there and fix the thing?"

"Yes. I've done harder things than that, since Rodman left."

"Rodman—what sort of a fellow?" he asked tersely.

"Rodman—is twenty-one!" she said, after a moment of hesitation. "He's a good boy, too. But you can't blame a youngster for growing tired of such a life as this, can you?"

He shrugged his shoulders.

"I'm goin' to fix that roof!" said he, and he marched straight to the task.

As he went, his heart swelled. When he looked about him at the signs of wreck and ruinous age, it no longer made him hopeless, but instead, it filled him with determination; and when he sat on the roof looking over the task to be accomplished, he already, in his mind's eye, had repaired every flaw, had covered the land of the ranch with cattle, had enlarged its boundaries, and placed a hired man in the garden, a cook in the kitchen, and put Elizabeth at a tea table in the living room in a pleasant summer frock.

He roused himself from this reverie and took more careful note of the condition of the roof. It was very bad. The shakes had in part worked loose, rotting away around the nails that held them, and in part they had been clean stripped away by strong winter winds.

So he went down the ladder and began carrying up bundles of shakes.

It was stiff work. The big bundles weighed a hundred pounds and more apiece, and as he toiled up the ladder, the hot sun made the moisture pour down his face, down his breast and back. Wood dust, too, fell down his neck and began to set up an itching, and before he had brought up two burdens, his fingers were filled with splinters.

However, he set his teeth, paused only to swear at the extraordinary heat of the roof, which had been well-baked in the sun, and then set about laying the shakes.

He put on half a dozen.

It was not a simple task, no matter how it looked. He knew that Elizabeth Furneaux would have done the thing ten times as quickly and ten times as well as he; but the craft which enabled him to juggle five knives at once seemed utterly useless for the purpose of handling a hammer. He barked his own fingers twice, and the nails bent under his strokes as though they were made of wax.

He began to swear, slowly, softly, but with intense viciousness!

He went down the ladder, after a time, for a drink, and walked to the house to get it fresh and cold from the windmill. The water was like ice, with a delicious taste, and he drank deep of it. Then he sat down on an old bench and took off his hat. It was very pleasant here! The coolness soaked into him; water was dripping, and the wheel high above him whirred and hummed, while the pump rod heaved busily up and down. The water it raised poured with hollow-sounding bursts into the almost emptied tank, and to this music he listened with wonderful content, thinking how delightful it was for the very wind that blows to be harnessed to the works of man! There might even be machines invented, one day, for the covering of roofs with shakes and shingles; and he busied his mind for a moment with a rather formless conceiving of such an affair. His idea grew gradually more dim—and presently he wakened to find Elizabeth Furneaux standing before him, saying, "It's lunch time, Carrick!"

# VIII

## • A GOOD START •

CARRICK started up with a spinning brain.

"Why—I just sort of dropped off—" he began.

"You shouldn't have tried work to-day," said Elizabeth. "You're not fit, yet. It's much too soon after your accident!"

She turned toward the house. "Come along!" said she.

"Wait a minute, Elizabeth," he begged. "Turn about and look at me, will you?"

She obeyed, and he looked searchingly into her face to try to discover scorn, and contempt, and disappointment in it. There was no shadow, however. She was as bright and as cheerful as ever.

"Elizabeth," he said, "is it possible that you really aren't disgusted with me?"

"For what?" she said.

"For starting to do so much. I was going to cover the roof of the barn—all sorts of things—and I've sat down here and gone to sleep!"

"You're tired," said she.

"I'm mighty near always tired," he answered, "when there's any work to do. Nothing like the idea of work to keep me in bed of a morning, for instance!"

She smiled at him and nodded; then she shook a warning finger.

"Don't try to grow conscience," she said, "because it's the one crop that a Carrick Dunmore never could raise, I'm sure."

"No," he admitted, "I've got on without being bothered much by it until now—"

He paused.

"Have you forgotten what I told you about Carrick Dunmore the First?" asked Elizabeth.

"I'm remembering. He was a man."

"Who never worked! Do you remember, Carrick? When the earl first saw him, he was juggling in the street of the village—"

He started.

"Don't tell me that you're a juggler, too!" Elizabeth exclaimed.

He wiped his forehead.

"Don't matter," said he. "But—Elizabeth, tell me one thing. Is there anything I can do to help you—that's not work? It makes me pretty sick to have to admit that, but I'm not a worker. I've got no strength for it—no strength in the brain, I mean!"

He was taken by an impulse that made him stand close to her and catch both her hands.

"D'you think I'm talkin' like a fool?" said he. "Or—"

She was serious at once.

"You've no obligation to this house, Carrick," said she.

"Then why's my picture hanging inside it?" said he.

Her eyes wandered; then they came back to his face with a snap.

"The fact is that you might walk into a lion's den for me, Carrick," she said, without smiling in the least.

"Give me the street and number of the lions," said he, "and tell me what was in the purse you dropped there?"

"I'll tell you," said she. "There's a twenty-one-year-old boy now herding with Jim Tankerton's gang. Go get him and bring him safe home before he has a chance to commit more crimes—hanging crimes, Carrick!"

Suddenly, she was trembling.

"Don't answer quickly! Don't answer quickly, Carrick. But think—think a moment!"

"Tankerton?" he repeated slowly.

"Yes, Tankerton. Jim Tankerton. You couldn't find a harder man to deal with!"

Instinctively he turned toward the mountains. The brown foothills rolled away into smoky blue, which was spotted here and there with streaks of white which might be the gleam of a cloud or of the snow on a distant peak.

Carrick Dunmore laughed softly. "That's my road, Elizabeth," he said. "That's Tankerton's hangout, isn't it?"

She looked white and sick, and her mouth twisted a little to one side as she watched him.

"Yes," said she faintly. "Heaven forgive me for letting the idea come into your mind! Oh, you know of Tankerton, but you can't know all that we do in this part of the world. There is no other evil, no other supreme, overmastering, and exquisitely complete evil except Tankerton!"

"I've heard a bit about him, here and there," said he, "but you see how it is? What right has he got over there on my ground?"

"What ground, Carrick? What do you mean?"

"Why, Elizabeth, I mean the blue, yonder, and all the roads that climb out of sight into the horizon blue. That's the land of the first Carrick Dunmore, and I'd say that I'd ought to have the same right, eh? Don't you think no more about it. I'm off."

"Not before lunch, Carrick!"

"I wouldn't trust myself," he said bitterly. "I might start to thinking about the long, hot trail that's lyin' ahead of

me, and the first thing you know, you'd have to wake me
up for supper. No, no, Elizabeth, I'm startin' now. As
quick as I can make up my pack and slap it onto the back
of Excuse Me!"

She did not speak another word in dissuasion but went
meekly about working on the pack. She put up a quantity
of food for him, since, as she pointed out, he would be following a road which rarely touched houses, and he would
probably have to sleep out in the open night. So the pack
was made up, wrapped securely in a tarpaulin, and lashed
behind the saddle upon the back of Excuse Me. She accepted this new burden with an angry stamping and rattling of her bridle, but she did not attempt to buck it off.
Then Elizabeth Furneaux opened the corral gate for her
champion to get out onto the road.

She stood beside the open panel with the same troubled
look and white face which he had seen before, so he
checked the mare close beside her, as he came out, and
leaned above her.

"Look here, Elizabeth," said he, "I'm going to tell you
something that you can write down as true, and all true.
It's about me. I've never done a square day's work in my
life; nor a half day's work, I've been a loafer, a hard drink-
er, a dead beat, borrowin' money and never payin' it
back—I've been a tramp, that's all. So no matter what
happens to me on this trail, there's no difference. You ain't
takin' the bread out of no child's mouth, and they's no girl
that's gunna break her heart because I never come back."

She listened to him with an attempt at a smile, which
failed.

Then he added: "But I will come back, after all. That's
my country; if I can't get on in the horizon blue, I'll never
get on anywhere!"

"Dear Carrick! Bless you!" said she.

He went past her into the road; then the mare stretched
into a gallop as long and as easily rhythmical as the swing
of a wave. He looked back only once and waved his hat to
the figure which was dwindling at the gate. His glance
could embrace all the place—the barn, the sheds, the land,
the trees, the house white above them.

Then a hilltop swelled behind him, and all was lost to
him.

He fell into an odd dream; and rousing himself from that, it seemed to him as though he actually had passed into a new world.

This sense, perhaps, came to him because already his mind was casting forward into mountains through which he never had ridden before. And it might also have been that he was now really feeling the impact of the shock which he had received that day, when he found that his face was the face of the first of the Dunmores.

It took his breath; it gave him an odd sense of disaster impending; but it also gave him a prodigious feeling of liberty as though, in very fact, he were now the possessor of some feudal castle, and of a hard-riding band of retainers, who would follow him wherever adventure and loot seemed in sight. And to that blue land of the mountains he turned his face with a strange assurance, and rode the mare eagerly on, even leaning a bit in the saddle, as a child might do, hurrying home.

Hoofs rang on the road behind him. Two hard-galloping riders pulled up beside the mare.

"Hey, Carrie! Is that Excuse Me? Did she turn out a square one after all?" asked one of the riders.

"She's turned out pretty square," he told them.

"I'd pay five hundred just for the looks of her!"

"She ain't for sale."

"That's what you always say. I remember when you had the gray hoss that jumped so well. But when you're broke and tight, you'll sell, right enough, and not for five hundred!"

The second man broke in: "Look here, Carrie. They want you over to the crossroads. You'll have free drinks there! They still got the knives sticking in the wall just where you left 'em after drawin' the silhouette of Pete Logan with 'em. Hey, Carrie, come on along. It won't be no piker's party. It'll be just the kind that you want to sit in on!"

"I can't go," said Dunmore. "Can't even think of goin'. But who's there?"

"Who's there? Why everybody, I tell you! There's Bill Clay, and the Guernseys, and Oliver Pike, and the Jensens, and Captain Patrick—"

"Is the captain there?"

"Why, sure, it was him that sent us over to get you, and Miss Furneaux, she said that you'd gone up the road this way for a little outing on Excuse Me."

"Captain Patrick? How is he getting on?"

"He's flush," was the eager assurance. "And he says that he'd rather have you across the table from him than any other gent that ever tipped a glass in the world! He's got a belt of gold dust that you could wrap around you twice, and it's loaded, every inch of it. He's so heavy with gold that his heels hit hard when he walks. He goes upstairs like he was carryin' a hod. Come on along, Carrie. You might as well get in on some of it as the next gent, eh?"

A whirl of wind raised the dust on the road before them and whirled it into the face of Carrick Dunmore. It was very hot, and the way dipped up and down interminably, and, after all, a man about to undertake such an important enterprise ought to relax a little—

"There's snow on old Digger Mountain, ain't there?" asked one of the pair who had overhauled him.

He looked in that direction, and saw the gleam of the snow strike through the horizon blue of his new-found land, his own country. And suddenly he touched the mare with his heels, and she bounded away like a deer.

That was his answer. A very rude one, and one that allowed no answer, for the pair could not match strides for one minute with the gallop of Excuse Me.

# IX

### • KNIVES THAT CUT SILENCE •

IT had just rained in Harpersville, and "Chuck" Harper, builder, proprietor, and manager of the town hotel, author, also, of its name and principal reason for its existence, came out from his hostelry and sat in a chair which he gripped with his knees, as though it were a horse. In this position, with his hat on the back of his head, he set to work whittling a stick of sugar pine, and to this he gave his utmost attention. He was not trying to reduce the stick to any definite design; he was working with such pains merely to see how thin a slice he could remove with the knife, which was sharp as a razor. The long, translucent whittlings were so light that they almost floated in the wind, and they fell one by one about his feet.

Every ten minutes, punctually, he raised his head and showed a massive, sullen face. He cast a gloomy look up and down the roads which were wound about the mountainside and entered the village and, bending his thick neck, he returned to his whittling.

There was a rattle of rain among the trees every time the wind slapped them; but the clouds had long ago melted, and the sun was raising steam from the pools and the silver streaks of water which lay in the ruts along the road. But Chuck Harper gave no heed to the face and form of nature. He watched the road, and communed with his own dark mind.

Presently, the door of the hotel banged. His wife, a raw-boned half-breed of his own age—which was less than forty—sang out in a nasal voice:

"Hey, Paw!"

He did not answer.

"Paw!" she shouted.

A touch of contentment appeared upon the savage face of Chuck Harper.

"Paw!" she screamed. "Are you gunna hear me?"

"I hear you," said the giant, without turning.

"You hear me, do you? Then I wanta know, are you gunna cut that wood for me?"

He squinted down the stick and removed a shaving as thin as a feather.

"Paw, I'm askin' ye are you gunna cut that wood for me?"

He raised his head, but did not answer.

"Paw, confound you, are you gunna cut that wood!" she shrieked.

"Naw," said he, and resumed his whittling.

This brief answer brought the woman to the verge of a veritable insanity of rage. For a time she lingered at the door, her clenched hands raised above her head, speech-less with the imprecations that crowded up into her throat. Then the door crashed heavily as she went inside.

Her husband raised his head again, and there was almost a smile of contentment upon his face.

At this moment, a rider came about the bend of the road on a dark, dappled-chestnut mare, a thing of such deerlike beauty that even the brutal eyes of Chuck Harper glimmered a little as he watched the animal come closer. She trotted with a movement so sweeping and soft that the rider hardly stirred in the saddle, and Chuck Harper turned his attention to the face of that rider for a single moment, and saw a man who smiled as he came.

Down dropped the head of Chuck again, and once more he whittled.

"Whoa, girl," said the stranger, drawing rein. "Is this Harpersville?"

Chuck did not hear.

"I'd like to know," said the other, "if this is Harpersville?"

Chuck did not speak. But his heart was eased by this new opportunity to annoy another. The daily torture of his wife was monotonous and would have been hopelessly so if it had not been that he knew that, sooner or later, she would try to slip a knife between his ribs while he slept. But strangers were a fair game, sweet to the tooth of Chuck.

His silence, however, was presently matched by the silence of the newcomer. Chuck, interested, saw the man dismount at the watering trough and watch his mare drink. Then he turned and stretched himself.

He was not a giant like Chuck, but he was big, and there was a peculiar sleekness about his neck and shoulders that suggested useless bulk and softness. This in turn was more or less denied by the extraordinary lightness of his step. Chuck observed these details not because he was greatly intrigued, but because he could not help noting every physical detail, any more than a hungry wolf can help being alert. There was one deathless craving in the soul of the hotelkeeper, and that was for trouble.

"Steady, Excuse Me!" said the stranger to his horse.

He turned from her, and at that, she followed him like a

dog at the heel. Chuck regarded the pair with disgust, because he looked upon horses as stupid means of travel and had no more affection for them than he would have had for a machine.

The stranger, however, spoke gently to the mare as he went toward the end of the water trough where there was a massive stone, one that had rolled down the mountainside the year before and luckily lodged here. It was of enormous weight and, if it had come faster, would have plunged straight through the hotel, from front to back.

The stranger, going to it, leaned, patted it, and bent over. Then Chuck was aware that the man was straightening; there was a sound of suction, and the burden came free.

Next, the fellow was bearing it, straight toward him walking slowly, but without bulging eyes, or a convulsed face, or any sign that this was a crushing burden.

He advanced. Wonder and awe leaped into the soul of Chuck, and he started up from his chair. The other came straight on and dropped the rock beside the chair.

"Sit down," said he. "Now we're fixed comfortable for a chat."

Chuck Harper sat down.

Amazement still flodded his soul, but he was enraged because he had been so startled by this exhibition of uncanny power that he had not been able to control his emotion. It was the first time since he could remember that he had been so unmanned, and fury gathered in his heart.

So, as he sat down, he resumed his whittling, and said nothing.

"This is a pretty good sort of a hangout," said the other. "I'll introduce myself. I'm Carrick Dunmore."

He waited. Chuck said no word.

Side by side they sat, silently.

"I'm Carrick Dunmore," said the newcomer.

And still Chuck was silent. He felt that this would be the beginning of a fight, and that was what he yearned for. The lust of battle was as hot as fire in his brutal heart, and already his lips were twitching at the corners, like the lips of a bulldog when it sees an enemy.

The stranger did not persist in his introduction.

Instead, he took from his belt a knife. It was a long,

rather straight-bladed affair, looking quite unlike any hunting knife that Chuck ever had seen before. This weapon, Dunmore flicked into the air. It sailed up fully thirty feet, hung for an instant in a sparkling whirl, then dropped rapidly down.

Such a knife, with so sharp and narrow a point, could drop through the skull of a man as though it were pricking an eggshell, and Chuck Harper instinctively ducked to the side.

The knife fell, but landing in the hand of the stranger it was flicked up again, and at its heels another followed.

Chuck Harper, disgusted because he had allowed himself to exhibit concern again, ground his teeth, and turned a violent red, but, nevertheless, he could not help feeling an interest in the work of those knives.

A knife was, indeed, a weapon which he favored even over a gun. It might produce less harm at long range, but at close quarters or in a crowd it was the very delight of his heart!

This stranger was a master worker. The knives flew up as a pair and descended together, and then flicked upward again, crossed in the air, and dropped almost simultaneously into the right hand—almost simultaneously, but not quite, for that cunning hand was able to give each an upward impulse again.

And then the two big knives were snatched from the bright sun and disappeared. Big Chuck Harper gasped audibly. Then, looking down at the belt of the stranger, he saw that the knives were actually in the leather sheaths which fitted there, one beneath the other, yet he could have sworn that no human hand had placed them where they belonged.

"You were saying about your name?" said Dunmore.

"I'm Chuck Harper."

"Chuck, I'm glad to know you. When a gent has been sashaying around through these mountains and not meeting anything but a squirrel or a rabbit—just enough company to keep him from starving—it's pretty good to run into a man, again. Mighty good to hear some conversation, and all that."

Chuck, brooding darkly, said nothing. He was contemplating two conceptions, both of which were painfully bright in his mind—one was the power which had lifted that bulk of stone. The other was the speed and craft of hand which had made the heavy pair of knives float and dance like bubbles in the air.

"If you're Harper," ran on the other with the same good-natured smoothness, "then I suppose that this is Harpersville?"

He hardly waited to appreciate Chuck's silence, but went on: "Of course, it is, and that means it's where Jim Tankerton comes for his vacations, as one might say. Is that right?"

Chuck Harper pressed his lips together and gathered anger in his heart.

"That bein' so, here's where I hang up my hat, but I might as well put up the mare, first. I'll just take her around to the stable."

He stood up and went to the mare.

"The stable's full," said Harper.

But now it was Dunmore who did not seem to hear. He broke into a whistle and started around the corner of the hotel, the mare following.

"There ain't no room for her!" called Harper.

"Why, any little corner'll do for her," said Dunmore, and went on his way, the corner of the hotel quickly shutting him from view.


# X

### • A ROOM WITH A VIEW •


CHUCK HARPER fidgeted in his chair.

Above all things, he hated to take note of any stranger. Indeed, there was only one human being in the world whom he feared and respected, but now he felt that he had been pressed into a corner, and that he would have to respond!

He first slid a heavy Colt from an armpit holster and

saw that it was in good working order. Then he rose, shrugged his shoulders more comfortably into the loose raincoat that covered them, and tugged his hat lower over his eyes.

Then he went with long strides in pursuit of the new-comer.

When he came to the door of the barn, he could hear the rustle of hay being forked down out of the mow, and the whistling of the stranger in the loft. And when he stalked down the aisle of the stable he found cause to stop with a jolt; for in the one box stall of which he boasted there now stood not the tall and powerful bay gelding which had been there in the morning, but the sleek and lovely mare on which Dunmore had just arrived.

He rubbed his eyes, hardly believing what he saw, and now the stranger came down the ladder from the mow and dropped lightly to the floor.

Chuck Harper laid a heavy hand upon his shoulder.

"You changed them hosses, you—" began Chuck.

He stopped himself, there. For his gripping fingers were working upon a mass of rubbery muscle. Suddenly, he understood that this young man was not sleek with fat but with sheer might, and it discouraged Harper's rage at once.

Dunmore shrugged his shoulders, and the hand of his host fell away.

"Sure I changed 'em," said he. "You take this here part of the world, partner, and, of course, you know that a gent always gives room to a lady. When I seen that big hoss standin' in there all by himself, I took a look in his eye, and plain as day he was sayin' 'Ladies first!' 'Thanks, old boy,' says I. I put him in that next stall and tied Excuse Me in here. She just seemed to fit, as you can see for yourself. Where's the grain bin?"

Mr. Harper had grown a dark and swollen purple, but somehow it seemed impossible for him to find the proper word with which to answer.

"Here we are," went on Dunmore. "Thanks!"

He lifted the lid of the big oatbin in the corner and dipped out a large measure, which he carried into the box stall, and dumped into the feedbox there.

"Look here—" began Harper.

"Yes, look at her!" said Dunmore, sleeking the neck of the mare with a fond hand. "Look at her try to stand on her head in that feedbox! Greedy pig, ain't she? But I never seen a hoss worth his oats that didn't want to swaller them alive!"

He came out from the stall.

"I'd better go and see about rooms now," said he.

"They ain't no room for you in that house," said Harper grimly.

"Why," said Dunmore cheerfully, "where I roll down my blankets is no worry to me!"

And he shouldered his pack and stepped lightly past his big host, and through the door of the barn toward the hotel.

Chuck Harper could hardly believe his eyes or his ears. He thought first of rushing after this youth and falling upon him with naked hands. Those mighty maulers of his had beaten many a strong man to a pulp, but something checked him now. It was the thought of the lifting of the great rock in front of the house.

For that matter, the thing might not be as difficult as he imagined!

His next impulse was to snatch out his revolver and send a bullet through the back of this calm-mannered interloper. But he remembered what the judge had said about "self-defense" the last time he was in court, and the memory made Chuck snarl like a savage but half-cowed dog.

Finally, he hurried from the barn in pursuit, but already the stranger was at the back door, speaking to Mrs. Harper.

"Keep that gent out!" roared Harper.

But at that moment Dunmore had stepped through into the interior.

"What's your name and what you want?" Harper heard his wife shrilling. "You git out of here! Chuck don't want you!"

Harper could hear a polite murmur in response. Then a door banged, and he came up into the kitchen with a leap, to find that his wife was raging at the dining-room door, and shaking the knob of it furiously.

"Chuck, he walked through here and locked the door

after him. I never seen anything like it. It's drivin' me crazy! What's he mean? Who is he? Is he drunk? I'd like to scratch his eyes out!"

Chuck Harper laughed. In the pure excess of passion he laughed, and that laughter died into a whining snarl. He tried the knob of the door, assuring himself that the impossible was indeed possible. Then he flung out of the kitchen.

His wife clutched at him and was dragged a little way with the rushing bulk of him.

She stammered: "Don't you do no murder, Chuck! Mind you, Chuck, don't you pull no knife on him———"

"I'm gonna bust him wide open!" gasped Chuck Harper, and raced around the corner of the house.

At the front corner, he slipped, such was the recklessness of his abandon, and fell heavily to the ground, skinning the palm of one hand.

It was like giving the spur to a runaway horse. He bounded to his feet again with a groan of intolerable anguish. It seemed to Chuck that he was entering a dark mist, a fog of sooty smoke, so did his emotion master him.

And, with a bound, he came to the front door and wrenched at it.

The heavy bolt answered him with a jangle and crash. That was all!

He recoiled for a step.

"My own house, too!" said Chuck.

It was one of his favorite diversions to work himself into a towering rage about trifles, about nothing at all. It was the one constant cup of joy for him to see others cringe and cower, not knowing why he was so maddened. But now he found an excuse for every violence.

For the first time in his life, murder itself would be justifiable, nay praiseworthy!

For what court can reprove a citizen for defending his hearth and home from the aggression of a stranger? He would be applauded, men would shake him by the hand, his own wife would smile upon the deed of valor———

And Chuck Harper threw his arms above his head and cried out in a stifled voice of joy.

Then he rushed for the first window.

He jerked it up a few inches, but there it stuck, for the sash was warped and would not run in the groove.

"By grab," said Harper, "the whole world's gone crazy!"

He, at that moment, heard the stranger pass with a light step and a whistle into the front room, the big room, the room which the great Tankerton himself honored with his presence when he deigned to come here for the night, and at this, the brain of Chuck Harper was somewhat befogged again.

He leaped for the next window, jerked it wide, and sprang in.

His Colt was in his hand as he crashed up the stairs.

He was so drunk with fury that at the landing he lurched into the wall and careened back against the railing, but he paid no heed to this. He felt in himself power enough to rip the house apart like a matchbox to get at the insulting man who called himself Dunmore.

So he came to the upper hall, and the boarding groaned and creaked beneath his weight as he plunged down the corridor of the corner room, the chosen room, the room from which he and his wife so gladly had removed themselves and their belongings in order to make way for the great James Tankerton.

The door was wide. He drove in, gun in hand, with a bellow like the roar of a bull as it closes in battle with a peer.

But suddenly he saw that the room was empty!

He whirled about.

There beside the door stood the stranger, still whistling softly, and carelessly, hip-high, he held a revolver that pointed straight at his host.

"Gosh!" ejaculated Chuck Harper, and remembered suddenly that life was sweet!

The gun slipped from his unnerved fingers and dropped upon the very pack which Dunmore had flung upon the floor.

"You're pretty modest about your place," said Dunmore gently. "I guess I figger out how it is. You'd like to have a bang-up, fashionable hotel, with hot and cold runnin' water in every room and all that, but for an ordinary cowpuncher like me, I don't see anything wrong with this little old room. It just about fits me, take it all in all!"

He made a gesture, and Chuck Harper saw that the gesturing hand was empty of any gun. He thought for an instant that he had imagined the sight of the leveled weapon of the moment before, but then he knew that he could not have dreamed the thing. But by some mysterious sleight of hand the other had conjured the gun out of view.

Perhaps it was merely shaken up his sleeve, and ready instantly to drop again into his fingers.

"This here room," panted Harper in a hoarse and shaken voice, "is already took."

And suddenly he realized that what he said would make no difference. This genial, pleasant-mannered fellow would simply help himself to what he chose, and smile for answer to every argument.

"You've got other rooms for him," said Dunmore. "But I'll tell you how it is—I need sun. And this here room has a south window. I need a view, too, and it's got another window that looks over the mountains yonder."

Deliberately he turned his back and walked to the nearest window and looked out.

Chuck Harper could not believe his eyes. Here was a man who turned his back upon him, and stood at a window without a gun in his hands, and on the floor at Harper's feet, rested his own gun, the handle invitingly toward him! It would be an instant's work to scoop up that weapon and use it. And yet Harper hesitated; and gradually his blood turned cold. What could an ordinary man do against a magician! He only bawled out impotently: "You know who's got this room, young feller?"

"Oh," said Dunmore, "Tankerton won't want to have any trouble with me!"

# XI

## • STICKY STUFF •

IT was a week later that Chuck Harper walked in the woods behind the hotel with a little dark-skinned man, a handsome little fellow, if it had not been that his eyes were like the eyes of a ferret, so brightly twinkling and so ill at ease.

He wore a continual smile, and had a habit of keeping his eyes fixed upon the ground, as though he were hunting for something there, then lifting them suddenly as though he had found it in his companion's face. Despite his smallness, Chuck Harper treated him with the greatest respect, for this was Lynn Tucker, who, in any other part of the world, might have been considered a very proper head for the most formidable gang of desperadoes. But this was the domain of Jim Tankerton, and, therefore, Tucker was not in command; men rated him as a sort of second lieutenant, beneath Tankerton himself and that wily old snake of wisdom and poison, Doctor Legges.

Chuck Harper knew all that others knew about Lynn Tucker, and, therefore, he talked chiefly when questions were asked of him. Already he had told of the coming of Dunmore, and Tucker had surveyed the great rock and even tried to budge it with his own lean hands.

"He's quite a man," said Lynn Tucker calmly.

So they went back into the woods and continued their talk.

"What does he want?" asked Tucker.

"That I dunno. Sometimes I think that all he wants is to live here free! I asked him for his week to-day, and he says that he's hurt and plumb surprised that he should be asked for his money before he's been here a month."

"Did he say that?"

"He did. Says that he wasn't used to being treated that

way, and that he would hate to begin now to have his credit doubted, but seein' as I was livin' away up here in the mountains, where they didn't understand the latest way of doin' things, he'd be glad to forgive me and overlook it."

"Does he talk that way?"

"He don't talk no other way, at all. If you was to go up and swear at him, he'd admire the fine flow of words that you had and ask where you'd studied it out, and was it all original, and did nobody help you with some of the big ones."

Tucker nodded and smiled at the ground, as usual.

"D'you think he has money?"

"I wished I thought so, but I figger that I'm keepin' him free of charge!"

"What makes you do it? You got the law to help you."

The landlord hesitated and then scratched the stubble on his chin.

"The law and me ain't chums," said he. "We've never been pals, and the further off that I keep from it, the better it suits me, I'll tell a man!"

"It's a pretty hard case," said Tucker.

"He eats me out of house and home. He's a hog! You could feed four men and a boy on what he pours down his throat every day. The wife, she sets up a feed for him, and he eats it and then he says he knows that she's holdin' back a little surprise on him. And he walks over and unlocks the pantry door——"

"Why don't you keep the key out of the lock?"

"He's gone and made himself a master key that fits every door in the house! I say, he opens the pantry door and goes in and comes out with a saddle of venison.

" 'Leave that be!' sings out the wife.

"He shakes his finger at her.

" 'You're gunna surprise me with this beautiful venison on Sunday, Mrs. Harper,' says he, 'but right here it's a pleasant enough surprise. What with walkin' over the hills and all, I've worked up a pretty fair appetite!'

"And then he slices off some steaks a couple of inches thick and fries them himself, or broils 'em over the stove."

"And while he's got both hands full, you wear a gun, old son!"

"I've seen him keep five things in the air!"

"Juggler, eh?"

"He is! Knives, and such, is his specialty. Knives sharp as a razor and——"

A gun barked in the distance, and the long echoes rebounded dimly along the forested slopes. Lynn Tucker lifted his head.

"Who's that?" he said.

"That's him, of course. Goes out every day and comes back with a batch of squirrels. Says that he's fond of squirrel meat, and he orders up a stew of rabbit and squirrel. Eats about ten pounds of it at every set-down!"

Lynn Tucker looked through a gap in the trees across the depth of the gorge, soft with blues in the hollow, and at the white mountains of the distance, gently veiled with blue, also.

He nodded.

"I begin to get a sort of an idea of this here gent," he said, in his quiet way.

"Maybe it'd give you a mite clearer idea," said the landlord, "if you was to know that the ways that he kills those squirrels is with a Colt!"

"A .45?"

"A .45 is what he uses, son!"

The other clucked, as though to encourage a tired horse.

"We'll have to see to this here!" said he. "I'd better keep out of sight till evenin,' maybe!"

That, accordingly, was what he did, and remained hidden, in fact, in the cellar of the hotel until the dark came, and then until a tap came at the door at the head of the stairs.

He stole up, soundless as a shadow, and Chuck Harper opened the door for him. Chuck carried a lantern, and above it, his face was pale and his little eyes staring.

"Are you ready?" asked Chuck excitedly.

"I'm ready. How long ago did he go to bed?"

"About an hour."

"Is he asleep?"

"Asleep, and snorin' like a pig."

"I like a man that sleeps as hard as that. It's sort of

honest!" said Lynn Tucker, and he smiled in such a way that his host smiled in answer.

They went into the kitchen, and there Mrs. Harper, looking grim and hard as an image of stone, poured out a cup of black coffee for the gunman. He thanked her pleasantly, and sipped it, warming his hands alternately above the stove in order to get the chill of the cellar from his bones.

Presently he said:

"I'd better be steppin' on. So long for a minute or two, folks."

The others looked fixedly at him, but said not a word in reply as little Lynn Tucker slipped through the doorway and went very softly up the stairs.

He moved not very slowly, but with infinite care, walking always close to the wall, where there is less chance of a footfall making the boarding creak. And so he came to the door of the sleeper.

Here he paused, and listened contentedly to deep, regular snoring. After that he tried the door and was delighted when he found that it had not been locked.

This reduced everything to the utmost simplicity. Already he knew every detail of the room. He had paced it off, also, and his accurate brain knew how many steps and a half to the foot or the head of the bed from the door, and the exact direction, and how many steps to the window opposite, and where the chairs generally stood. A blind man hardly could have been more at home in the darkness than he was when he pushed the door open and stepped into the room, with the snoring resounding soft and deep about him.

He paused, once inside the door. There was only one thing that bothered him, and that was an odd feeling about the floor on which he stood, as though it were covered with something softer than carpet. So he shifted his gun to his left hand and with the right hand he touched the floor.

To his amazement, it was very sticky!

And at this moment he was aware that the snoring had ceased. Something fanned him with a gust of wind and the door crashed behind his back, while a broad flood of light snapped into his face.

Lynn Tucker, thoroughly trapped, did not give up.

He lurched for the floor, and, as he fell, he transferred the revolver to his shooting hand.

Falling, too, he noted several other things with the rapidity of a wild animal. One was that there was a quantity of gleaming liquid on the floor about his feet; another was that every article of furniture had been altered in position to exactly the opposite of where it had been before; and third was that a shadowy form was rising from a bed in the rear corner of the room!

At that form he fired, but his sticky fingers could not work easily on the gun, and the next moment a hulky shadow sailed through the air and fell upon him.

He fought out from beneath the feather bed, and as he did so, the cold muzzle of a revolver pressed upon the nape of his neck. He knew that he was lost; he knew that he was dead!

And a very pleasant voice said above him:

"Well, well, partner, you must've been walkin' in your sleep, eh what? You might lay aside that gun, because it looks like it had the habit of explodin' sort of careless."

"Stand up, stranger," came the next gentle invitation, as Tucker tossed the Colt away.

And he rose with some difficulty.

By the feel and the smell he now knew what he had fallen into. It smudged his hands and knees, and for the gripping of any weapons, those hands of his were now altogether useless! So he stood dismayed, bewildered even in his ratlike, active mind, and looked at the mildly smiling face of Carrick Dunmore.

"That's a pity," said Dunmore. "That glue spilled on me, and I was gunna clean it up tonight, but I got plumb sleepy. A mighty pity! It'll take you a lot of cleanin' to fix those clothes."

Lynn Tucker said nothing, but took note of a string that ran from the bed to the door. By that string it had been jerked shut and he had been securely trapped. It was something like the snaring of a wild beast! He waited for his doom, but Dunmore went on:

"Must've scared you, sort of, when you found yourself in the wrong room, and I sure don't blame you for pullin' a gun when you stepped into that and tripped! I won't keep you from gettin' cleaned up. But I'd like to know your name, stranger?"

The other did not hesitate. There was a slight ring of meaning in that last question, and he said instantly: "I'm Lynn Tucker."

"Well, well," said Dunmore, "I'm mighty glad to meet you. Tell your boss that I'm still hopin' to see him down this way some time soon, will you?"

# XII

# • LIKE A BULLET THROUGH THE BRAIN •

IT was nearly another week before another emissary came to Harpersville from Jim Tankerton. This time it was a man with a reverend white beard and a serene face, as white and pink as the face of a baby. He was tall and heavy, but he was mounted upon a small mountain pony with a pot belly and a powerful set of limbs, which carried him along actively.

As he entered the street of the village, two women saw him first. He took off his hat, and as he bowed to them, the wind of his gallop blew out the white hair across his shoulders. They made their faces bright as they saw him, and bowed and waved in answer to his greeting, but the instant he was gone by, they scowled darkly to one another.

"Heaven help us," said one of them, "if Doctor Legges has come down here to take one of our men!"

"It'll be that lout of a Morgan, that went to the band and would not stay in it. Legges has come for him, and mark my word on it."

But it was not the lout, Morgan, that had brought the doctor down to Harpersville. Instead, he went straight to the hotel, and there he found Harper himself wielding a great ax and chopping up wood for the stove. He swung an ax of double the usual size, and his strokes were so great that they rang through the thin mountain air like the explosions of a rifle in the near distance.

Doctor Legges dismounted, and the pony, like one familiar with the place, trotted off at once to the stable.

Harper himself, at sight of the visitor, cast off all his usual sluggish discourtesy, and hastened up, tipping his hat.

"Man, man," said the doctor to him, in mild disapproval, "do not raise your hat to me! That is a salutation which the devout leave for their Creator, and the fond for women as they meet. Give me your hand, Brother Harper, and I praise Heaven that I see your honest face again!"

This greeting he spoke in an unctuous tone and a still more impressive manner. He talked like a revivalist in a less fiery moment. His voice had the ring and the resonance of a public speaker, and it was said that the doctor had, in fact, saved more than one erring soul before his practices were found out and he was hunted out of society by a sheriff's posse!

The good doctor wrung the hand of Harper in a powerful grip as he gave him this greeting, and so much was Harper impressed by the coming of this famous evildoer that his eyes actually sought the ground. He begged the doctor to come inside for a cup of coffee or a bite of food, but the doctor refused.

Instead, he whistled, and a lean-sided hound came running up to him and played about his feet. The hound had run down from the higher mountains at the heels of the doctor, and now the old man leaned and patted his head.

"Danny's feet are all muddied," said Doctor Legges, "and I wouldn't be putting your good wife out of temper by letting such a muddy dog into the house."

"As you please, Doctor Legges," said Harper. "Would you've come down here to talk to me about young Dunmore, sir?"

"Dunmore? Dunmore?" said the doctor, in affected absentness of mind. "Ah, is that the name of the youth? But first of all I wanted to ask you about our dear friend and good brother, Lynn Tucker. We haven't heard from him since he came down here."

"No," grunted Harper. "You won't hear from him for a while, because he'll be off in the woods, waitin' until his shame has settled down in his boots a little out of his heart!"

"Shame is a good Christian feeling, brother," said the doctor. "But how was Lynn Tucker shamed? By this same young Dunmore?"

"Aye, by him!" said Chuck. "And may trouble overtake him! Because when Lynn went up to his room with a gun that night, Dunmore was ready for him. He caught him with glue on the floor, the way that you might catch a bird with a limed twig."

"How did he know that Tucker was here?" asked the doctor with a touch of sharpness.

"How can I tell? Unless he read the minds of my wife and me as we sat at the supper table! Who knows how he finds out what he knows? But know it he did, and got ready a trap!"

"What did he do with Tucker?"

"Talked soft to him, the way that he always talks, and said nothing at all to him!"

"Where is he now?"

"Lyin' up in his room, sayin' that he's tired, and that he's gunna rest there, and wants his supper carried up to him——Givin' orders like he was a lord!"

"He wants his supper carried up to him, does he?" said the doctor, again leaning and patting the head of the dog. "And do you wait on him like that?"

"I would see him starve first," said Harper, "but the wife has come into a strange sort of fear of that man. She says that he's no man at all, but a rank demon, and I'm half thinking that she might be right! So we work for him and we wait on him hand and foot, and we never get a penny for it!"

"He doesn't pay?"

"Never a penny!"

"Ah, ah, ah," said the doctor, "I'm greatly afraid that he's a bold and bad young man! But this night let everything be done as he wishes it to be done. Give way to the wicked, my friend. When a man bids you walk with him a mile, walk with him two, and pray for his soul. Let your good wife cook him an excellent dinner, but before it is carried up to him, let me see it. I may wish that it should carry a peculiar blessing. Hark, man—can he see me from any window, now?"

"He may not see you now," said Chuck Harper, "but he's apt to know that you or someone's here. He can see through walls, my wife says, and I'm kinda thinkin' the same way with her!"

They finally went for a walk into the woods, and it was dusk when they returned. Then Harper went in first and learned from his wife that the stranger was in his room still, and had not come out. After this, the doctor was brought in, and the cooking of the supper was quickly concluded.

There were two thick venison steaks, and fried potatoes, bread, sirup, and a pot of coffee for the guest of the hotel. Mrs. Harper glowered as she set out the food.

But the doctor smiled on the big tray.

"What will he relish most?" he asked.

"The meat, the meat!" said Mrs. Harper. "He can eat half a cow a day. He's got a winter famine in his stomach all the day long! He's a pig, and not a man!"

"Gluttony is one of the deadly sins," said the doctor. "Now Heaven forgive him for it, but, after all, the sinful must have their lessons and their privations; spare the whip and spoil the soul of the wrongful man!"

He spread his hands above the meat, and as he did so, a little shower of white powder descended upon it.

"What is it?" asked Mrs. Harper. "What've ye done to the meat, doctor? Chuck, Chuck, I won't carry the tray up, now that this is done to it!"

"I'll carry it to him myself," said Chuck. "What do I care? This'll stop him hungerin', maybe!"

So, with a set face, he started to leave the kitchen, but the doctor cautioned him: "Smile, man, smile. There's more to be done with a smile in this world than with a cocked gun or a sharp knife!"

So big Chuck Harper went up the stairs, with the hound, Danny, scampering behind him after the smell of the meat. Presently Chuck came down again, grinning in very fact with a true malice in his face.

"He rubbed his hands when he seen that venison!" said he, "and I last seen him dabbin' the salt onto it, and slicin' off a hunk—doctor, what'll we hear? What'll he do?"

"You'll hear nothing but the sound of a fall. The wicked are up, but they must be put down," said the doctor. "That's a lesson to be learned from this, Chuck, my young friend. The wicked are up but they must descend again, and Heaven have mercy on their souls!"

He turned to Mrs. Harper. "Now, my dear," said he, "let us have a little more of that same steak, but this time we'll let salt be the single blessing on it. Where's the dog, Chuck?"

"I dunno," said Chuck, "I didn't see. He went up with me. I had something more'n dogs to think about," he added significantly. "Tell me, doctor, will it kill a man quick—like a bullet?"

"Quick—like a bullet! As much of it as the head of a pin on the tongue of a horse would kill him instantly!"

New venison steaks were now hissing and steaming in the pan as Doctor Legges went on cheerfully: "What did this foolish young man want? How was he trying to establish himself? Ah, well, that will be a thing to be determined later on, when——"

The door opened from the dining-room side and Carrick Dunmore came in, and struck a white silence upon every face.

"Go on talking, folks," said he, while Doctor Legges noted that the footfall of this man made no sound upon the floor as he crossed to the stove. "Go right on talking and don't let me upset you any."

From the nerveless hand of Mrs. Harper he took the big fork and with it turned the venison steaks; and Doctor Legges, as the man's back was turned, glanced sharply, inquiringly at Harper, as much as to say: This is the time to strike!

However, he did not have to look twice at Harper to understand that Chuck was sick with awe and fear, and incapable of raising a hand. The good doctor even slid a hand covertly inside his coat, for though he was old, he was not much more slow than an aged cat, say.

But just as the burning thought entered his mind, and his hand had crept into the breast of his coat, Carrick Dunmore turned about the stove and waved the big fork toward them.

"Nothing in the world like fryin' meat for a hungry

man!" said he. "The smell of this here, it came up to me sweeter than incense. You won't mind if a hungry man takes this turn, will you, Mrs. Harper?"

Even in her fear, her hatred mastered her and wrinkled her face as she answered:

"You got your steak already—a three-man piece of meat, too!"

"Ah, and beautifully cooked, and it sure was seasoned to the queen's taste," said Carrick Dunmore, with continued good cheer. "Only," he went on, "it wasn't me that ate it."

"Not you?" cried Mrs. Harper indignantly.

"You see, there was that little Chilton boy that had got into the house, and he come runnin' down the hall——"

"Ah—Heaven!" exclaimed Mrs. Harper, with a sick face.

Carrick Dunmore paused, and for one instant his eyes centered upon the woman's face and burned her to the soul.

"And when I went to speak to the little boy," he concluded slowly, "the dog, Danny, got at the meat. It killed him—like a bullet through the brain!"

# XIII

## • A GRATEFUL GUEST •

THE hand of the doctor froze upon the butt of the revolver within his coat, and there it remained; for the glance of Carrick Dunmore had now turned upon him and rested brightly, but steadily, on his face.

"You're a newcomer, I guess?"

"Yes," said the doctor.

"When I heard someone calling for the dog by the name of Danny, was that you?"

"No."

"You didn't own him, then?"

"Yes, I owned him."

"Well, sir," said Dunmore, "I'm mighty sorry that he died, that way. It'll cut you up a good deal. That's why you're so silent, right now, I suppose," he continued, looking with a softened eye upon Legges. "I guess if one comes right down to it, they's a lot of men that you'd rather see dead than that dog, eh?"

Though he said it in ever so casual and sympathetic a manner, the eye of the doctor gleamed with fear and then was blank again. But he merely nodded, and did not speak. He could not help noticing that, in spite of his very careless manner, this young man had the big fork always in his left hand, the right remaining free for emergencies.

"I don't know what could have happened to him. Choked on too big a bite, maybe? But choking takes a little time, eh? What would you say could've killed him?"

"Heart disease, no doubt," said Doctor Legges calmly.

"Heart disease?" said the other. "Why, sure! That must've been it. Got himself all weakened from running around in this here thin mountain air. Maybe he run up the stairs too fast, just now, and then he had the excitement of pitchin' into that meat——"

He paused.

Having made the picture as ridiculous as possible, he kept a mildly pleased eye upon Legges and added: "You must be a doctor, to've thought of that! And they's only one doctor around here, I understand, and that's Doctor Legges."

He crossed the room and held out his hand—his right hand.

"I'm mighty glad to meet you, doctor," said he.

Legges, glancing over the shoulder of Dunmore, looked straight into the eyes of Harper; for the man's back was once more turned upon his host, and this surely was the time to strike!

But, as he looked, he saw Harper's jaw sag down, and he drew the back of his hand across the loose lips. Suddenly Legges knew that Harper, against the curious guest of his, would be of no more help than a figure of wood. The woman, too, was frightened.

Therefore, the doctor held out his hand and took that of the younger man.

"Glad to know you. You're Carrick Dunmore, that Harper has been telling me about."

"Harper's mighty good to me," said Dunmore. "So's Mrs. Harper."

He went toward the stove again—once more turning his back upon the doctor, and again the latter gripped his gun, but somehow could not use it. It was as though an icy breath struck him, and the fear which possessed the Harpers also seemed to be stealing into his veins.

"Nothing that they don't do for me," said Dunmore, turning the steaks in the frying pan again. "They ain't happy unless they're doing some little thing. Mrs. Harper, here, she sews on my buttons, and brushes up my clothes, and keeps my boots a-shinin'. And Chuck Harper, he's always searchin' for something to do for me. The boss hotel-keepers of the world, I'd call 'em! Look at Mrs. Harper, here, insistin' on me taking these steaks that she was cookin' for all of you! That's kindness, ain't it? She's got a big heart for a hungry man, has Mrs. Harper!"

He smiled on her, and she, attempting to smile back, made a horrible grimace.

"A great cook, too," went on Dunmore smoothly. "And fine at seasoning. Look at the way she'd fixed that steak—so's it broke Danny's heart with joy when he tasted it! That's what I call a cook, Doctor Legges."

The doctor drew a long breath. He began to wish that he were far away from that kitchen. And yet he was held here by a great curiosity, also.

"If you're Doctor Legges," went on Dunmore, "you're the best friend of Tankerton. Is that right?"

The doctor was silent, for it was a forbidden name.

"And that bein' the case," said Dunmore, "I'd be mighty happy to have you take a message to him for me."

"What message?" asked the doctor.

"Why, you tell Tankerton that I'm mighty surprised that he ain't come to see me. You tell him that it was a real pleasure to see his friend, Lynn Tucker, down here. And it was a sure great pleasure to meet Doctor Legges, too. But I'd like to talk to Tankerton himself! Will you go and tell him that, partner?"

Malice suddenly mastered the doctor.

"Young man," said he, "are you sure that you want to see James Tankerton?"

"Nothin' that I want to see so bad," said Dunmore.

"Very well," said Legges. "I think that can be arranged. Tankerton himself will call on you, Carrick Dunmore!"

"Thanks," said Dunmore.

He raised the frying pan from the stove and carried it, contents and all, toward the door.

There he turned.

"You won't forget that the dead dog is still in my room, Doctor Legges, eh?"

Then he passed out and left three silent people staring at one another. But all had been differently affected.

Mrs. Harper was convulsed with the most savage anger, so that she trembled with it.

Her husband was loose, and white, like a man about to faint.

And the eminent doctor was mopping his forehead with an automatic motion.

Then Mrs. Harper spoke. "And here's what we get," said she, "after the years that we've slaved, and fought, and starved, and gone through suffering for Jim Tankerton! Here's what we get in the way of help when we need to get out of a——"

Her husband grasped her by the shoulder and shook her most violently.

"Shut up, you!" he gasped at her. "Ain't he apt to be behind that door now listenin'?"

"Listenin' and laughin'!" said the wife, undaunted, because now fury completely mastered her. "Listenin' and laughin' is what he's doin'! Laughin' at a great, fat-faced noodle that ain't man enough to be the master in his own home, but that lets a low, sneakin', dead beat come in and trim him to the bone, and take the food off of his table——"

"Will you quit it?" asked the gentle Chuck, lifting up his massive fist.

"Be quiet, both of you," said the doctor, with an air of authority and impatience. "I can console you both by giving you my personal assurance that young Carrick Dunmore will be dead before the week's out!"

# XIV

## • A MAN'S KINGDOM •

JAMES HAMBLE TANKERTON came over the mountains to Harpersville.

He had the mount on Gunfire, on this day, and therefore he came fast, for that was the only way that Gunfire knew how to travel.

He had his name from the sound of his flying hoofs upon the road—like rolling gunfire, a certain sheriff had said, as he had his posse spurred hopelessly up the dark of a road in pursuit of the brigand.

Now, on Gunfire, he flashed down the slopes, and trotted up the rises, and swung away in a long gallop down the easier going which brought him to Harpersville.

On the hill which stood above it, he halted his stallion and surveyed the surrounding country, with hand on hip, like a king looking over his kingdom. And this, in fact, was what that countryside was to James Tankerton.

In this wilderness of heaped mountain ranges, split across with great canyons, and darkened with trees of the most enormous size, he was the undisputed prince.

It was not a rich domain. Those who lived here were as a rule the poorest trappers and hunters; or else they worked patches of farmland in the bottoms. But this was all the better for Tankerton. For the poorer his people, the more easily he could exercise his power over them.

In fact, he drew no revenue from his kingdom, but rather it was a source of expense to him continually. What it returned to him was constant support and protection. All who did not love him, feared him, and both the one class and the other needed him. What little money many of these families received from their farms, their few cattle, the sale of pelts, was in many cases almost doubled by the handsome gifts which Tankerton made right and left. He

66

gave with apparent recklessness but with real care, and though he adopted a magnificent and paternal manner, yet his hand could fall heavily when he chose. More than one mountaineer received a sudden message advising him to flee to the plains beyond, and always that warning was heeded. If not, the body of the obdurate one would be found before many days lying in the woods with a bullet through brain or heart.

"Accident while hunting," the coroner would give as verdict. But every one understood and took the lesson darkly home. Those who were true to Tankerton had his support and money at their command in a strong measure. For a friend in need, he was known to have organized a band of raiders and ridden two hundred miles to break open a jail in the secure heart of a town. With that rescued man he returned, and the mountains rang with the deed.

Such acts gave him the right to rule as a king; the people accepted him; and if he was a robber by profession, none of his plunderings occurred in the mountains where he lived. But, now and again, a band gathered somewhere in the valleys, and a dozen or a score of beautifully mounted men rode out into the foothills or the level, rich lands beyond. There they struck at a bank, a jeweler's stock, a train, a stagecoach richly laden, and whirled back into the mountains to squander their loot; and that squandering poured out more money into the laps of the mountaineers! So it worked for them in an eternal circle!

The rule was by this time established. No sheriff or marshal, riding on the trail of Tankerton, could penetrate into the mountains with any success. The lips of all men were sealed, the ears of all men were deaf, there was no hospitality, no help, for the men of the law, but a screen of scouts and spies rose up before the posse and continually spread around them like waves spreading from a dropped pebble in a pond. In a few days, the whole region of the mountains understood the nature of the posse, knew descriptions of the individuals, and well comprehended that if any of these men should suddenly be missed from the ranks and found dead among the rocks or the trees, Tankerton would not be offended! In fact, the people of the mountains were his militia, and they had served him so extraordinarily well that the army of the law no longer reached after him. It meant long and hard riding, bitter weather, hard trails, and in the end nothing but broken-down men and horses and an emptied pocketbook!

These thoughts drifted through the mind of Tankerton as he rested his horse upon the summit of the hill and looked over his domain. He felt assured and fixed upon his throne, and he would not have traded his place for any scepter in the world. This was his own realm, the place he knew, the air with which he was familiar, where every road was traced in his memory, and where hardly a sapling could fall without his knowledge. He had all that a sovereign could wish for in the fear, the obedience, and the love of his subjects. He had the additional joy of the gambler who plays a winning game against great odds!

It was wearing toward the latter half of the afternoon, and, therefore, the light already was growing stained with blue in the bottoms of the valley; the canyon seemed deeper; the snow upon the mountains in the distance looked through the mist with a gleam like the glitter of swords; but all was slowly being overcast with blue.

The vapors ascended from the gorges, from the forests, and blew down with the melting of the snows, and wherever the mountain mist appeared, it was blue of the sky, faintly breathed among the trees, or deeply pooled in the hollows; and the kingdom of Tankerton was the kingdom of the blue horizon!

He filled his eyes with the noble picture, and then he gave Gunfire his head again, and the black stallion swept down the slope.

Tankerton came to the rear of the hotel and saw a small boy coming up the trail beneath him. There he paused, with Gunfire turned into a black statue among the bushes and the poplars, until the youngster had come close enough for him to see the child's face.

It was a brown little mountaineer of twelve or fourteen years, wearing his father's trousers, worn to shreds that hung halfway down the scratched calf of his leg, and with a single strap passing over his shoulder by way of suspenders. He lugged a heavy shotgun of ancient make, and his face was dark with disappointment.

However, as he came closer, it seemed to Tankerton that he could recognize the features. He could not be expected to know every man, woman, and child in his dominions, but he followed the example of Caesar as nearly as he could. He did not think he had seen this boy before, but he ventured that he knew his father.

So he waited until the lad, coming within five or six steps, suddenly halted and looked with bright, suspicious eyes about him. He had not seen anything, but like a wild young animal, he seemed to suspect that eyes were fixed upon him from the covert. Tankerton rejoiced in the sight of him. He was as ragged, as rough, as unkempt as a bear cub; but he had a bear's keen senses, a bear's courage, and one day he would have almost equal strength. Such boys as this would grow into the men who would assure him a long reign, for Tankerton knew very well that the permanence of his power did not depend upon the crew of lock breakers, yeggs, thieves, confidence men, and plain gun fighters and murderers, who brought him in his immediate revenue. It was the mountain militia which enabled him to keep his standing army from being broken up by the arm of the law.

"I'm here!" said he suddenly.

The boy whirled and jumped the butt of his shotgun into the hollow of his shoulder, before he saw who it was that sat the horse half shrouded among the brush.

"Hey!" he said then, and the gun almost dropped from his hands. "Jiminy! Look what I nearly done!"

Tankerton rode out into the trail.

"Do you know me?" he asked.

"Sure I do," said the boy.

"Who am I, then?"

"You're Jack Timberline," said the boy.

"I'm Jack Timberline?"

"Yep."

"And what else do you know besides my name?"

"You got a bad pair of lungs," said the boy. "That's one of the things that I know about you."

"What makes you think that I have a bad pair of lungs?"

"If you wasn't a lunger," argued the boy, "why would you be hangin' around here in the mountains, except it was for your health? Maybe you're one of these here scientists that studies bugs, though, or flowers. I dunno. But I'd say that Jack Timberline was something special!"

Tankerton could not help smiling.

"I know your father," he said.

"No, you don't," said the boy.

"Are you sure?"

"He's been dead for ten year. You might know Cousin Bill, though."

"Do you look like him?"

"Do I look like a hog that's run wild?" said the boy.

He sneered with disgust. "I'd tell a man that I hope I don't look like him!" he said.

"How old are you, sonny?"

"I'm old enough to shoot a buck," said the boy.

"And skin him?" asked Tankerton.

"Aye, and skin him, and cut him up. No butcher could do it no better!"

"Are you sure?"

"Ain't Bill the butcher at Harpersville?"

Suddenly Tankerton remembered the humped shoulders and the long, bestial face of Bill, the butcher at Harpersville.

"That's Bill Ogden. He taught me how to cut meat. He always sets in the sun and swaps lies with Chuck Harper."

"Your name is Ogden, then?"

"Me? I hope it ain't! My name is James McVey Alderwood Larren."

"It's a good long name."

"My pop was a good long man, and he figgered it that the Larrens oughta have at least one name for every couple of foot of 'em!"

"And Bill Ogden was related and took you in——"

"He took me in proper, he did! He ain't hardly done a stroke since I arrived."

A big mountain partridge, hiding beneath a bush, thought that it had crawled far enough from the sound of the voices and now rose on whirring wings. Instantly, James McVey Alderwood Larren wheeled and discharged his shotgun. It was a quick shot, but it went home, for the partridge staggered in its flight, thumped against a tree trunk, and then fell to the ground.

The boy marked the spot and then let the bird lie. He

turned back to Tankerton again, and assumed a careless air.

"That was a bully good shot," said Tankerton. "You'd better pick it up."

"I guess I'd better," said the boy. "A good thing for me that I slammed that feller on the nose," he resumed, as he came back with his burden. "I'd 've got a whanging from Cousin Bill, otherwise."

"Does he whang you when you come in without any game?"

"Sure he does. He knows how, too. He's been a tanner."

The boy laughed carelessly. "It don't do me no harm," he said. "Along about last year I learned not to holler, and that takes a lot of the pleasure away from Bill, when he don't hear me yap."

"It toughens you up, I suppose," said Tankerton, rather wonder-stricken by the philosophy of this lad.

"Don't it, though?" said James Larren brightly. "When I get into a fight with some of the other kids, don't seem like I can feel it when they punch me! They can wear 'emselves out punchin' me, but I knock their teeth down their throats in the finish, darn 'em!"

He grinned, and his white teeth flashed.

"Bill isn't your uncle, then?" said Tankerton.

"Him? He ain't much more related to me than a swaller is to a bald eagle, though both of them is birds. There was never but one Ogden that went out and got himself famous by bustin' in and marrying with a Larren. And there ain't gunna never be another. But girls is funny, Mr. Tan— Timberline, as maybe you've noticed once or twice yourself. They go a lot more by faces than by fun!"

"Ah, but I'll wager that you have your share of 'em, Jimmy? They know a man, even in the making."

"Thanks," said Jimmy, flushing with pleasure. "But I don't have nothin' to do with 'em. A lot o' gabbin', gabberin', squealin', wo'thless things that keep a boy mindin' that his shoes is wore out at the toes, and keep a man from readin' his paper peaceful of an evenin'."

He looked down and wiggled his toes thoughtfully as he said this. They were visible through great ragged gaps at the end of each shoe. Tankerton laughed again.

"You don't have much fun in Harpersville, I take it," said he.

"Aw, things is all right, because you can get shut of the town so quick and have this for your main street!" said the boy.

He waved to the great chasm of the canyon, and smiled at it with an air of possession.

"But lately," he said, "things has been lookin' up, since the new man come."

"Who is that?"

"Carrick Dunmore. He is a man!" said the boy, his voice softening with awed admiration. "You'd oughta see the stone that he lifted! He's got Chuck Harper lookin' like he'd just been kicked. And by Mrs. Harper's face, you'd think that she was just from seein' a ghost."

"A hard sort of a fellow, is he?" asked Tankerton with interest.

"Him? He ain't hard at all. He's soft. He's so soft you can't break him with a hammer, and he's so hard you can't cut him with a knife. That's him!"

Tankerton drew out a dollar and tossed it. It winged high in the air, but it was caught by the unerring hand of the boy.

"Will you do something for me?"

"I'll do a dollar's worth, and that'd be about five years' pay, according to the lights of what Bill Ogden pays me."

"Go to Harper. Tell him that I'll meet him on this trail. No one else needs to hear what you have to say."

The keen eyes of the boy flashed; he nodded, and was instantly off up the path at a run. Tankerton watched the sturdy legs flying, and thanked the providence which had furnished his kingdom with such man-material as this!

# XV

## • A GENT WHO MAKES YOU FETCH IT •

TANKERTON dismounted now, but, even so, he did not
relax his precautions, but rather redoubled them. He left
the horse in the center of the thicket, where the perfectly
trained animal stood without attempting to crop grass, or
the succulent ends of the twigs about him; he hardly so
much as swung his tail at the flies, or shook his bridled
head. Tankerton, for his part, went two trees back from
the trail and sat down to smoke. At this distance from the
path, the smoke would not be seen, and yet he could view
the way through gaps between the trunks.

He did not need to use these precautions. He was able
to ride where he pleased among the mountains, and he
knew it; on occasion he enjoyed showing himself boldly,
but his instinct was that of a hunted man, and in time of
peace he constantly prepared for war.

The noises of the forest closed around him—the drip
and murmur of a small stream near by, and the whisper or
rush of wind which carried with it bird noises, the squeak
of squirrels, and deep voice of the waterfall in the canyon,
and these sounds delicately intermingled with fragrance of
wild flowers, and the pure, sweet smell of the pines. In the
distance, all the mountains had turned blue.

Presently, he saw Big Chuck Harper coming down the
trail in huge lumbering strides, and he stepped out under
the shadow of the first tree. Harper halted at sight of him,
and then came on, half eagerly and half diffidently.

All the nature of Tankerton revolted at this man. He
was himself fastidiously, beautifully made, lightly and
slenderly; and the gross and shapeless bulk of Chuck
Harper repulsed him. However, he was not one to allow
such qualms to affect his attitude toward one of his most
valuable tools. The hotel of Chuck Harper was of peculiar

value. There were few like it, and no other hostelries with-in a full day's ride; therefore, it was sure to be used by people of every kind who traveled light; and for that rea-son he had to have Chuck Harper heartily in his service.

He went straight to the big fellow and gripped his hand.

"I'm glad to see you, Chuck," said he. "I'm sorry that Lynn and the doctor were not able to take care of this bus-iness for you; so you see I've come myself. He's a remark-able fellow, from all that I hear—too soft to break and too hard to cut, eh?"

Chuck balled his huge fist, and then the fingers loosely relaxed.

"I dunno. He's one of these here hypnotists, I guess," said he.

"Do you think he'll be able under any circumstances to hypnotize my gun, Chuck?"

Harper looked earnestly at his chief, and he seemed to be making a comparison which could not be decided in one glance, but rather he had to sum up many details in order to get at the crux of the matter.

Finally he said: "You know your own business, chief. Nobody ever had downed you, but if I was you, I'd never tackle this here gent alone."

"Is he as dangerous as all that?" asked Tankerton light-ly.

But though there was lightness in his tone, there was sinister care in his heart. And the rumor of the greatness and the power of this stranger bulked larger in his mind for the very reason that the man was unknown to him.

"I've seen him do things," said Chuck, unwilling to admit that his chief could be surpassed by any human creature.

He stared at the lean, handsome face of Tankerton. That of Carrick Dunmore was handsome likewise, but much fuller, with rather a sleek look. And both of them were smiling faces, but the smile of Tankerton was that of superior intelligence, or assured mastery of men; whereas that of Dunmore was the smile of one engaged in a pleas-ant game, who knows some secret that may presently make all that an enemy does appear absurd. Each had a wonderfully steady eye, but the steadiness of Tankerton was the steadiness of a vast and self-conscious will;

whereas the strength of Dunmore's glance was that of one who reads a very entertaining page. But, finally, the regard of the hotel-keeper rested upon the towering, swelling forehead of his master, and that convinced him.

"Somehow you'll be able to handle him," he said doggedly. "I guess you'll be able to do that. But I've seen Tucker and Legges turned into pulp by him. He ain't no common man—that's sure!"

That bitter conclusion the chief was willing to agree with.

"Doctor Legges," said Tankerton, "also advised me to bring down some of my best men and attack our friend Dunmore."

"Doctor Legges is a gent with good sense," said Chuck.

"But," said Tankerton, "I want you to understand, Chuck, that I never have avoided single men who cross my way, and I don't want to form the habit of an old man, while I still can walk without the aid of a crutch."

Chuck blinked and nodded.

"This fellow is a lazy sort of a chap, as I understand it, who can lie in the sun and be perfectly happy."

"He can. For a whole half day," said Chuck.

"And also he can go out and walk fifty miles across this sort of country?" inquired Tankerton.

"He started out the other morning and came back by evenin' light, and he brung with him some twigs of red willow, and if that there grows any nearer than Center Creek, I'm a liar, chief. That's all I know about it."

"He carries his guns with him, too, and shoots small game with a revolver?"

"Aye, he do."

"What else has he been doing lately that's of interest?" asked Tankerton.

"Why, nothin'. I don't think they's anything in his head, except he wants to sit yonder in my hotel and get you, when you come for him. He's too lazy to start a regular hunt for you, but he wants the blood money that's on you. That's my way of writin' this here story!"

"Ah, well," said Tankerton, "a good many men might be tempted by ten thousand dollars, and a great reputation along with it. You must admit that, Chuck."

The little pig eyes of Chuck gleamed. But then he looked into the face of his master again, and his glance was abased.

"Now, then," said Tankerton, "I want to know the details of the last few days. Tucker has come in at last, and he and Legges together have told me the first part of the tale."

"He's been as usual. Lie around one day. Go off trampin' the next. Then fiddle around a good deal. Go and set and yap with some of the folks up and down the street. Went to the blacksmith shop and got an old plowshare, for instance, and brung it home."

"What did he want with that?"

"That's what I asked him."

"What did he say?"

"He says that it makes the boss mud scraper of the world. That's what he says. What does he want with a mud scraper?"

"Did he put it up?"

"No. No sign of him doin' that."

"That's rather strange, then!"

"I dunno that it is," said Chuck. "Ma thinks it's strange, too. I dunno why. He's jus' one of them lazy, shiftless kind. Gets an idea, and then goes to sleep and forgets about it. But what for would he want to make a mud scraper for my hotel? He ain't showed any signs of doin' anything else for me! He sure ain't paid his bill yet! But when the first of the month comes, I'm gunna have it, if I gotta take it out of his hide by burnin' the hotel down to scorch him till he melts, the skunk!"

He roared with his anger, and then caught his breath as he saw the slight frown upon the face of his leader.

"A dangerous man, Chuck, but you don't think that there's any great mystery about him?" asked Tankerton.

Chuck hesitated, his lips twitching as he controlled the angry words that came.

Finally he said: "It's like this, chief. You take that kind of a gent—I dunno how to put it. But they's been two men in the world that have give me a kind of a chill—he's one of 'em!"

"That's interesting, Chuck," said Tankerton. "And who may the other have been?"

"You!" blurted out Chuck.

Tankerton smiled again.

"No chills, Chuck. No chills. I'm your friend, I trust."

"I hope so," said Chuck with devout emotion. "But if you'd tie up with a couple more of your best—if you and Lynn Tucker and maybe that new young feller that you got—Furneaux—was to join up together——"

"And add you to the party, Chuck?"

Chuck rubbed his knuckles across his fleshy forehead.

Then he said, while he turned a dull red: "I wouldn't be no good, I guess. He—he's got me hypnotized, all right." Then he broke out: "And if I was you, I wouldn't waste no time. I'd go and break right in on him and not give his eyes no chance to work on you. That's the best way!"

"Of course it is," said the other. "And I'll do it alone."

"Are you dead set, chief?"

Tankerton waved his hand toward the mountains, as though on their hard faces could be seen the answer to his question. Then he said simply:

"A fellow like that will be a pleasure to meet. And if I have to die, it's best not to be dropped by the chance bullet which some fool in a posse fires."

Chuck blinked again, for this was a spirit to which he could listen, but which he could not very well comprehend. He knew that it was above and beyond him, and a new thrill jumped from his heart to his brain as he realized that his master was, indeed, utterly fearless. Sometimes, men were apt to say that he was a wily fox who put the burden of his labors upon the shoulders of others, and then collected the money and the fame at their expense, but Chuck could see now that this question was answered once for all. For his own part, he would rather have faced a fiery dragon than that pair of smiling eyes and that faintly smiling mouth of Carrick Dunmore.

Actually he fell back a pace and took a short breath.

"All right, chief," said he.

"Where is he now?"

"Up in his room. He's just made the wife bring him up tea and m'lasses and hot cakes. This time of day, will you think?"

"How can he make her, Chuck?"

"It's better to fetch him what he wants than to have him come and take it," said Harper.

"Very well," said Tankerton, "then I'll go to his room, rather then let him come to fetch me!"

# XVI

## • PARTNERS! •

BEFORE he left the screen of trees behind it, Tankerton paused and examined the hotel with care, for there was plenty of danger in crossing the clearing if some accurate shot waited behind the windows, rifle in hand. And the face of the building depressed him, as the sight of a new school does a boy on the first day of a term. However, he shrugged away this weakness and immediately stepped out from the trees to the open, crossing it with never an apparent look at the windows before him.

But as he went, he was deeply realizing what he had almost forgotten in the last few years—that his kingdom was built upon his own strength and courage alone. He had his little army of scouts and of fighters to deal with the heavy posses who rode up from the plains, but it never had occurred to him that a single man might quietly step through his outer defenses and sit down here in the heart of his power!

From the street beyond the hotel he could hear some one whistling "The Campbells Are Coming," and he wondered if this might be a signal that concerned his own approach.

The rear door of the hotel opened, and Chuck Harper was there holding it ajar and greeting him with a twisted grin and a white face. The big fellow was badly frightened, but viciously hopeful, and as for his wife, she looked at Tankerton as one who already smells a feast.

"If you take off your boots here," said Harper, "I'll

show you how to get up the stairs to his room without makin' no noise."

"I'll walk up in my boots," said Tankerton calmly. "I may be dying in a few moments."

"Don't talk about it!" said Chuck Harper in horror. "But the main thing is for you to get there easy. Now I could show you a way across the roof. He might be watchin' the door. He ain't so likely to look for a gent to pop in at his window."

Tankerton smiled.

"Do you think that I want to do a murder, Chuck?" he asked. "This is the way up, isn't it?"

Straightway he marched across the dining room and through the hall, and up the darkened staircase, his feet heavy with the knowledge that this day would make history in his life, and his heart strengthening itself for the battle. For the tenth time he loosened his revolver as he walked.

From the top of the stairs, Chuck Harper, who had stolen noiselessly up behind his master, pointed and whispered.

"Last door on the left—your room."

"My room!" said Tankerton beneath his breath.

Then he went forward with anger. There was enough anger, at least, to warm him thoroughly, and to make him grateful for the last remark made by Harper.

So he came to the door at a brisk walk, jerked it open, and stepped inside with gun in hand and a bounding joy that he had not found the door locked. He was taking advantage, but such advantages were permissible, according to his code.

As he snatched the door wide, he heard from the street the shrilling whistle of "The Campbells Are Coming" still in progress, and with the lilt of that music in his ears, he saw a man turning toward him from the window, and stepping out at him at the same time.

He saw every detail of this man in the burning concentration of the first glance. He saw the shoulders sleeked over with strength, the fine head, and, above all, a faint smile in lips and eyes—the stern joy of one who really loves battle!

The gun of Tankerton was poised as he entered; he

needed only to let the muzzle drop down upon the mark, and into the breast of the other he sent a .45-caliber bullet.

It was as though an invisible finger pushed through the shirt of the other from left to right; but he did not fall. And then the wink of steel which had appeared in the hand of Dunmore—plucked out of the air, as it were—exploded. A stifling breath struck the face of Tankerton, like the breath of a great beast of prey, with hot prickles of fire stinging his eyes blind.

Into the red-speckled darkness he fired blindly. The gun was wrenched from his hand and he himself embraced with such a might as he never had dreamed of. He reached for his second gun—it already was gone, and a cold muzzle was clapped under his chin.

At the same time the voice of Dunmore said loudly: "Well, Tankerton, it's a draw. Are we going to murder each other, or do we stop here?"

The brain of Tankerton spun.

"Answer, you fool!" said Dunmore in a whisper. "They're listening. You see no sense in murder——"

"There's no sense in stupid murder, Dunmore," said Tankerton.

"Sit down, then," said Dunmore, "and we'll talk the thing over."

Tankerton found himself lightly lifted and then deposited in a chair. In the hall, dimly, he heard retreating footfalls, rapid steps that ran away with such reckless haste that the floor pulsed with the impacts.

A fiery torment still blinded him, so that he saw only red-speckled blackness streaked across with dazzling white lights; but a wet cloth now pressed across his face gave almost instant relief. There was some soothing medicament upon it; his eyes cleared; and once more he could look about him, though somewhat dimly for the moment.

At least, he could see that Dunmore was on the opposite side of the room rolling a cigarette, which he now lighted.

"Have the makings?" he politely proffered.

"No," said Tankerton.

He was anxious enough to smoke, but he was afraid lest there might be a visible tremor in his hand. He was still shaken from head to foot by the shock of what had happened, and his very vitals ached from the grip of Dunmore's arm.

"Reckon that they won't be listening at the door," said Dunmore. "But they's quite a little ol' crowd gatherin' below. Hear 'em?"

There was a confusion of many voices which lifted to the ears of Tankerton, but all those voices were suppressed and kept down, as though by fear. Then his eyes cleared altogether; his mind at the same time could function again, and he realized that he had been beaten for the first time!

Dunmore, watching him critically, understood.

"Sort of a low-down trick that I played you, Tankerton," said he.

He undid his shirt at the neck, and, drawing over his head a loop of leather thong, he pulled out the broad, heavy blade of plowshare.

"I couldn't've taken the chance with a less straight shot than you, Tankerton," said Dunmore, "but I knew that you'd hit the heart, and you done it!"

He laughed a little as he indicated a bright streak across the rusted face of the iron.

"You hit it with a whang. That time, you must've heard the bell ring, Tankerton?"

The outlaw sat with head erect, leaning a little forward in his chair, and studying the other with a calm brightness of eye. Never before had Dunmore seen such a man, or felt in another such nerve of dauntless steel.

"The stuff I used on you," said Dunmore, "was not fair, of course. But it was better than knocking you over with a slug, wasn't it?"

Tankerton waved a hand, dismissing these courteous apologies and explanations.

"What are you after, Dunmore?" he said.

"A talk with you," said Dunmore.

"Did you have to run this mystery game at Harper's place in order to talk with me? You must have known that I'm always ready to talk with any man."

"This takes a little explaining," said Dunmore. "The fact is that I knew I could talk to you when I felt like it, but from my way of lookin' at it, it was a lot better to have you come to my office than for me to go to yours! Saved me from sendin' in my card, you might say."

Tankerton made another brief gesture.

"You have all the cards in the pack," said he, "so you can say how the game is to be played."

"Why, we'll each take half," said Dunmore.

"Half of what?"

"We'll make a merger, Tankerton."

"A merger? I want to try to understand you, Dunmore."

"I'll put it straight as I can. We each of us have something to give; we've each got something to get. For instance, you've got the mountains, here, under your thumb. I want half of that power. You've got a gang of hard-handed fightin' men. I want half of that bunch. You're the king, Tankerton. You can keep right on bein' the king, but I'm gunna be the grand vizier, or something like that. Instead of one whip, they's gunna be two!"

Tankerton waited a moment, flushing a little.

"I understand you now, I think," said he. "The point is that you will buy half the stock in my company."

"That's a way of putting it."

"Nearly everything in the world is for sale," said Tankerton. "I might point out that I've worked a good many years to build up this company. What price are you paying to let yourself into it on an equal basis?"

"What price did you pay to get it?" asked Dunmore.

"Careful planning, patience, and dangers faced and outfaced."

"I've paid in the same coin," said Dunmore. "I've come in and stepped into the tepee of a big chief with a lot of scalps already at his belt. I've hung out here while a gunman came down and tried to murder me in the night. I sat around until murder with poison was tried. And, after that, the king got off his throne and come sashayin' down here to polish me off. But he tripped. He didn't have the luck. And so he's settin' here thinkin' things over and decidin' that after all I'm talkin' business the right way."

Tankerton shook his head.

"Do you think that my men would follow you?"

"I got an idea that they'd learn to."

"I don't see the possibility," said Tankerton.

The face of Dunmore grew hard.

"Think it over, old-timer," said he. "You'll see that I'm right when I say that we'd better shake hands, and then go to the window and let the boys outside see us together!"

Still, Tankerton waited for a moment, his teeth clenched hard, but suddenly he rose and held out his hand. "I'll agree on the start," said he, "but you'll have to take care of your own finish."

Dunmore met the proffered grip willingly. "I never asked for loaded dice," said he.

# XVII

## • BEATRICE KIRK •

STANDING shoulder to shoulder, as though for mutual support, Chuck Harper and his wife saw Carrick Dunmore and Tankerton come down the stairs side by side, Dunmore with his pack across his shoulder; and the two were talking in the most amiable fashion!

Whatever Chuck had heard from the hall outside the door of Dunmore's room, he could not be prepared for this, and his jaw sagged loosely as he watched.

Tankerton went up to him with a smile.

"Why, Chuck," said he, "you might have known that you were mistaken about Dunmore. He's one of my oldest friends, and one of my best, come out here at my invitation to be my partner. But the scoundrel wanted to introduce himself in his own way; so long since we've seen each other that I hardly recognized him, at that. Eh, Carrie?"

"Well," said Dunmore, "it's the first time that Judge Colt has made old friends recognize one another. What's my bill, Harper?"

"Seventy-four dollars and fifty cents this morning," said Chuck, "and——"

"Pay him for me, old fellow, will you?" said Dunmore

to the outlaw. "Don't generally carry such small change as that around with me."

Tankerton flashed a grim side glance at his companion, but he immediately took out a roll of bills and peeled off two of them.

"Here's a hundred, Chuck," said he. "You keep the change for luck, will you?"

Chuck, trembling with emotion in all his great bulk, drew the other aside. He was breathing so hard that it was almost impossible for him to speak.

Finally he could say: "Him? A friend of yours, chief?"

"We played together when we were youngsters," said Tankerton easily. "He's all right, Chuck—only a little eccentric, you know, and that doesn't matter among old friends! You see that you've been paid for what he's eaten."

"Paid?" echoed Chuck hollowly. "I couldn't be paid with a million dollars, unless the money was printed on his hide!"

And he jerked about, presenting his back to his master and striding away.

This was an act of open rebellion that would have called for quick disciplining at any other time, but Tankerton had now many important details to occupy his mind, and let the trifles slip. He heard Dunmore saying good-by to Mrs. Harper, and watched her face turn yellow with disappointed malice. In their own way, Tankerton felt that there were no two more evil characters in the mountains than this precious pair, and it seemed that Dunmore had been at pains to bring out every ugly phase of them.

He was saying now:

"This here is a sad time for both of us, Mrs. Harper. But that's the way of things. Smooth goin' for a little while, and then we get the bumps. Don't you take on, though, little woman. Because all the time that I'm away, I'm gunna be thinkin' of you every time I see a wild flower, like a flowerin' cactus, say, or a prickly pear. I'm gunna be reminded of you constant, and that'll help me to bear up. Shake hands, little woman."

She jerked her hands behind her back.

"I'd—I'd ruther touch a toad!" she gasped at him, and fled from the room.

"They hate you, Dunmore," said Tankerton, looking after her.

"Look here," remarked Dunmore. "Would you take it for a compliment to have that sort of a crowd like you and want you in the middle of the family?"

Tankerton shrugged his shoulders, and went with Dunmore out the front door of the hotel.

The light of the sun, sloping through the great trees from the west, sent long splotches of shadow across a crowd of fifty or sixty people who were gathered there; Harpersville hardly could have collected a greater number. And when they saw Dunmore and the outlaw as friends, side by side, they gave back, with an awed and bewildered murmur. Tankerton stood on the steps of the hotel and made a little speech.

He said, briefly: "Friends, I'm mighty glad to see you all here, because I want to introduce you to an old companion of mine who has come up here to be my partner. We didn't recognize each other at first, and it came close to being a bad meeting; but good luck made us both miss, and we're glad of it. If you see Dunmore after this, look on him as being as much a friend of yours as I could be."

He said this quietly, cheerfully; but Dunmore could see the pallor of the man's face, and recognize the forced quality in his smile. By those tokens he could guess at the shame and rage and hatred which were gathered in the breast of the outlaw, and he could prophesy the danger which must lie before him. And yet he was amazed by the honesty with which the man fulfilled his pledge.

In all his life he had not seen a more savage-looking crowd. They looked like rough hunting dogs leaning on the leash, and one word from Tankerton, one gesture, even, would have launched them in a wave at Dunmore. Yet Tankerton refrained. It was pride, no doubt, that held him back. He would not admit that he needed the assistance of any man in single fight!

The manner in which the assemblage took the speech of their patron was typical of their rude, half-savage natures. A sort of growl ran through them; then they swayed into groups, facing the two main objects of interest, but muttering and mumbling among themselves. It was plain that when they heard of the arrival of Tankerton, they expected that swift destruction would overtake the impertinent stranger, and they could not accommodate themselves to the disappointment. Yet they eyed Dunmore with some admiration, and a great deal of wholesome respect.

As the horses for the two were brought around to the front of the hotel, such a space had formed in front of them that Tankerton turned to Dunmore and said with a smile that was for the benefit of the crowd, and a bitterness of voice that was for the man beside him:

"I've lost this day as much as I've won in the last three years. I owe that to you, Dunmore."

"Take me as you find me," answered Dunmore. "A month from to-day you may be glad that I've joined you!"

Tankerton allowed his smile to slip into a sneer for an instant, and then looked down the street toward the form of a rider who was coming up at a furious speed. It came closer and grew from a blur of dust and haste into the figure of a flying bay horse, dust-coated, and flecked with foam. In the saddle was no man, in spite of this furious speed, but a girl. As she came up, the speed of her gallop furled the brim of her hat, and so it was that he had his first view of Beatrice Kirk, dark-skinned, dark-eyed, and beautiful.

Straight into the crowd she rushed her horse, so that they scattered with yells to each side. A man would have been dragged from his horse and flogged for such conduct; but they laughed at her recklessness.

For her part, she paid not the slightest attention to them, but drew in hard on a wicked Spanish curb that threw the bay on his haunches. So he skidded to a halt in splendid style, and a gush of dust spurted over those who were standing near by.

"It's Beatrice Kirk!" Dunmore heard a voice say.

He thought it a lovely name; and though the horse no longer stirred, it seemed to him as though the beauty of her face were sweeping on strongly into his mind.

All was delicately feminine in her fashioning, all was lightness and grace; but in her expression he could see neither humility, nor patience, nor kindness, nor friendship, nor timidity, nor any of those domestic and shrinking virtues with which most men fit out their ideal. She was all fire, passion, contempt, pride, courage, and a sinister dash of cruelty lurked about her mouth and eyes, Dunmore thought.

She flung out of the saddle and stood panting before them.

"Is it all over and I'm too late, Jimmy?" she said to Tankerton. "I rode like the mischief to get here, because I wanted to see that fight. But now you've finished it and I'll only see the Dunmore corpse!"

She panted out the words, making a savage little gesture of disappointment.

"Dunmore?" said Tankerton. "Does he look like a corpse?"

He pointed at his companion, and the girl, turning with a start, stared full at Dunmore. He felt as though he never had been looked at before those hard, bright, and searching eyes were fixed on his. It was as though she did not see his body, his clothes, his face, but only demanded: What is in the soul of this man?

And suddenly he felt empty, and a little frightened.

She had turned back to Tankerton, as suddenly as she looked on Dunmore.

"Bah!" said she. "He won!"

A world of ringing disappointment and contempt was now in that voice of hers.

Dunmore said hastily, "Nobody won. We were introduced with a couple of shots, and we found out that we were old friends."

"Old friends," said Tankerton, repeating the idea, and it seemed to Dunmore that he spoke with a touch of desperation in his voice. "Why, Beatrice, we played together when we were kids!"

She looked at him; then flashed her bright eyes at Dunmore and never had he seen such disbelief and such contempt commingled.

"Well," she said, "your guns have scared the two of you into a mighty good story. Jim, is he going back with us?"

"Yes," he answered with an unwilling drag in his voice.

"He is?" she snapped. "Well—give me a hand up. I'm going to ride on ahead."

"We're all going back the same road, Beatrice," said he, well-nigh pleading.

"Are we? Not unless you can go faster than the bay will take me."

"What's the matter with you?" Tankerton demanded.

"I want to be alone," she answered bitterly. "I want to be alone, so that I can have a daydream and think about one real man. There aren't any wearing boots in these mountains!"

## XVIII

### • JIMMY LARREN JOINS UP •

At several things Dunmore wondered.

He had seen proud girls, and pretty girls, before. He had seen them treat men with all the contempt of that tyrannical power which beauty gives into their hands; but never before had he witnessed such a thing as this. And, most marvelous of all, the proud Tankerton submitted to this abuse in the face of the crowd, and actually was offering his hand to mount her. More wonderful still, the crowd did not seem offended, or to find anything ridiculous in this submission, but they merely looked upon Beatrice Kirk with wondering and admiring eyes.

There was an interruption just as she was about to put her foot into the hand which Tankerton was offering. Out across the street from the butcher shop lurched a big man, Bill Ogden. He had humped shoulders, and a long, brutal face; he looked, in fact, very much like Jimmy Larren's description of him—a swine that had run wild in the woods.

He carried a stout stick in his hand, and singling out Jimmy in the crowd, he brought the cudgel down on his shoulders.

"You little brat!" yowled Ogden, even louder than Jimmy's yell of surprise and of pain, "I'll teach you to go gaddin'! I'll learn you manners! I'll——"

Jimmy dodged away like a flying bird into the open and

took to his heels, but the club reached him again as he darted off, and this time it grazed his head with sufficient force to make him stagger.

Dulled though his wits were by that stroke, still he had intelligence enough to know that he could not get away in the open after receiving such a blow, so he wheeled and staggered back into the crowd.

They seemed used to this brutality, and gave back, roaring with laughter, while the youngster fled on with contracted, desperate face, and the monster gained rapidly behind him, one hand outstretched, his mouth grinning with expectant joy.

At the first shout, the girl had turned from her horse; now she leaped in between Jimmy and his persecutor, with her quirt slashing through the air like a sword. It fell straight across the leering face of Bill Ogden.

"You wild cat!" yelled the butcher, staggering back. "I'll—I'll teach you! I'll——"

She leaped straight in at him.

Dunmore could see her face and it was on fire with a savage joy, a sort of animal ferocity.

"You brute!" said she through her teeth. "I'll teach you to grunt and howl among human beings!"

And with almost every word the rapid quirt slashed and lashed over the head, the face, the guarding hands of Bill Ogden.

Once he actually lurched forward at her; but at the same moment he saw the leveled revolver in the hand of Tankerton, and received a blow that drew blood from forehead to chin. Howling like a beast with pain and with rage, Bill Ogden turned at last and fled with a bleeding face to the shelter of his shop.

Beatrice Kirk, watching him out of sight, went back toward her horse, saying: "Bah, bah! The filthy pig! Why do you let such creatures stay here, James? Why do you do it?"

"I don't think that he'll stay long, after this," answered Tankerton.

"Where's the boy?" she demanded. "I want to have a look at him."

Out of the crowd, some one found young Larren as he was skulking away, and brought him back to her. He was rubbing his injured head, but the expression of his face was calm enough.

"Are you hurt, sonny?" said she.

And Dunmore, listening for some feminine touch of pity and gentleness, thought that he recognized none whatever in the voice of the girl.

"Well, whacha think, ma'am?" said Jimmy.

She laughed, seeming much pleased by this sharp answer.

"Not hurt bad, though," said he, philosophically. "He didn't bust anything. Otherwise, I don't care a rap."

"You don't? D'you get many of these beatings?"

"Enough to keep me toughened up pretty good," said he.

Again she laughed. She drew nearer to the ragged lad and laid a hand on his shoulder.

"Look me in the eye," said she.

"Aw, I can look at you, all right," said Larren.

He tilted his head a little, for he lacked a good deal of her height, and the pair confronted each other. Dunmore surveyed them with a peculiar interest. It was this same lad who had whistled "The Campbells Are Coming" under his window and roused him from the bed where he was drowsing; roused him just in time, and cleared his brain to meet the sudden attack of Tankerton.

Steadily she eyed the boy, while the crowd watched curiously.

"Well," she said, "what's your name?"

"Jimmy Larren."

"Was that your father?"

"Does that look it? He don't, and he ain't!" said Larren.

"You're not very grateful to me," she suggested.

"Aw," said he, "I'll get everything that you saved me from. I'd rather you had let me alone. Because then he would have finished in one bust. This way, he'll spread it on thick for a month. He'll whack me every time the cuts on his face hurt him."

Then he added, with a boy's sense of justice: "You meant pretty good, though. I thank you for that, ma'am."

"James!" she said suddenly.

"That's me," said the boy.

"No, it isn't," she retorted, as Tankerton came up.

"Why don't you take this boy along with you? He's not living with his family."

"You don't mean it, Beatrice!" said Tankerton.

"Why don't I? I'll take care of him. Besides, he looks like something real to me. Not a fake!"

And she looked insultingly into the face of Tankerton, and then straight across at Dunmore.

At that, his heart rose hotly in him, but shame and yearning immediately followed.

Tankerton had stepped back.

"Youngster, do you want to come with us?"

"Me? Why not?" said Jimmy.

"You know that we move about a good deal?"

"Well, you've had a good look at my speed just now," said Jimmy, grinning.

At that, the crowd laughed, except the girl and Dunmore. She was too busy watching the boy's face; and Dunmore in watching the keen, almost grim, expression of Beatrice Kirk.

When the laughter died down, Tankerton added: "You understand, Jimmy? You'll hardly have a steady home with us?"

"Say," said Jimmy, "I ain't used to a home. I been raised in a butcher shop."

"Don't make any more objections," commanded the girl. "I want him. He's a good boy. Maybe he will be a man! Give him a horse, James, and we'll start together."

This high-handed command Tankerton mildly obeyed, and at once. A mustang and a saddle were on hand in five minutes, and Jimmy Larren was mounted; his clothes, in obedience to a message from the outlaw leader, had been tied in a bundle and flung through the window of the butcher shop into the dust of the street. These were tied on behind the saddle, and the four were ready to start.

As they mounted, Dunmore heard Tankerton say to the girl: "Where's the boy?"

"What boy?" she asked.

"Young Furneaux. D'you mean to say that he let you ride out of camp without tagging along?"

"Oh, Furneaux's all right," said she, "but I'm tired of him. He started to come along, but I chucked him in the woods, and it'll take the greenhorn a whole day to find his way back!"

To that, Dunmore listened with sharpened ears, but now they began to move out from the crowd, and presently they were jogging down the road, raising the dust in lazy drifts behind them. The sun was very low now, and crimson was appearing in the eastern sky, low down between the blue mountains. Up from the gorges, more blue was welling, the very trees were entangled in it, and it seemed to Dunmore that he was riding, truly, into the blue kingdom of the horizon to where Carrick Dunmore had ruled so many hundred years before him.

The girl and Larren went in front, and Tankerton and Dunmore kept to the rear, Tankerton deep in thought, and now and then biting his lip.

"Is she one of you?" asked Dunmore at last, tormented into speech by his curiosity.

"She? Beatrice?" said Tankerton absently.

Then he explained: "Her father was Judge Kirk's son. The great Judge Kirk, I mean. The one who was run out of Tennessee by the Hodgkin-Kirk feud. His son took that to heart. They'd lost everything, you see. And Phil Kirk— that was the girl's father—after his father's death, went back to Tennessee to settle a lot of overdue accounts. He killed three men, or four, I think."

"Fair fight?"

"Why, I suppose so. That doesn't matter so much in a feud, I guess. At any rate, he killed 'em, and they didn't leave it to the feud law. They called in the police!"

"And ran him out?"

"Ran him straight into these mountains. He was working a patch of land, taking a few pelts every winter, and living like a beggar, he and his girl, until I came along eight years ago and showed him how to find an easier life for himself, and an education for Beatrice."

"She's been educated?"

"About everything that money can do for her has been done," said Tankerton, almost drearily, "but——"

"But what?"

Tankerton did not answer, but looked down the road before him as though he were seeing some new and strange sight approach.

Dunmore did not press his last question, for he had seen and heard enough to partially understand what a problem the girl could be. He soon found himself staring ahead into the riches of the eastern sky, and at the noble, blue mountains that rolled to either side in rank on rank.

## XIX

## • JIMMY LARREN, PHILOSOPHER •

WHERE the road took a sharp turn around the shoulder of the mountain, with the big pines walking up from the lower slope, and the jumbled stumps left by a forest fire standing like black-hooded figures of misery, two men started out from the woods on active little mountain ponies and swung into the trail with raised hands.

Tankerton spurred instantly to the lead.

"Who's there?" he called.

"Hank and Lew Deacon," came the answer, and the riders drew slowly closer, as though to prove that they were not dangerous but came in peace.

Dunmore saw two bulky figures of young men, looking in the dull glow of the sunset as large as the horses they sat on. Both stepped to the ground from the saddle, rather than leaped down, and they stood before Tankerton.

"What do you want with me?" he asked.

"We want half a minute of your time, Mr. Tankerton."

"What is it?"

"We been wranglin' two years about a piece of ground down there in the river bottom. Our uncle died and he left no will. He owned the ground, and he'd promised it to Lew, because he always favored Lew over me. But I'm the older. And there wasn't no written will. So I claim one half the place."

"Why shouldn't you let him have it?" asked Tankerton of Lew.

"I'll see him hanged first," said Lew. "He's a sneak, and

a fool, and too yaller to be willin' to fight it out, man to man."

"It's a lie," said Hank. "I'll fight you now!"

He said it quickly enough, but his voice was a shade unsteady.

"There'll be no fighting," said Tankerton. "You two split the land in two parts and keep each to his own share."

"And the house?" said Lew. "Is that to be carved in two? Besides, it'd make me sick to see the face of him every day!"

"How many acres are there?"

"Forty."

"What are they worth?"

"More'n two thousand dollars, and the house and the barn and the rest of the stuff, like hosses, and what not, would bring in pretty nigh onto three thousand more."

Tankerton said quietly: "Lew, go back to the house and pack up your things. You leave that farm, and Hank will pay you twenty-five hundred dollars for your share."

"Why," said Lew, "I'd let him have it for two thousand, but he ain't got that many cents!"

"He'll pay it to you a fifth part with interest every year. D'you hear, Hank?"

"I could manage that pretty good," said Hank.

"I'd take anything to get shut of him," said Lew.

"Then," said Tankerton, "you can go down to the Erickson Lumber Company and tell the boss that I sent you along. Or else I could get you a place in the plains working at——"

"I'll take the lumber, thanks."

"I'm going on. Mind you that I'm the witness that this agreement has been made, and I'll hold you both to it. There's one last thing that I have to say to you. How long since you've shaken hands?"

"Us? Why, I dunno that we ever started!"

"You'll start now," said Tankerton. "The pair of you, shake hands in front of me."

Hank reluctantly held out his hand, but Lew started back.

"I'd rather touch mildew!" said he savagely. "I'd rather take a dead man's hand!"

"What!" exclaimed Tankerton with sudden force. "Do you think that those big shoulders of yours and the strength in your hands make you able to despise other people? I tell you, Lew, that no man has any power, except that which his friends are willing to give him. And where are you to pick up friends if you can't get them out of your own family? A man full of hate is like a house with the shutters closed. He can't see out, and no one else can see in! Shake hands with Hank, and no more words about it!"

Lew did not answer, but, making a slow step toward his cousin, he reluctantly held out his hand, and gripped that of Hank.

"Good night!" said Tankerton. "And remember that if you're proud of your own blood, you ought to be proud of each other!"

He rode on, but the two cousins made no answer to him. They stood silently facing each other in the dark of the increasing dusk. Then Dunmore found that Tankerton was no longer at his side, but went in the lead with Beatrice Kirk, while Jimmy Larren was now knee to knee with him.

Jimmy was chuckling softly.

"What's the joke?" asked Dunmore.

"Why, Tankerton's the joke!" said the boy.

"I thought he did that job mighty well, sonny."

"Aw, sure he did. Them two, they'll be cryin' on each other's shoulders the whole of the way home. But that ain't what I mean. I mean Tankerton, there, the way he treats her. Look at 'em now!"

With a sudden whoop, the two leaders darted away down the road and disappeared around the next bend.

"Aw, he'll let her beat him, too," said Jimmy Larren. "Even let her beat Gunfire, he would!"

"Why not, if it makes her happy? She's only a girl, Jimmy."

"Say," said Jimmy, "if you was to raise a dog like a wolf, would you call it a dog because it looked like one, or a wolf because it killed calves and was like to cut your own throat?"

"What do you mean by that?" said Dunmore, gradually guessing what the youngster had in mind.

"Well," said Larren, "here's you and the chief that meet up and make friends, and along comes that girl and gives you both a dirty look, and horsewhips Cousin Bill, and takes me off to the camp."

"You ain't grateful, Jimmy, for that?"

"Aw, sure I am. But no man could've acted more rougher nor more prouder than her. You take the way that she hands lip to the chief, what would he do if she was wearin' trousers instead of skirts? He'd give her a whackin'! Does he give her a whackin'? Naw, he treats her like she was a cross between an angel right down from the sky and his own grandmother."

"You gotta learn to be polite to ladies, Jimmy."

"Everybody oughta get what's comin' to 'em," said Jimmy. "And if a mule plays hoss, he's gunna be rode with spurs. But when this here girl comes along and kicks you and the chief in the face, you both get on a kind of sick, moony look, like you'd swallered a spoonful of honey and it turned out to taste like castor oil! Nope, I dunno what happens to a gent when he gets about eighteen. Seems to lose all holts when he sees a girl with a pretty face or fine figger. And when along comes one like Beatrice Kirk, as slick and as fine as a blood filly two-year-old, stampin' on the ground, and runnin' in the wind, it plumb paralyzes the brains of all kinds of important gents. There's the chief looking like a lost calf every time she comes around, and there's that Furneaux, that would like to go straight ag'in and climb back onto a high chair and be a bank clerk, or something, but he can't get himself away from her!"

Dunmore started in the saddle. He began to bless the moment that had put him in touch with young Jimmy.

"Where do you learn all this stuff?" said he. "Or where do you think you learn it?"

"Aw, you take somebody as young as me," said Jimmy Larren, "and it don't make no difference what you say right in front of me. A kid like me, he ain't got no brain. And if you want to dodge me, all you gotta do is to use big words and give each other a funny look!"

He chuckled at the thought, and Dunmore laughed aloud.

"Who is this Furneaux?" said he.

"He's one of these men that always rides straight up and never pulls no leather," said the boy. "He's got an idea about how he'd oughta act. If he was to ride five mile without gettin' blood on his spurs, he'd be plumb ashamed of himself. He's gotta wear a sash, like a greaser, and his hat cocked on one side, and pearl-handled guns, and if he was to tip less'n a dollar, it'd keep him awake all night for ten nights runnin'!"

"He's a fake, then?" asked Dunmore.

"Him? Aw, he wakes up every morning, and tells himself that he's a desperado ten times before he puts on his boots. And when he goes to bed at night he says: 'I ain't shot nobody down, or faced nobody down; this here is a wasted day!'"

"I sort of get your drift," said Dunmore. "What started him?"

"He got sight of Beatrice Kirk, and he says to himself that the only thing to do is to turn wild. Finer than ice cream! Well, wild he turns, and he's had so much cream that he's hankerin' after steak and fried potatoes!"

The boy snorted with disgust.

"Hey," said he, "what's the matter with growed-up men that they can see something in her so doggone fine and rare?"

"She did something for you to-day," said Dunmore, "that no other woman would've done."

"Well," said the boy, "that proves that she's a pretty good sort of a man, then, don't it?"

Dunmore did not answer, but he took the words of the boy home to his heart and considered them.

Ever since he had seen Beatrice, there had been a hopeless ache in his heart, and he had found himself sighing deeply. It was like nothing so much as homesickness, to his way of thinking, and it gradually dawned upon Dunmore that he was at last thoroughly, wretchedly, miserably in love!

And now it seemed to Dunmore that the dusky road was changed, and the great woods around him began to be loftier and more majestic, brushing their tops against the stars, which were just appearing, and what he had heard from this ragged urchin seemed to Dunmore the profoundest wisdom.

She had been something beyond touching, beyond comparison; she had been like a blade which is all edge—something to dazzle but not to be grasped. But now perhaps this lad had fitted a handle to the problem.

So Dunmore raised his head and drifted on with the smooth and sliding trot of the mare, while Larren bumped beside him on the back of his mustang.

"Hey!" said the boy at last, "are you gunna jolt the lungs out of me, Dunmore? Or are you jus' ridin' in your sleep?"


# XX

## • SECOND PLACE •


THEY came up with Beatrice Kirk and Tankerton after a time, and from the first words they overheard, it was plain that the boy had been right. The two had raced, and Beatrice had won with her bay.

She said with perfect assuredness: "You don't jockey your horse enough, James. You ride him too straight up."

"You're a lightweight," he told her.

"What does weight count in a short sprint like that?" she demanded. "Look at the light they're winking on the shoulder of Mount Tom!"

Dunmore, looking to the right as she waved, saw a rapidly blinking light, obviously spelling out some message. The leader was sufficiently interested to draw rein.

"I hope Legges is in camp taking that down," said he.

"They wouldn't go on chattering if they hadn't had a signal back," said she.

"More business! More business!" sang out Tankerton, quite cheerfully. "There'll be something for us to do before long."

"Then I'm going to ride with the boys," said she.

"You?" cried Tankerton.

"You promised me!"

"That I'd let you ride on the next trip? Are you wild, Beatrice? You teased it out of me, but you knew that I didn't mean what I said."

"If I don't go," she raged, "I'll never have a thing to do with you again. I'll—"

"Look here," broke in Tankerton, at last annoyed sufficiently to protest against this tyrant, "you're not fair! You want me to let you put on trousers and be a man."

"I'd make a better man than half of you," said she. "I can ride as hard and as far; I can shoot as straight; I'm not afraid, and—I don't knock myself silly with redeye! Why can't I go with the party?"

"Don't talk any more about it," said Tankerton.

Instead of answering, she twitched her horse off the road and dashed noisily through the underbrush, disappearing at once among the big trees beyond.

Tankerton turned his horse as though to follow, but, thinking better of this, he reined back onto the road with a curse, and then spurred up the trail rapidly.

"It ain't all turkey for Tankerton," laughed Jimmy Larren. "I bet many a time he wishes that he was runnin' a little farm, even if he had to get chilblains all winter and sunstroke in the summer."

"He's the king, however," said Dunmore.

"Sure he's the king," said the boy, "but he's settin' on tacks all the time. Mostly when she's around!"

They jogged on after the dwindling figure of Tankerton until the trees parted before them and they came into a clearing with a big fire in the center. By the light of the fire, they could see four log shacks built around the verge of the open space and, at the doors, or lounging around the fire itself, were fifteen or more men.

Dunmore, instinctively, drew a tighter rein on Excuse Me.

He had known beforehand into what company he was riding, but no amount of mental preparation could altogether brace him for this scene. Nearly a score of men were there; all were armed; all were experts professionally with their weapons; and all obeyed Tankerton with an absolute faith. And a gesture from him would be the end of Carrick Dunmore.

Dunmore could see reasons why the bandit would delay

the business until the camp was reached. The mob of Harpersville was one thing; but here in the camp his killing could be executed far more privately and cause less talk. But of one thing at least Dunmore was assured. Tankerton would not admit a partner to his greatness without making some much more desperate and prolonged struggle than that in the hotel at Harpersville.

So he checked the mare and she pranced uneasily, while the boy sheered close to him and gasped:

"You ain't gunna go in, Mr. Dunmore?"

Carrick threw a grim glance at the youngster, for the exclamation came as a sudden and unexpected reinforcement of his own feelings. The boy went on: "I thought— that you was just gunna be—the first gent that ever had a firsthand sight of Tankerton's gang, but—are you gunna go on in?"

Dunmore looked aside, and there he saw leaning against a big stump a tall fellow with a rifle in his hands, watching him attentively. If he whirled Excuse Me and strove to bolt, that rifle would bring him down!

His coolness deserted him, then. He had to grit his teeth to make himself go on, and coming within the circle of the firelight, he swung lightly down to the ground.

Out of the darker shadows in the background, Tankerton's voice came harsh and grating upon his ear.

"Boys, the doctor and Lynn Tucker were all wrong. Dunmore is an old friend of mine; I've brought him back to be one of us!"

That was all. There was no talk about division of authority, partnership, or even a lieutenancy placed in the hands of Dunmore. But the latter wisely decided that this was not the time to press the point.

As he was introduced in this casual fashion, he saw every face around the fire lifted, while all eyes examined him for a single blazing second with the utmost fervor; men stepped out from the cabin doors, as well. But after the first scanning, they regarded him more covertly, as though not wishing to offend him with a stare.

He waved his hand to them and then started off to find the horse shed and put up the mare; but it had been made plain to him that his name was familiar to the gang. Whatever other consolation he was to get out of the situation, this was a grim one—that they must have talked over his affairs more than once, and perhaps the three expeditions which had been made against him had every one been the subject of many surmises. Each day they had expected to see the champion come back victorious; twice their men had been foiled; the third time, the chief brought him in.

In what manner would they take this? As a victory on the part of the leader, or as something which Dunmore had forced Tankerton to do? No doubt, the former would be the way of it.

He found little Jimmy Larren at the stable before him. The stable was a long lean-to, built beneath the shelter of the trees and anchored against them, and inside there was a single row of horses.

Jimmy carried the lantern before him down the list, and he found himself looking over animals of two types. There were little sharp-backed mustangs for mountain work, and there were long-legged blood horses for expeditions farther afield. Toward the center, he found a vacant stall and put the mare into it; the boy scrambled up into the hay and forked down a feed, while Dunmore found the grain bin and brought a measure of clean oats.

Tankerton was waiting for him near the entrance to the stable.

"I'll show you where you sleep," said he, and marched Dunmore off to the largest of the four cabins. Inside, there were ten bunks fixed against the wall, a stove in the center of the room glowing with a fire, for the mountain night was always chilly, and a table at either end piled with tattered books and magazines whose covers had disappeared, and whose leaves were frayed, curled up with much reading, and yellowed with exposure to the sun. Between the head and foot of each bunk were a number of pegs, making a sort of clothes closet. He noted that every "closet" was well filled, usually several extra pairs of boots appeared on the floor, several hats of different kinds topped off the display, and on the whole there was a sense of much well-being, for men leading such lives. The cabin walls, too, seemed solidly built, without unstopped chinks through which the winds could pry, and though in the winter it might be difficult enough to be comfortable here, at this season of the year, it was better than most ranches.

"Here you are," said Tankerton. "That bunk there in the center is empty. That's yours. I'm busy now. So make yourself at home."

Of course, it was unsatisfactory. After the promise of divided sovereignty which Tankerton had made in Harpersville, there should have been more ceremony, more opportunity to choose. But Dunmore had made up his mind to accept the present for what it would bring. He said nothing, but nodded and carried his pack into the room, while Jimmy Larren followed, dragging his own bundle of rags, and took an apparently free bunk at the foot of Dunmore's.

There appeared to be no other person present, at first, but by light of a lantern which burned at the foot of the room, Dunmore presently saw in the farther corner a slender youth who lay in his bunk reading a magazine. This he now lowered, as though feeling Dunmore's eyes, and looked fixedly at the newcomer.

So Dunmore crossed to him, and coming nearer, saw that the left arm and shoulder of the reader were swathed in bandages.

"My name is Dunmore," said he.

The other extended his right hand.

"I'm 'Bud' Arthur," said he in a curiously soft voice.

He waited without another word, his calm, cold eyes fixed steadily on Dunmore's face, but the latter, with a nod, turned away. For the name shot many pictures across his mind's eye.

Bud Arthur never had appeared off his father's ranch or in the public prints a year before. Since then, he had stood in a mask before a stagecoach and plundered the boot; he had walked into a bank at midday and nearly got off with a fortune; he had then returned to his home town to shoot down a marshal who had made certain poisonous remarks about him; and had escaped from the town, hotly pursued.

Since, he had passed into oblivion, so far as the public was concerned, and the reason now was clear. The omniscient Tankerton could not afford to overlook a lad who had killed four men in the space of six months, and, therefore, he had stretched out his hand and taken in the wounded youngster. Another week or so and this hawk would once more be on the wing, flying at the whistle of

Tankerton. For such were the ideal citizens of the blue kingdom of the horizon where Dunmore now must sow and reap, and once more his mind grew dark with the way that lay before him.

As he went back to his bunk, young Larren grinned suddenly aside.

"What's eating you, Jimmy?" he asked.

The latter clucked as though calling to a hen yard.

"Chick, chick, chick!" said he. "You got some raw wolf meat to feed to these here chickens, big boy? They're plumb tired of raw dog, the way they look!"


# XXI

## • LET DUNMORE DO IT •


A GONG sounded loudly and rapidly across the clearing, and a high, singsong voice intoned: "Come an' get it, come an' get it, boys!"

So Jimmy Larren and Dunmore went out of the bunkhouse and headed in the direction of the clamor. From the other houses, other streams were heading in the same direction, and presently Dunmore entered a low cabin which had a long table stretched down its center, the men taking their places on either hand.

There was plenty of light. Two lamps were hung by iron chains from the roof, and they threw an illumination which enabled him to see all the faces around the table clearly. The men were filing in with cheerful words to one another, until Dunmore appeared—after which came a moment of silence until the cook, a broad-faced fellow with a face as scarred as that of a pirate or a German student, called out: "There you are, new man. There's your place down by the foot of the table. Set down!"

All cooks are tyrants, but Dunmore overlooked the order entirely. Tankerton was taking a place at one end of the long boards, and Doctor Legges was about to take the other end, when Dunmore tapped the doctor on the shoulder.

"Did you aim to set down here, doctor?" he asked genially.

"This is my place, my young friend," said the doctor. "And it's good to see you among us at last, Dunmore. Idleness, idleness is the greatest sin, Dunmore; and it pleases me that you're about to set to work!"

"Thanks," said Dunmore, feeling that all eyes were on him and the doctor—men even refrained from dragging back their chairs, as though they would not risk shutting out a word of the conversation by their noise. "Thanks, doctor. There ain't a thing in the world that's better than good advice. It's a better present than money, because money can be swiped, eh? But now I'd like to do something in return. Look here, you were going to sit down where the draft is blowing straight in on you through the window cracks! It's no place for a man of your age, doctor."

The doctor blinked, as though not understanding what was meant.

"There's no draft here," said he at last. "Not a stir of air!"

"Listen to you!" said Dunmore in gentle reproval. "You'd set right down here and sacrifice yourself for the sake of keepin' a younger man out of this here chair! You'd set here and take rheumatism and lumbago and a chill, and all for the sake of sparin' a mighty lot younger and stronger man from the same troubles. But I wouldn't let you, doctor!"

Softly he pushed the doctor away.

"Down there by the stove is the right place for you, doctor," he insisted. "That's where you——"

"This," said the doctor, turning red and then white with anger, "has always been my chair!"

"There you are!" said Dunmore. "I got no doubt that's what's aged you—settin' in a draft, givin' up your health for the rest of the boys. But I'm gunna save you from that after this. I'm gunna take the chair—and keep it!"

With that, he sat down, but no other man in the room stirred. All looked fixedly at the doctor, thus ousted from the second place of honor at the table; and the doctor himself seemed to waver for a moment between a desire of battle and fear of the new enemy.

But at length the genially smiling face of the younger man overcame his own power of will. He turned with a nod and an assumed smile.

"As a matter of fact," said the doctor, "there is a chilly draft of air blowin' at that end of the room. We gotta get hold of some weather strippin' to shut out some of the wind from this room."

With a murmur and a scraping of chairs, the rest sat down, and Tankerton seemed to be busying himself with talk with Lynn Tucker, who sat at his right, studiously avoiding the eyes of Dunmore at the farther end of the room. As a matter of fact, all the others avoided the attention of Dunmore, but there was a good excuse for this, since huge platters of beef-steaks, of potatoes roasted in ashes, of corn pone, and of ham, were borne in and carried about the various positions of advantage, where the long arms of the hungry men could reach to the food.

Dunmore was liberal to his own plate, but he could not claim any instant precedence in such an assemblage of eaters!

While the first clatter of plates, and of steel forks grating on tin, was still at its height, Tankerton said suddenly:

"We have bad news. Our friend and bunkie, Chelton, has been nabbed!"

It was a new name to Dunmore, but the announcement made a sensation among the others. They stared at one another and at their leader. Eating paused for an instant.

"How was he got?" someone asked.

"He wanted hotel food in a big town and he went all the way to Clifford Springs to get it!"

"I've had that hankerin'," said a ruffian close to Dunmore, though he was not addressing his words to the latter. "I seen a time when I'd 've paid its price in gold for a table set out with a white cloth, and a waitress in a white apron and a clean pair of hands to bring on the chuck and ask how many lumps of sugar would I have in the—"

"Who got him?" interrupted another.

"Why, nobody but that Ban Petersen," said Lynn Tucker with a fury in his voice. "He's gunna be got, is Ban Petersen, and he's gunna be got good!"

"He's ridin' us!" said another.

"They say he keeps a special picture gallery in his home-town jail, all filled with our pictures!"

"I'd like to make a fire of them pictures, and toast Ban on the top of the pile."

"What's gunna be done?" demanded another.

Tankerton raised his head a little, and though he kept his voice quiet, every other sound and movement instantly ceased throughout the room.

"What's going to be done?" he asked acidly. "Why, no doubt you have an idea, Jeff. You want something to be done, of course; and of course I expect all of you to have brilliant ideas. When you go out and get yourselves tangled in barbed wire, you are always able to get out. You don't clamor for me then and expect me to come. You don't blame me and your own luck if I can't get you free without tearing your clothes and pricking the skin. No, by Heaven!" said Tankerton, his lips growing stiff with passion. "When you're well and flush there's no thought of Tankerton, that slave driver. You go off as Oscar Chelton did. You throw yourselves over a cliff, and you expect me to be standing by beneath, ready to catch you!"

He snapped his fingers in careless fashion.

"I'm tired of being nursemaid to a crew of half-wits!" said he, and sternly ended his speech.

The others did not rebel against this sweeping condemnation, but they looked studiously down at their plates, avoiding the eye of their leader, even avoiding the eyes of their table companions.

And, when this had gone on for a few moments, there still remain a silence over the table, which was broken by the sound of angrily disputing voices.

"There's our Beatrice at it with young Furneaux again!" said Doctor Legges. "If they keep it up, it will have to be a case either of marriage or of murder."

Dunmore could hear the voices clearly as they disputed. Young Furneaux was making no effort to keep his temper or his voice within bounds, but he exclaimed bitterly: "You've made a fool of me again, Beatrice. This is the last time. You've tricked me and dodged me because you're tired of having me around. Well, I'll never bother

you again that way. I'm through with this absurd business,
I tell you!"

"You won't listen to me," said the girl. "You're simply
trying to make something out of nothing!"

"Is it nothing to ramble half a day through the woods,
shouting for you?"

"Dear Rod," said the girl, "how I wish I could have
heard you!"

"I suppose you do, but this is the last time that I'll be
such an ass as to think that you can treat any man as a
serious friend!"

"Hush! They'll hear you inside the chuck house."

"What if they do?" They've known for weeks that I've
been raving mad about you! It's one of their great jokes!"

The girl appeared in the doorway, and as all heads
turned toward her, Dunmore saw her wink broadly upon
the crew, as though to invite them into her confidence.

"Uncle Jim," she appealed to Tankerton, "here's Rodman saying that I'm a liar, and I don't know what else!
Are you going to sit by and listen to such things?"

"Of course I am," answered Tankerton. "Because he's
right, and you know he's right."

"Harder for you to tell the truth, Beatrice," said one of
the men, "than it is for a snake to make a straight trail on
the ground!"

"There you are!" said the girl, taking her place at the
right hand of Tankerton. "Every one of you hates me, and
every one of you slanders me. I'm going away! I simply
won't stay here!"

"Why, honey," broke in a Southern drawl, "the heat
you raise would melt yo'se'f right out of any other place
but this."

Furneaux went gloomily to a chair and jerked it back,
looking to right and to left as though he would have wel-
comed trouble on either hand. Then he sat down.

He looked somewhat like his Aunt Elizabeth. There
was the same lean, aristocratic face, the same pride, the
same bright, clear eye. No other at that table seemed
worthy of being placed beside young Furneaux, and Dunmore could not regret that he had come to win such a fellow back to an honest life. But though the task seemed
worth while, it also appeared trebly difficult the instant

that he laid eyes on the boy. It would be like guiding a hawk in the middle air to attempt to handle this lad.

The girl in the meantime, by no means had given up her attack upon Furneaux, but Dunmore, carefully watching, saw her eyes rest more than once half sadly, half dreamily upon the face of the boy. The instant the latter became aware of her gaze, she pretended confusion, dropped her glance, and talked busily with Tankerton. And presently Furneaux was neglecting his food and looking straight before him into vacancy.

Dunmore smiled. It was plain that she had won him back again.

"And now for Chelton, boys," said Tankerton suddenly.

"How are we to help him? Let's have ideas?"

Doctor Legges said instantly: "Why, Jim, there's your man. He's so careful to keep us out of drafts that he'll be sure to nearly break his heart to keep any of us out of prison. Let Dunmore handle the job!"

## XXII

### • TWO ODD PASSENGERS •

SHERIFF BAN PETERSEN had two qualities which were invaluable in his profession: In the first place, he knew how to shoot straight. In the second place, he had no sense of humor.

In all men who laugh, there is a strain of the easy-going, and those who go easily, gently through life are not always prepared for the worst which they may find in the human nature of others. It was very different with Sheriff Ban Petersen. He was always ready to look to the bottom of any problem of crime, and no motive was too small or too mean to escape the keen eye of the sheriff.

In the same manner, he never thought that any jail was "safe enough" or that any guard in it was "honest enough."

He trusted in this world nothing but himself, and the result was a career which grew more and more brilliant.

But of all that he had done, nothing promised so much for him as the bit of luck which made him the captor of that famous member of a famous band—Oscar Chelton. Good fortune had thrown Chelton into his hands, and the sheriff was determined that nothing on earth should get him away! Having got his man, it only needed that the sheriff should deliver him at the right place. Thereafter, his name would be among the immortals. He could be sheriff forever; and no man would dare to run against him! But that was only true if he kept Chelton from slipping through his hands.

In this case, he did not depend upon himself alone, but he occupied the rear of the smoking car on the train with his prisoner and a hand-picked posse of six men. They were mountain men, these, and they were armed, therefore, not with revolvers but with rifles. For his own part, the sheriff had not much faith in revolvers when they were used by any one less expert than himself, or a Tankerton, say. Rifles were the safe bet.

"A slow shot but a sure shot is what we want!" he was fond of saying.

But even with the prisoner manacled to his own left arm, and with six hardy riflemen about him, the sheriff was not perfectly at ease, but examined every platform of every station that the local passed through, searching for suspicious faces in the groups that were often standing there.

The curious, from time to time, came back into the smoking car, and the sheriff regarded all these intruders with an intense interest. He would have been very glad to have the smoking car entirely to himself, but since this could not be, he had to content himself with warning the passengers to keep three seats away from him and his armed escort.

Even so, he sometimes unfastened Chelton from his arm, clamped the manacle to the side of the seat, and went forward to overlook any man who appeared to him a possible danger.

It was at one of the smallest flag stations that the blind man got on board.

Even this fellow the sheriff insisted upon examining, while the posse smiled covertly. For it would have been hard to imagine a more decrepit case of invalidism than this. The old fellow came well bent over, with a grizzle stubble of beard an inch or so long on his face, looking as though it had been trimmed with a sheep shears. Dark glasses covered his eyes; his trousers were a sort of rusty green-black, and the frayed seat had been literally patched with sacking, stitched in with sack sewer's yarn. His boots were very old; and because one foot was troubled with rheumatism, perhaps, the toe of that boot had been cut away and the foot protruded, wrapped in a dusty rag. He carried a stout stick, as well to feel his way as to support him in stepping, but even with it, his sight seemed so completely gone that he could not have made progress except for the boy who led him along. He was as ragged as his elder, but he was a blithe and chipper as a sparrow, and seemed to be winking at the world to invite it to join him in laughter at the poor old derelict.

However, no sooner had those two steered to a seat than the sheriff disengaged himself from his prisoner and going to the two, he said: "Who are you, partner?"

The blind man cupped a hand at his ear and barked in a screeching voice that rang through the entire car: "Hey?"

The sheriff started. The posse and the other passengers laughed loudly, and perhaps it was this, or perhaps because he really had detected something in the appearance of the old man that made him suspicious, but at any rate the sheriff at once plucked the glasses from the face of the other.

The old fellow raised a hand to shade his eyes, as though whatever bit of life remained in them were dazzled by the sudden radiance in which he found himself, and the sheriff leaned over and squinted sharply at him.

"Sonny, sonny, what mought it be?" quavered the old man.

The sheriff replaced the glasses he had just removed.

"Maybe you're all right," said he, "but you got a mighty young-lookin' pair of eyes to go with the rest of your makeup. How old are you?"

"Hey?" screamed the old man again, leaning closer with hand cupped behind his ear.

The sheriff started back a step, thrust away by that horribly raucous voice.

"You, kid," he said to the grinning boy, "what's his name?"

"'Pop' Cumberland is his name."

"What does 'Pop' stand for?"

"Grandpop."

"What's his front name?"

"I dunno. His old friends they all called him 'Squinty,' and Gramma, she called him Josh."

"Joshua Cumberland," translated the sheriff. "Where you come from, kid?"

"Up at Kilrainie, in the hills, where Cousin Jack has a place with—"

"Whatcha doin' away down here?"

"When Pop started for Tulma, Cousin Jack, he said it'd be better to break the trip by stoppin' off at Cousin Maggie's down here at—"

"You drove down?"

"Cousin Jack, he was sending down the wagon to cart back some two-by-fours for the buildin' of a new corral, because Jack, he's gunna catch mustangs for the market next year and he wanted to yard 'em up where they wouldn't—"

"So you're goin' to Tulma?"

"Yep. Cousin Joe, he's willin' to take on the old man for a couple or two years, he says, and then—"

"You got cousins all over the face of the map?"

"You just oughta see!" said the boy with enthusiasm. "You take an old gent like Pop, here, and he's got 'em right down to great-grandchildren, and all of 'em has married, and all has got children, and them children has married, and what with cousins by birth and cousins by marriage, it's a regular clan, Pop says, that he started all by himself."

"I've heard of the Cumberlands," agreed the sheriff, "but I never knew there was such a herd of 'em!"

"Ain't there, though? If you could see 'em come and pool together along about Christmas—"

"What are you gunna do at this Cousin Joe's when you get the old man there?"

"They say that I'm gunna go to school. But they got another guess comin'!"

The sheriff laughed.

"I guess you're all right, the two of you," said he, and he went back to his seat, while the passengers and the posse covered their smiles again.

However, Sheriff Petersen was able to detect the amusement in some of the faces, and he explained sternly:

"A lot of you that think this is queer, I wanta tell you that they wouldn't be so many trails run to the ground, if it wasn't that folks looked under stones, now and then, instead of just on top of 'em. That old gent, Cumberland, I guess he's all right, but when he stumbled comin' down the aisle, it looked to me like he recovered himself right smart and easy."

"He's a mountain man," said one of the posse.

"Sure he is," agreed the sheriff, "and, take it from me, a mountain man loses his brains a long time before he loses his legs."

With this, he leaned and looked out the window. The train was approaching a small station beyond which the track led on in a broad bend into rough hills. His eyes narrowed as he looked ahead, and then, pulling back his head from the window, he turned to the prisoner, whose arm once more was manacled to his captor's.

"How you makin' it, Chelton?" he asked.

"Aw, I'm fair," said Chelton.

"Ain't hungry, or nothin'?"

"I could use some food.'

"What'd they give you last night an' this mornin' at the jail?"

"Rice'n molasses."

"Hey? Rice an' molasses? Well, I wouldn't feed a Chinaman on that kind of chuck. But we're gunna stop at this here station of Last Chance, and I reckon that we can pick up some sandwiches or something."

"That'd do me fine," said the prisoner, who maintained a quiet, but not a broken attitude.

The sheriff looked him over with approval.

"You ain't made no trouble for me, Chelton," said he, "and you've acted like a man right straight through. I'm gunna see that that counts for you, in the windup!"

"Nothin' is gunna count for me, much," said young Chelton. "The windin' up is gunna stretch nothin' but my neck and a rope!"

"I wouldn't be too sure," suggested the sheriff amiably. "They's a lot of ways of dodgin' that, and the judge might give you a spell in jail——"

"Jail?" said Chelton. "Look here, Petersen, would you want to live on if you had to change into a hog?"

"Why, I dunno what that has to do with it."

"It's got a lot. I'd rather be a dead man than a swine barred up in a pen! I been in the pen before. Even the smell of it is worse'n death to me, I tell you!"

He said it contemptuously, sternly, and the sheriff looked askance at him and nodded, with rather a dreamy look in his eyes, like one who perceives something far off, and cannot tell whether it be horizon cloud or lofty mountain.

Then the brakes began to grind for the stop.


# XXIII

## • FAST AND SHOOTING •


THEY were pulling into the station at the small town before them, and it appeared that most of the other passengers in the smoking car dismounted at this place, for they were thronging forward toward the platform, the laborers carrying their blanket rolls. The sheriff took note of a number of buckboards and riding poinies gathered near the station, and in front of the station building were half a dozen men waiting. No doubt they had come to meet the cargo of laborers and take them off to ranches and farms.

Well assured of this, he looked to the other side of the track through the opposite windows, and saw that the railroad gate had closed there, in the face of another pair of buckboards and a rider or two.

When he had seen these things, the sheriff stood up

from his seat, dragging his prisoner with him. With a motion of his arm, he gathered the posse about him.

"Now, boys," he said, "I'm gunna tell you something that'll explain why I wanted so many of you along to help me guard Chelton, here. I ain't in the habit of needin' so doggone many to watch one man, but this here case was different. It wasn't Chelton that bothered me none. It was Tankerton and his gang!"

This announcement caused the posse to look solemnly at one another.

"We've got the news accurate and full," said the sheriff. "We've got it from a inside man. They're gunna put one man aboard this here train at this here town, right in front of us. And it ain't gunna do us no good to search for him. Likely, he'll put aboard on the brake rods and climb up from them, or else he'll be blind baggage as we pull up into Running Hoss Gulch. There he'll stop the train, and when he stops it, they's gunna be a swarm of crooks charge us out of the brush on each side of the road.

He paused.

Then, having examined the faces of his hearers carefully, noting the degrees of resolution or of fear which they showed, he went on:

"Some of 'em will probably split for the baggage car. The rest of 'em will come pilin' straight for us. They want money out of this job, but more than that, they want Chelton! They'll come fast, and they'll come shootin', and maybe I don't have to tell you that Tankerton's men can shoot straight?"

He stopped again to examine the grim faces of his men before he continued: "They got a new man up there among the Tankertons, and he's gunna have the charge of his job. That new man is gunna try to win his spurs, as they say, and he'll fight like a wild cat, for one. Now, boys, I could've taken twenty men instead of six. But if I took twenty, probably the Tankertons would've heard about us, and they wouldn't make the charge. As it is, we'll have a chance to warm up our rifles. Keep cool, and shoot to kill! You'll have the sides of the car to cover you. You'll have the window sills to rest your rifles on. We're gunna give the Tankertons such a pepperin' that they'll wish they'd never been born

to see this day! And when the smoke clears off, maybe
we'll have a new cargo of dead men and men that are sick
with bullets to take with us. I ain't talkin' to you about the
glory only, but they's a price on pretty near every head
among the Tankertons!"

"And what about them that go for the baggage car?"
asked a voice.

A deep snore was heard at this moment. It came from
the aged Pop, whose head was sunk upon his breast in the
most profound slumber.

"The old reptile!" growled the sheriff, at this interruption. "Well, boys, them that goes for the baggage car ain't
gunna feel so pert, neither. Inside of that car, they's a safe
and a money shipment. But they's also locked up there a
Federal marshal and four of his men, loaded all down with
repeatin' rifles, and such. If the Tankertons bust open that
door, they're gunna feel like a dog that's stuck his nose
down a rabbit's hole and has a wild cat come bustin' out at
him, all teeth and claws!"

There was a grim chuckle in response.

"It looks like a pretty good plant!" said one.

"Don't it?" answered Petersen. "I tell you, it's a plant
that can't help but work, if you boys will do your share.
We've come in with one Tankerton. Give us a mite of
luck, and we'll have a whole bag full of 'em, and your
names'll all be remembered, besides the solid hard cash
that you'll get out of it!"

He waved his hand toward the exit platform.

The brakes were grinding as the train shuddered to a
stop.

"Leave your guns here," the sheriff added. "Go out
there on the platform and take a turn up and down and
steady yourselves with a good deep breath of fresh air and
then hook on when we pull out!"

Said one: "You gunna stay here alone with Chelton?"

The sheriff grinned.

"I reckon that I'll be all right, unless the old man and
the kid come back and take him away from me!"

There was a laughter at this, and the posse swarmed out
of the train as it halted.

Voices sounded from the platform, then, as the laborers
found their employers here and there, and as soon as the

train was halted, all currents of air roused by its motion ceased, and the still, blasting heat of the Western sun poured through the windows and choked the passengers.

"It's hot," admitted the sheriff.

Chelton did not answer.

He sat rigid, his eyes fixed before him, his lips set, and plainly his mind was far forward in Running Horse Pass, among the shadowy forms of his fellows who would be waiting there! Of this the sheriff took note, but not with pity. Not that he was a hardhearted man, but he lacked imagination, and could not get out of his own skin and into the lives of others.

Here Pop Cumberland wakened with a start and rose.

The boy clawed after him. "This ain't our station," he said.

"Hey?" answered Pop, in his peculiar screeching voice.

And he continued down the aisle toward the sheriff and the prisoner, fumbling his way along from one seat to another.

The boy rose and went in pursuit.

"Old man," said the sheriff, "this ain't the way out of the car, if you want to get out."

"Hey?" said Pop, and he leaned above the sheriff for an answer.

"I say," began the sheriff, "that this ain't the——"

He got no further. Pop Cumberland darted a ponderous right hand to the jaw of the worthy sheriff, and Petersen lurched senseless against the shoulder of the prisoner.

"Keep your hat on," said the quiet voice of Dunmore to Chelton. "We'll soon have you out of this."

With accurate fingers he dipped into the vest pocket of the sheriff and took out a key, and with a turn of that key he made Chelton, for at least that moment, a free man. The manacle which fell from the arm of Chelton he next clasped over the iron side arm of the seat, and tossed the key out the window.

Then they started.

As for Chelton, he had not said a word, but a great tremor ran over him, and he made a single gasping sound, like a man who has risen to the surface after being under water for a long dive. Then he grasped one of the rifles which had been put aside by the posse. Young Jimmy Larren, escort of the aged Pop, had taken another, and Dunmore a third.

They bolted for the platform, but Dunmore, going last, paused long enough to see the sheriff open his eyes and look around without comprehension—then close them again!

From the platform, they descended on the side opposite to the station, and then hurried down the track toward the railroad gate beyond which the two buckboards and the riders waited. Dunmore gave quiet directions, as Chelton suggested that they bolt for it as fast as possible.

"The minute you start running, you'll start trouble," said Dunmore. "Take it easy, Chelton. When we get past the gate, cover that right-hand gent on the cream-colored hoss. That hoss looks as if it could step. I'll take the bay on the left, if I can. It don't look so fast, but it's pretty sure to have enough power to carry my pounds. We'll slice the near hoss out of that team of buckskins and dump Jimmy on it. He can ride anything that steps."

A wild yell arose from the smoking car behind them; a gun clanged like the closing of a metal door, and a shower of cinders kicked against the calf of Chelton's leg.

"Time's up," said Dunmore, as they reached the gate. "Charge 'em, boys!"

And he dived over the gate with a yell.

That yell began and ended the battle for the possession of the horses. Here were half a dozen peaceable citizens who suddenly found a pair of ruffians, to say nothing of a savage-looking boy with a rifle, rushing at them with provocation, while other armed men rushed out of the smoking car of the train and plunged toward them.

The good citizens tumbled out of their saddles as the rifles covered them. Ground never had felt so good as it did now beneath their feet. They bolted for the fences, hopped over them, and kept on running.

"Drop a few shots around that posse—you don't have to shoot to kill!" called Dunmore to Chelton, as for his own part he slashed the chosen horse out of the buckboard team.

The posse, bewildered by the sudden alarm which had called them to this side of the train, their ears stunned by the yells, the orders, and the imprecations of the manacled sheriff, had nevertheless tried to acquit themselves as brave men should do, and had lunged straight for the railroad gate behind which the fugitives were securing mounts. They were a few steps away when Chelton opened fire.

He had been told not to shoot to kill, but the nearness of the men of the law drove him mad. The nearness of his own death was still a taste in his mouth as of ashes and lye.

Therefore, he put a .38-caliber bullet through the thigh of the leading posseman, and as the fellow tumbled with a cry, he slashed the shoulder of a second with another shot.

Standing behind the gate, his rifle resting upon the top bar of it, he made himself at ease, and his deadly work took the heart out of the posse with wonderful suddenness.

They split to either side and rushed back for the shelter of the train, while Chelton, his cruel heart eased, kicked up the cinders behind them with accurate malice.

One man, he who had been wounded in the thigh, lay groaning and cursing, waiting for his finish. But of all the rest of the armed men who were on the train, those in the baggage car never got out of the car, bewildered by what they had heard, but convinced that it was their duty to wait for trouble to come to them. And the cowpunchers and farmers stood by in disinterested fashion while the three fugitives swung onto their stolen horses and galloped down the road.

There was no pursuit. The dust rose behind the three; when that dust dissolved, they were out of sight among the hills.

# XXIV

## • WILL DUNMORE COME? •

THERE was only one place in the camp of Tankerton where privacy was fully assured, and that was the little cabin where Beatrice Kirk lived alone. As for the bunkhouses, someone or other was sure to be loitering about in them, and for that reason the councils of Tankerton usually took place in the cabin of the girl.

On this night there were assembled here Tankerton himself, Doctor Legges, and Lynn Tucker, while Beatrice Kirk poured coffee for them from the pot which simmered on a crane over her open fire. Otherwise, she loitered in the room, listened to the talk, interrupted it when she chose, or lounged on the couch which Tankerton, at huge expense, had brought up from the lowlands for her comfort. She was in all respects like a spoiled child; and like a petted favorite she was treated by the others.

They were discussing, on this occasion, the plight of Chelton, Dunmore, and little Jimmy Larren, who had escaped from the train, but apparently had been cut off from their flight to the upper mountains and the refuge there.

"They'll never break through," said the doctor. "The last word is that between Griswold and Channing Station there are five hundred men strung out."

"Any man of brains can break a string," said the girl.

"A string of Winchesters, my dear?" asked the doctor.

"A man like Dunmore?" she countered.

"She's lost her heart to Dunmore," commented the doctor softly. "I thought that that would happen."

"Sure," said Lynn Tucker, grinning sourly. "He's the newest man, and she ain't had a chance to get tired of his line!"

"He doesn't waste his time chattering," said Beatrice.

119

"Have some more coffee, Lynn, and thaw that mean look out of your face, will you?"

He held out his tin cup with a grimmer expression than ever. Of all who had succumbed to the beauty of Beatrice, none had been more thoroughly overcome than Lynn Tucker.

"You sure make the whole camp at home," said he.

"How is that?" said the doctor.

"Because she gives the woman's touch to the whole bunch," said Lynn Tucker, glad to explain. "She's got claws enough to go all around!"

"I keep you healthy, though," she retorted.

"Are you a tonic, dear?" asked Legges.

"I keep the fat off your brains," said Beatrice, and turning her back on them, she threw herself on the couch and picked up a magazine, which she pretended to read, but every now and then her head was raised, and her dark eyes were fixed upon them.

"Dunmore's a resourceful fellow," said Tankerton, "and by himself he might break through. But he has the other two with him. Chelton will still be half sick with the prison shakes. And little Jimmy's only a boy."

"There's more man in Jimmy than in the whole rest of the camp," threw in the girl.

Lynn Tucker flung an ugly glance at her.

"My part," he declared, "I don't give a hoot what happens to Dunmore——"

"If you want to be disagreeable," said the girl, "go out where the horses are. I won't have you talking like that in here."

"It doesn't matter about the rest of us," put in the doctor, with his smile, "but she doesn't like to have you talk like that of Dunmore."

"Dunmore! Dunmore!" shouted Lynn Tucker furiously. "If he's such a man, why didn't he live up to the plan and keep goin' on until the train was in Runnin' Hoss Gulch? Then we'd've had some money for our troubles! But he had to make his break before—he had to play his lone hand and act up all by himself——"

A galloping horse drew up at the door and a hand beat upon it.

Beatrice herself ran and opened it, and panting voice said: "Is the chief here?"

"Yes."

She turned to Tankerton: "It's 'Biff' Laurie," said she in introduction. "He's boiling over with something."

A hot-faced boy of twenty stood in the doorway and waved his hat at them.

"Dunmore's through!" he called.

"He ain't!" exclaimed Lynn Tucker. "It's a lie. He couldn't do it, with Petersen and all the rest in line!"

"He went straight through the line. I got it straight."

"How?"

"Why, a doggone simple way! The three of 'em held up a load of hay and got into it. Dunmore laid there behind the driver with a rifle lyin' in the holler of his back, and that driver come right on through the lines——"

"The blockheads!" broke out Tucker. "That trick's the oldest in the world and——"

"So's four aces, Lynn," said Beatrice, "but it still wins a lot of money!"

He glared at her. "Of course, I'm mighty glad they're through," he muttered.

"You look it," she sneered. "You better have some more coffee, and make it half sugar, this time. You need sweetening, beautiful!"

"Where did you hear this?" asked Tankerton.

"The word just passed up to Chuck Harper's place. He was bettin' three to one that Dunmore never would reach the mountains, this trip. In come Chris Lane, with the news, on a dead-beat hoss."

"Where's Dunmore now?"

"Comin' up from down Rusty Gulch way."

"He'll be here before the morning, then," said Tankerton, "if he's mounted. And there are plenty of people to mount them in that part of the mountains. Go find yourself a bunk, Biff. Thanks for the news. It's mighty welcome to all of us!"

The door closed on Biff, and as it did so, Beatrice, on her couch, broke into a subdued chuckling.

"What's so funny?" snapped Lynn Tucker.

"This yarn in the magazine," said the girl.

"Let us in on it, will you?"

"Sure. It tells about three pikers who were grouchy because they couldn't set up the cards on a tenderfoot."

"Meaning us, I suppose?" demanded Tucker.

She threw the magazine into a far corner and sat up with gleaming eyes.

"Ah, don't try to make a baby of me!" she exclaimed. "I see through the set of you. You'd all like to take his heart out and peel it like an orange to see what's inside. You want to see what makes it go."

"You tell us, Beatrice," said the doctor. "You know a great deal about anatomy."

"I'll tell you what makes it go, sure," she answered. "Nerve!"

At this, there was a chorus of shouting from the men in the clearing, and immediately afterward the door was jerked open without ceremony by an excited member of the band who shouted: "He's here! He's just come in! Dunmore, and the other pair with him, and——"

Beatrice Kirk leaned for her magazine, and having reached it, she threw it accurately at the head of the messenger.

"What the——" gasped the man, barely ducking in time, as the magazine flew like the flutter of a bird's wings past his head.

"You knock before you enter here, you long-legged half-pint of moonshine!" she said amiably.

The door was jerked shut by the angry man, and the doctor, smoothing his beard, remarked: "That's to make us think she doesn't care about him! Oh, Beatrice, you're a clever child! I'd be proud to have you for a daughter!"

"He's here, then," said Tucker, "and I can ask him why he didn't carry out his promise to stop the train in the gulch and——"

"You'd better come along and find him then," said the girl. "Because he won't come in here! He's not the kind to go around blowing trumpets!"

"He'll be here in two minutes," said the doctor with assuredness. "He just wants to brush his hair and dust his boots for you, honey!"

"What's the bay horse that I ride worth?" she snapped.

"I paid eight hundred for him," said Tankerton.

"How long have you had him?" asked the doctor.

"Not two weeks!"

"Then he's probably half broken down. Not worth a penny more than four hundred now. What about it?"

"You mossy old dead beat," said Beatrice. "The bay against a hundred that I'm right about Dunmore coming here, and that you're wrong!"

"A hundred dollars? My dear, I'll have my saddle on that horse in the morning."

"You take me?"

"I do."

"The bet's made," she said. "You witness it, James. You'll see Father Time, there, crying into his beard and paying me the money, before the night's over!"

Suddenly they were silent, waiting. The fire crackled. The smoke fumed slowly up from the doctor's pipe.

"Look at the doctor, breathing hard," said the girl at last. "This strain is going to tell on him!"

"It's ten minutes," said Tankerton. "She's right, Legges."

"She's not right. Give him time!"

Again they were silent. The girl picked up her magazine and lay back among the cushions, humming to herself, and that soft sound of music made the three men look scowlingly askance at her.

At last Tankerton murmured unwillingly: "It appears that she's right, doctor."

"She knows men," growled Lynn Tucker.

"Why shouldn't she?" barked Legges in sudden passion. "She's held enough hands and——"

The girl did not look up, but with her eyes on the magazine she lifted one forefinger.

"Steady, doctor," she said. "I'm just reading about a fellow who had to eat red-hot coals. And—he had dyspepsia the rest of his life."

The doctor rose with a groan of impatience.

"Well, let's go find him," he said, "and let Lynn Tucker ask him his question."

# XXV

## • HE'S A MAN! •

THEY could not find Dunmore.

He had vanished, and no man knew where he had gone from the camp, but they could and did find Chelton in the middle of the bunkhouse with a circle of excited listeners about him. He himself talked in a husky voice, roughened by a cold, and this gave him a peculiar monotony and lifelessness of speech. Besides, now and again he interrupted himself, coughing, so that what he had to say was spoken in a tone of almost mathematical abstraction. Immediately every one felt that there were no imaginings in this story; they felt that it was rather an understatement than an exaggeration, as the recovered member of the band went on with his narrative.

Sometimes they broke in upon him with feeling questions and remarks.

"Settin' there on the seat, ironed up to Petersen, that must've been rough!"

"Mighty nigh as rough as a rope fitted around your neck," said Chelton.

"You done some thinkin' about that same rope, old son."

"I went through the whole job, over and over. I'd start at the time I faced the judge for sentence, and then sashay into the death cell, and then eat my last meal, and smoke my last cigar, and then waltz out onto the platform and make my last statement——"

"What would you say in your last statement, kid?" asked one of the older men, who himself actually had once been in the death cell for a week, before a prison break.

"I always told 'em all to go shoot themselves," said Chelton, and paused to cough again.

124

"Go on, kid, and tell us what happened after some of 'em left the car."

"Well," said Chelton, "they'd all gone out except the sheriff that was buckled to me like a spur to a boot, and three or four others. Was it three or four?"

Chelton turned toward Jimmy Larren. "How many was it, Jimmy?" he asked. Jimmy looked at the ceiling. "Four," said Jimmy.

"The sheriff and four more. That makes five altogether," said someone. "That's what I'd call a crowd!"

"It was a crowd, all right," said Chelton. "And me with the iron on me!"

"I bet you felt as cold as sweatin' iron inside, kid."

"I didn't feel no other way," assented Chelton. "Now, as I was sayin', there was the five of 'em, and right down the aisle was the kid and the blind man. I told you how Petersen mighty nigh smelled out the truth about that blind man."

"That was a squeeze!"

"But I gotta admit," went on Chelton, "that I hadn't guessed anything. I thought Petersen was a fool, and so did the rest of the posse. They was clean throwed off of their guards! And now up gets the old blind man and comes fumblin' aft, with the kid clawin' at him and tryin' to tell him that that wasn't their station. But he wouldn't stop and listen. The sheriff bawled out to him, but just then, he got to the posse and let out at 'em——"

"With two guns?"

"He don't need guns, when he's got two iron dukes like his. He slammed a red-headed sucker in the mouth so hard that you could hear the teeth go rattlin' down his throat, and then he made a half turn and poked a fat yap from Montana under the chin and lifted him through the windowpane and halfway out of the window——"

He paused and coughed again.

"Go on, kid! What was the others doin'?"

"Why, what time did they have to do nothin'? Dunmore was dealing punches faster than 'Mississippi Slim' ever dealt a poker hand. The third gent was just on the rise with his gun, when Dunmore shoved a bunch of fives into his face and spread his nose across both cheeks. Then he reached for the sheriff, and the sheriff had his gun out, but he was too late. He turned as soggy as a half-filled sack of bran."

"Ain't you leaving something out?" said Jimmy Larren.

Chelton looked with blank and fixed eyes upon the boy. Then he said slowly: "Sure, I'm leavin' something out. I'm leavin' it out on purpose, to put it at the end. The fourth gent was about to send a slug through Dunmore's back that would've busted him in two, when Jimmy Larren, here, dived between his legs and put him down. His head it clipped on the iron bindin' of a seat, and he was out for good!"

"That must've made enough noise, that fight, to let everybody know what was happenin'?" asked a voice.

"Sure it did. Made as much noise as a brass band all made up of nothing but slide trombones, and for the cymbal crashes, there was gents knocked through windows of the car, and that kind of thing. The rest of the posse and about a hundred other gents piled into the car."

He stopped again to cough.

"Go on, Chelton! You can cough all night, after you've finished."

"He's gotta have a chance to think a little," some one suggested dryly.

But this suggestion was received with favor. There was no man more feared and hated by the long riders than Sheriff Petersen, and they rejoiced in this tale of his downfall.

"Go on, Chelton. Don't mind that leatherhead, Borrow. He don't know nothin'. They was pilin' into the car, you said——"

"Well, there was three of us, then," said the undaunted Chelton in the same monotonous voice. "And with Dunmore first, we cut through 'em like nothin' at all. The thuddin' of Dunmore's fists sounded like the beatin' of a drum! We got out and sprinted for the other side of the track where there was the hosses an' the buckboards that I told you about seein'. Dunmore got the hosses, while I popped three or four of the hombres that was follerin' and made 'em duck!"

"Didn't kill none?"

"There was one that won't kick no more," said the indomitable Chelton. "I'd say there was one, wouldn't you, kid?"

Jimmy Larren shook his head gloomily.

"There was one they'll have to bury," said Jimmy, and rolled up his eyes as though appalled at the thought.

To this much of the story, the girl and her three companions had listened, but now Lynn Tucker broke in with:

"It was kind of a pity that Dunmore didn't wait until the train got into the pass before he made his bust! D'you think so, Chelton?"

At this, Chelton turned gradually red; his eyes bulged a little in the extremity of his wrath.

Finally he said: "Tucker, you done the plannin' of that job, I guess?"

"I done it, and what was wrong with it?" asked Lynn Tucker.

He said it aggressively. There were only two men in the world from whom he accepted checks, and their names were Tankerton and the doctor. Perhaps Dunmore was now to be added, and it made his heart sore to think that he now stood fourth on the list! But as for the rest, even such a fellow as Chelton, he regarded them not at all.

"I done it," he said to Chelton. "Could you've fixed it up any better, young feller?"

Chelton stiffened. "You planned it for Runnin' Hoss Canyon?" he inquired.

"I did. Would you've picked an open plain, if you had been me?"

"If I had done the pickin' and the choosin'," said Chelton, "I would've talked to myself and not shot my face off all over the world, old-timer."

"Who did I talk to, except the chief?" said Tucker, more savagely than before.

Chelton turned a bit and faced Tucker.

"Then maybe it was you—or maybe it was Tankerton himself—that sent down word to Petersen to double-cross the boy that was layin' in wait in Runnin' Hoss Canyon— and to get Dunmore caught in a trap, and hanged alongside of me, in the finish! Which of the two of you was it?"

As for Tucker, his lean face turned gray, but not with fear. It was wildest anger that worked at him and made his mouth tremble and twitch. Tankerton merely took out a pipe and filled it carelessly, looking from Tucker to Chelton as though the affair were entirely theirs.

"I ain't gunna say that this here is a lie," declared Lynn Tucker, after a moment. "I'm gunna wait to hear what else you gotta say, before I tell you the hat size of the champeen liar of the world, and the worst fool. Go right along, Chelton, and when you get to the end, lemme know!"

Said Chelton calmly, with the calmness of truth:

"I heard the sheriff make a speech to his gang, and in that speech he told the boys that the Tankertons was ready and waitin' for them in the Runnin' Hoss Canyon, and how they would tackle the baggage car and the smokin' car to get money and me. And how he had a Federal marshal up there in the baggage car, and how they was all to get their rifles hot, as soon as the Tankertons rushed the train! He talked about head money and the rest. But he sure knew all about the plan that Lynn Tucker made. Now, I say, how did he find it out?"

The rage of Tucker disappeared, and left him so blank of eye that, first of all, he stared toward his chief, from whom he usually received the decisive tip in case of need. But Tankerton merely was lighting his pipe and seemed rather like a visitor than an active member of the gang.

It was a role which he was fond of assuming, so that he really appeared to be looking on at affairs from the outside.

In the meantime, this was not a matter which could be dropped. It was something even more vital to all the members than the actual deliverance of Chelton, for that which had kept the Tankertons together successfully had been their mutual good faith, and if there were a leak in the society, a single treacherous member of the gang, they were near the rocks.

So every man darted a sudden glance of suspicion at his neighbor; his own bunkie, for all he knew, might be the traitor!

Chelton went on: "Whoever it was that spilled the news, he knew all the inside plans. And I ask you how Dunmore must've felt when he sat there in that car and heard the yarn? What would anybody else've done? Why, he would've quit cold on the job. But not Dunmore! He changed his plans and tackled them right there!"

After this, there was a moment of thoughtful silence, and then a deep voice exclaimed: "Aye, he's a man!"

So they accepted Dunmore and stamped him with their approval.

# XXVI

## • CAT AND MOUSE •

THE following morning Tankerton stopped at the cabin of the girl and tapped at the door.

"Halloo!" she called.

"Are you up, Beatrice?"

She opened the door.

"Why should I stay late in bed when there's a real man come to camp?" she asked him.

Tankerton half frowned and half smiled. For, in part, he understood her, though in part she was Greek to him.

"Are you going to throw your cap at that fellow?" he asked.

"If he'll notice me," she said. "But he won't. He's too important!" And she raised a hand to pat her hair into shape.

Tankerton nodded at her. "Every good fisherman likes practice," said he.

"You don't think I'm serious?"

"If you were, you wouldn't tell me. I want to talk to you about something that means more to me than anything that has to do with young Dunmore."

"Oh, he's old enough," said she.

"Is he?" smiled Tankerton. "I'm here to talk Furneaux to you."

"What do you want me to do about him now?" she asked, scowling. "Haven't I done enough already with him? Haven't I kept him here tied hand and foot?"

"What have you done for him?"

"Let him hold my hand, once. And picked him out to smile at, now and then."

"Is that a lot?"

"It's enough."

"Don't you like him?"

"He's moody, not so bad."

"You've got to do more with him, Beatrice. He's slipping away from us."

"Look here, James," she asked him, "tell me straight—what does this moony fellow mean to you?"

"He means a lot," said Tankerton. "He's what we need in the crew. We have to have tone, my dear girl. That's a reason that you're priceless here. And another reason used to be 'Gentleman Charlie' Bender. When they shot Charlie they shot half of the respectability out of my boys. Weed out the boys of good family, breeding, the natural gentlemen, and you make us into a gang of ruffians, thugs, and jailbirds. But keep a few Benders, or Furneaux, and the mountains respect us and liken us to Robin Hood. I have to have Furneaux! Besides, he's everything that he should be—a straight shot, a good rider, brave as a lion, and perfectly true to his friends. He never could have treacherous thoughts——"

"Like the doctor?"

"I said nothing about the doctor. Will you do it?"

She sulked. "I'm tired of doing the dishes for you," said she. "I'm tired of the dirty work. Rod is a good boy. I'd rather see him go home."

"Will you do it, nevertheless, Beatrice?"

"What does it mean to me?" she snapped at him.

"All that it means to me, I hope," said he. "We work together, my dear. Whatever I have is yours, and you know it. And if you'll let me, one day we'll——"

He stopped.

"You nearly slipped then," said she, nodding.

"I've promised to keep off that subject," he answered. "But I don't stop hoping."

"Someday you'll marry me," observed Beatrice Kirk, thoughtfully. "In the meantime, I'm the fisherman's fly. I catch the fish and you handle the line! I'm sort of recruiting agent for you, James!"

"You like the sport, yourself," said he.

"Suppose I have to go off and get engaged to that boy to keep him with us—besides, you haven't said why he wants to leave?"

Because he's learned that he has a chance to go back to respectable society and——"

"In spite of all the killings that have been chalked up against him?" asked Beatrice incredulously.

"Newspaper killings, my dear, and apparently the governor knows the truth about them, at last!"

"Well——" she drawled.

"Will you do it?"

"No," she flared at him. "I'm sick of this job, and sick of you and your ways!"

She slammed the door.

Tankerton reached for the knob, but changing his mind, he shrugged his shoulders and walked away, whistling softly.

She, from a chink near the window, watched him go.

"He's sure of me!" said the girl.

And she gripped both hands and burst into a silent tantrum that left her, at last, sitting tense and bowed upon the couch.

However, her passions rarely lasted long, and now through her mind drifted the words of Tankerton. It was quite true, in a sense, that whatever he gained, she gained also. For in the district over which he was a king, she was a queen, through all its valleys, and its hamlets, its logging camps, and its solitary ranches. Her word was law. Guns would be drawn at her bidding as quickly as ever they might be at that of Tankerton.

Whatever made firm his hold, made hers firm, also. Moreover, she admired and respected Tankerton. On some days, she told herself that she almost loved him. For being a creature of action herself, nothing was so dear to her as the man of indomitable courage of wits and strong hands. And in all the blue kingdom of the mountains, there was no one to compare with Tankerton for power. He, an unsceptered king, was absolute in his mastery. To serve such a man was no shame, and particularly since her logic and his told her that she would be serving herself as well.

It seemed to her, to a degree, a crime to flirt with Furneaux; but flirtation never can be a serious crime to a young girl.

However, she went slowly to the window, still filled with her doubts, and Providence at that moment brought the tall and dignified form of Furneaux stalking across the clearing.

She did not hesitate another instant. But with a gambler's love of a "hunch," she was instantly out the door, and waving to him.

He turned and came to her at once.

"You look like thunder and lightning," she told him. "Where are you going to strike?"

"Somewhere on a high stool behind a counter, keeping books, probably," said Furneaux. "I'm leaving all of this and going back to twenty dollars a week."

She dropped her head, as though the blow had bowed her, and she was unwilling that he should see her emotion; but she did let him see a tightly balled fist.

"Well, it's better for you to go," she said.

The shadow of Furneaux fell over her as he stepped closer.

"Are you playing cat and mouse with me?" he asked her. "Do you care a whit, Beatrice?"

She dared not let him see her face; she merely put out a hand that fumbled blindly and finally came to rest upon his arm. That was her answer, while the corner of her eye trailed about the clearing and saw no one there except little Jimmy Larren, who was busily grooming the mare of Dunmore. She was very glad that she was not observed.

"I can't talk to you here," she told him. "I—I'm a little dizzy, Rodman."

He was on fire with excitement at once.

"We'll walk back into the trees," he said. "Beatrice, if you're acting a part now, Heaven forgive you!"

She merely pressed his arm closer with her hand, as they went on. Her heart was racing with a sort of gambler's pleasure; there was a great fear in her, as well, for she felt in this man a grim and relentless earnestness. The first dappled shadows of the trees brushed across them, and in another moment he had halted and, taking her face between both his hands, turned it up and stared down at her with a scrutiny half stern and half anguished with hope. Her very soul quaked in her, then, and she wished with all her might that she had not stepped so far in this affair; but now she could not withdraw, and she softened her glance so that all he could see of her soul of souls was a film of mist!

"Beatrice," he said, "do you really care about me? Do you love me?"

"I don't know," she answered. "I care about you more than the others that I've ever seen. I don't know that it's love, but it made me dizzy to think that you were about to leave us! If you——"

At this, a clear voice rang from the camp, calling: "Furneaux! Furneaux!"

It was Tankerton, and the girl could guess that he had watched her departure with Furneaux, and wished to give her a welcome interruption.

"It's the chief," said Furneaux gloomily. "Will you try to see me again in a moment, unless Tankerton is sending me off on a trip?"

"I'll wait for you here," said she.

He made a step away from her, then turned back.

"Furneaux! Furneaux!" called the chief.

"If you care a whit for me—if I am anything to you," said the boy, "wear this for me until I come back."

He slipped a ring into her hand and then remained for a moment hanging tensely over her. She saw that he was about to sweep her into his arms, but bracing herself to endure that, she kept her eyes melancholy and wistful as they met his.

He left her as Tankerton called again, hurrying away through the spotted shadows, and turning once on the verge of the sunlight to look back at her. She was expecting that, and, therefore, she was ready with a smile and a wave; then Furneaux disappeared.

A moment later, from the verge of the clearing, she saw him mount and gallop off. She had known it would be so, for Tankerton would send him on some small commission to get him out of the way for the day. And she remained holding in her hand his ring. The gem was a little ruby, like a drop of blood.

# XXVII

## • JIMMY ON THE JOB •

TANKERTON, as she came from the verge of the trees, met her with a smile.

"Did I give you long enough?" he asked her.

For answer, she held out the ring, loosely fitted upon her finger.

"Hello!" said he. "Did you get yourself engaged to him? I never meant you to go that far."

"I'm not engaged," she said, "but I'm on the dizzy edge of it. You called just in time to save me from a tangle. I've more than let him guess that I'm in love with him—and I hate your politics, James! Let's not see each other again, today."

She left him, aware that he was smiling and nodding after her, and hating him for his coolness. But yonder she saw Jimmy Larren, who was now combing the mane of the dapple-chestnut mare, and she went toward him, hoping to forget in talk the disagreeable scene through which she had just passed; for she felt as though she had been smudged and stained by the artifice which she had used.

"Hello, Jimmy," she said. "Have you turned yourself into a stableboy?"

He turned his keen, twinkling eye on her.

"I ain't a stableboy," said he. "I'm just gettin' acquainted with Excuse Me."

"Riding her would be a better way, wouldn't it?" she asked.

"I tried it this mornin' early," said Jimmy. "Mr. Dunmore, he gave me leave. But Excuse Me is like gunpowder. She hoisted me so far in the air that I thought I'd never come down. I hung up there like a bubble for a while and then I come down with a whang. I hit the ground so hard that it sounded hollow!"

He laughed.

"So I've taken up conversation with Excuse Me, till she gets more used to me."

"How did she get her name?" asked the girl.

"Why, she got it from excusin' herself when any gent tried to ride her. She slammed everybody on the ground and then she used to try to eat 'em. She had the same kind of manners as a mountain lion, d'you see?"

"But Dunmore rides her."

"Him? Aw, sure. He fixed her. He can fix anything, if you come down to that!"

"Is he a great friend of yours, Jimmy?"

"Him? I wouldn't go around saying that. But I'm working to make a friend out of him."

"Well, I don't know that you'll get much out of him, if he gets you to do the grooming of his horses for him!"

"He's gotta get his rest," said the boy seriously. "That's a mighty pretty ring that you got on!"

She doubled her hand, instinctively, to hide it.

"Is he still asleep this beautiful morning?"

"He says that one hour's sleep is worth ten hours of anybody's scenery!" answered Larren.

"I don't see how he can sleep so long, though."

"He puts on sleep the way that a camel puts on a hump. Then when he's slept up, he can go a month without hardly closin' an eye."

"You haven't really known him for a full month, Jimmy."

"Why," said Jimmy, "you don't have to read him for a month to tell what he's like. Nobody else could teach me nothin' like Dunmore."

"About horses?"

"Hosses, and trails, and guns. But knives is his main holt!"

"I've heard that he's very clever with them."

"He could easily draw your picture, heavin' knives into that tree," said the boy.

She looked around her at the waving of the trees in the wind, at the royal blue of the sky, and one cloud blowing west, like a ship across a sea.

"Still in bed?" said she.

"If you wanta talk to him, I'll go see if he's awake," said the boy.

"Talk to him? Oh, I don't want to talk to him. Yes, I do. I want to know what's his price for Excuse Me. Go ask him, Jimmy."

Jimmy trotted to the bunkhouse and, entering, he found it empty, except for Dunmore, who was not asleep but even now was pulling on his boots.

Said Jimmy: "She's out yonder askin' the price of Excuse Me."

"Who is 'she'? Beatrice Kirk?"

"That's her."

Jimmy sat down on the edge of the bunk and began to talk confidentially.

"Shall I say that you ain't awake?"

"But I'm awake, all right."

"It ain't the mare she's after. She's after you. She's gone and got her one scalp already this mornin', and the takin' of it, it makes her hungry for more."

"What d'you mean, Jimmy?"

"I mean that ruby ring that Furneaux was wearin' the other day. She's got that on her, now."

"She has! Are they engaged?"

"Not by the look of him as he rode off on his hoss, a while back. But they're within throwin' distance of it, I guess."

"I'll go out and talk to her," said Dunmore. "Jimmy, you know why I'm here. If she becomes engaged to Furneaux, I've wasted my time. I'll never get him away from the camp."

"Aw," answered the boy, "nothin' that she does is honest Injun."

"What's that?"

"I used to make playhouses out of chips and mud. Well, half the fun was breakin' down what I'd built up the day before. That's the way with her. She'd get engaged one day so's to have the fun of gettin' unengaged tomorrow."

"Jimmy, you're a hard one on the girls. Wait till you get a little older then you'll feel different about them."

"Aw, sure," answered little Jimmy Larren. "I'll get to the meltin' point some day and thaw out as soft as mush;

but my brains, they still belong to myself! I can see her like she was made out of glass and sky blue."

"Go on," chuckled Dunmore. "What comes next?"

"How would she get herself engaged to one like Furneaux when she's got a couple of real men around the camp?"

"Furneaux is a gentleman, in a way of putting it," said Dunmore.

"Sure," said the boy. "But what difference does that make to her? She goes by money in the bank. I mean, it's him that shoots the straightest and hits the hardest and has got the most fox inside his brain. That pleases her."

"She's not as hard as you think, Jimmy."

"Well, she's cracked a good many already," said the boy. "I dunno that you would like to see it this way, but I'd bet you a dollar to your busted knife that they ain't no man in this camp that she can see between here and the sky line except Tankerton and you!"

"Hold on, Jimmy!"

"You wait and see. Besides, she likes new men; all them pretty girls do. You go out there and she'll melt in your mouth!"

Dunmore finished his dressing.

"I'll go out and have a chat with her," said he.

"Hold on! Hold on!" pleaded Jimmy. "Wait'll I go out first and talk a mite to her. I gotta break the trail."

He started for the door, and then turned about and came a few steps back.

"Chief," said he, "suppose you really wanted to get Furneaux out of this, dead easy? You take the girl away from the camp and he'll foller wherever you lay the scent!"

"Jimmy, you're crazy. You want me to kidnap her?"

"Aw, whatcha think?" asked Larren in disgust. "I didn't say nothin' about kidnaping!"

And he left the cabin in apparent disgust.

But Dunmore, remaining behind, rubbed his knuckles across his chin. The suggestion of the boy seemed ridiculous enough, but the taking of Furneaux from the gang seemed otherwise impossible. If it were true that Furneaux was engaged to Beatrice, he was bound to Tankerton with bonds of steel.

So, meditating upon the problem, Dunmore drew closer to the cabin door, and at last he could hear the faint tinkle of the voices of the girl and Jimmy on the farther side of the clearing, without looking out at them.

He heard the girl say:

"Still sleeping?"

"He's kind of half-awake, and lookin' at the mornin' with one eye," answered Jimmy.

"Did you speak to him?"

"Yep."

"Jimmy, don't be obstinate. What did he say?"

"About what?"

"About selling the mare, of course!"

"He said that you might make a meal for Excuse Me, but that oats was better for her."

"He didn't say that!" exclaimed she.

"Didn't he?"

"Is he coming out?"

"He says that he'll think it over, but in the mornin' he don't do his thinkin' none too fast!"

Dunmore leaned against the wall of the cabin, laughing silently. When he could control himself, he straightened again and was about to step out when he heard Jimmy Larren say carelessly: "They's only one reason that the boss might sell Excuse Me."

"What's that, Jimmy?"

"I'll tell you why. She's a mare. And he don't like nothin' female!"

"That's a strange idea, Jimmy!"

"Is it? It's the way with him. Hosses, dogs, or birds, he don't like nothin' female. And you take when it comes to women, he's got no use for 'em at all!"

"That's because he's young!" said Beatrice carelessly.

"Nope," said the boy cheerfully. "It's because he's growed really up. He says them that stop halfway is the ones that the women get!"

# XXVIII

## • THE START •

IT was a strange mixture of handicap and advantage under which Dunmore labored when he left the bunkhouse and advanced toward the girl and Jimmy Larren. He had been established in an unusual position by the boy; but it was a position which he hardly knew how to maintain; he felt just like a gambler who throws in the dark.

"I've been admiring Excuse Me," said the girl, "and I wondered if you'd like to sell her."

"I'd sell anything," said Dunmore.

"Well, then, what's the price for her?"

"I suppose," said Dunmore, "that she'd be worth as she stands eight hundred or a thousand of any man's money."

"I'd pay that," said Beatrice Kirk eagerly.

"But besides," said he, "there's a lot of other things that she means to me."

"You mean that you're fond of her?"

"I'm fond of her, and that would boost the price a good deal. Several hundreds, I suppose."

"Well, let's hear the price."

"There's other things to think about. The work I'm doing, a fast hoss might be the price of a man's neck! There's nothing in the mountains that can touch her, I suppose."

"What?" she cried. "Not Gunfire?"

"You beat Gunfire with your bay."

"That's because James rode Gunfire with one hand. Even with his weight up, Gunfire would have won if Tankerton had ridden him with both hands, as you might say!"

Dunmore shook his head.

"I don't think that Gunfire could live with her, no matter who was up on him."

"Not with a lightweight like me?"

"Not even with you."

"I'll make you a wager on that!" she cried eagerly.

"Anything you like."

"Anything I like? Then, what about making the mare the stake? She against Gunfire?"

"What would you do with her if you had her?" asked he.

He stepped to Excuse Me, and stroked her neck, and she turned her lovely head and touched his shoulder fondly.

The girl smiled and nodded.

"Jimmy tells me that she's a bad one, but I'd handle her."

"That's what a lot of people have said. When she gets you down, she tries to eat you."

"It'll take time. Time and kindness will beat any horse that I ever saw."

At this, Dunmore looked more closely at the girl.

There was an element of truth in what she said, and she shone with courage and with confidence, more than any man he ever had known. And it seemed to Dunmore that she was, in fact, a greater force than all the people he had met. She was filled with an indomitable spirit.

However, he shook his head. "Can't do it," said he.

"I'll lay you fifteen hundred cash," she said hotly, "against Excuse Me. And I'll throw in some boot, too, if you want it!"

"She's worth more than fifteen hundred to me," he answered. "What boot would you throw in?"

"Anything you like. If Gunfire doesn't beat her, I don't know horses!"

She waved her hand as she said it, and the ruby on her finger made a red streak in the air.

"Throw in that ring," said Dunmore. I'll take on the bet for that!"

"What ring? This ruby one?"

She clasped a protecting hand over it, almost as though she expected him to snatch it.

"All right," said Dunmore, "I ain't so keen on making this race, after all. You keep the ring, and I'll keep the hoss."

She glanced down at the little red jewel, and then, biting her lip, she stared at the mare.

And it happened that at this moment Excuse Me tossed her head, so that a ripple of light ran over her sleeked neck and across the rippling muscles of her shoulder, making her seem a thing made all of beauty and of light. Whatever her speed, her loveliness was a thing to wonder at, and the girl thought of herself perched on the back of the mare—fitted to Excuse Me by diving right, as it were, and stopping the hearts of all men by a double authority!

Then she said: "Fifteen hundred—and this ring? Why should you want this ring, Carrick Dunmore?"

He laughed. "I don't want it so much, but it hit my eye. That's all. I don't worry much about reasons and prices. But I see that you ain't so fond of taking the chance. It's all right. I don't blame you, because she's a runner."

At this, he could hear her teeth click.

"How far will you run?" she asked.

"Why, as far as you like—distance is all on your side, because Gunfire won't be carrying much weight."

She looked narrowly at Dunmore.

"There's a pair of pine stumps down the road to Harpersville. Will you run to that place, if you know it?" she asked.

"That's a couple of miles," he answered. "That's fair enough."

"But, instead of the ring, I'll add another hundred to the bet. Sixteen hundred against Excuse Me!"

He shrugged his shoulders. "I've already hitched my fancy to that ring," said he.

"Are you trying to dodge the race?" she asked him tauntingly. "I'll make it two hundred more—three hundred, if you like!"

"Why, it's all right," said Dunmore, watching her with hidden anxiety. "If you're fond of the ring, you hang onto it, and I'll hang onto the mare. That'll make it evens!"

He turned to Jimmy Larren, and saw the eye of that youngster wink in secret delight. "Turn her out, Jimmy," said he. "You won't have to hobble her, because she won't stray far from me!"

There was anger in the face of the girl now. He could

feel it without looking at her, and he was not surprised at the tremor of rage in her voice as she broke in:

"All right. If you want to have it that way, I'll race you for the fifteen hundred—and the ring!"

She hesitated. Her mind's eye seemed to conjure up the consequences if she lost, but then she shrugged her shoulders.

"I'll have Gunfire on the road in five minutes," said she.

And turning abruptly, she hurried from them and went toward the stable.

"She's pretty mad," commented Jimmy Larren. "She'll pretty near kill herself to win this race. But if you get the ring, what'll you do with it?"

"Wear it, I suppose."

"That'll make Furneaux wanta kill you."

"He might chase me for the sake of the ring, then?"

"I dunno. I guess not. But if he spoke to her, she'd about die for having given it away again."

Dunmore laughed.

"I'm beginning to see a good many things, Jimmy. Get me the saddle and bridle, will you?"

Jimmy brought them both, and Dunmore himself saddled and bridled the mare, looking to the cinches with care.

When he was on the back of Excuse Me, he saw the stallion, Gunfire, come to his hind legs out of the stable, filled with nervous fire, and the girl atilt in the saddle, wonderfully brave and cool. On the out trail he met her, while Larren on his mustang scampered past them, to get to the finish in time for that end of the spectacle.

Then Dunmore took note of the difference between the two animals.

The stallion was more imposing, more grand; the mare was more beautiful. But it seemed to Dunmore that she had greater strength, as well. She had not the proudly arched neck, to be sure, but her square quarters, and her long, powerful shoulders, and the shortness of her back told both of carrying power and speed. Gunfire stormed into the mind and royally demanded admiration, whereas the mare slipped more quietly into one's appreciation. But yet, as he surveyed the stallion and contrasted him with his own mental picture of the mare, he was more and more confident.

They came to the point where the various trails from the camp and its vicinity met and joined to make one established road that twisted here and there among the trees and led on toward distant Harpersville.

The girl ranged beside him at once.

She was as light in the saddle as a jockey, and the strong pull of the black horse seemed to be lifting her from her seat and straining at her arms. But that was mere semblance. He could tell in another glance that she was in perfect balance, controlling the stallion with a steady pull.

She flashed at Dunmore, at the same time, a glance that ran from head to feet, appraising him, criticizing him, taking note of formidable qualities, but at length leaving the mare and settling upon Dunmore alone.

He thought that he saw her nod a little, as much as to say to herself, no matter how fine the mare might be, the bulk of the rider would make the difference in a four-mile race. The same thought was in Dunmore's own mind.

Besides, he had a feeling that this day was the turning point which was to test the success or the failure of this strange embassy to the bandits. He knew he had gained enormously by the rescue of Chelton, but he was still unsure of his place among the outlaws. At least, whatever he did would have to be done quickly, before the malice and the cleverness of Tankerton finished him off one day. And in the race he saw his opening, if only he could win!

Beatrice leaned and patted the neck of Gunfire, and he tossed his head, in recognition.

"Straight away to the two stumps," she called to Dunmore. "And the shortest line is the best line?"

"All right," he said, "but——"

He was beginning to make a protest, for he knew nothing of any short cuts with which she might be familiar. However, she did not wait for him to make his protest, but seized on his first words as an agreement. He saw her eyes flash with triumph.

"We're off, then," she cried, and gave Gunfire the rein.

# XXIX

## • THE RACE •

IF he had been unprepared for the running of the race in a bird's line, still more was he unready for a sudden start, such as this. He had expected that some signal would be arranged between them, but she was half a dozen strides away on the stallion and going like the wind before he got the mare together in pursuit.

He was very angry, as they swept down the road. He had lost, now, an advantage that might prove fatal to the chances of Excuse Me. Moreover, not knowing the ways of the short cut, he would have to follow the stallion at any rate, and so he would put the mare to a greater and greater chance of losing.

He should have shouted that the start would have to be made over again, but a stubborn rage burned up in him, and he determined to continue as they had begun.

Gunfire leaped out of view into the trees, and he put Excuse Me after him.

It was only to see the tail of the stallion switch out of sight to the left, and he followed back onto the road again.

So the girl had feinted for the first time, and with an Indian cunning she had gained another precious rod of distance. Furiously the stallion ran, the clotted turf that he flung up dancing in the air and hanging there while the mare rushed on her way beneath. But she moved as smoothly as flowing water; and while the roadway slid away beneath her for the first mile, gradually and surely she overtook the black. Yet Dunmore was not pushing her; there was no need, since she ran eagerly, with pricking ears, and he must needs keep a steadying pull to rate her along. But it seemed to him that her stride was a shade longer and a shade easier than that of the black; in any

144

moment he was sure that a single hard burst of sprinting would carry them into the lead.

No sooner had he come to that conviction than the girl glanced over her shoulder and then swung the mare once more into the woods. The dappled shadows flowed over her, and she was gone from view. Dunmore did not hesitate. It might be another trick on her part, but he dared not risk the chance that she would be cutting away on a shorter course, and so he swung the mare in pursuit.

He found himself driving at once through very thick woods. The way, such as it was, twisted and turned in serpentine suddenness, here and there, and the branches reached so low that he had to keep a constant lookout. The girl and the stallion she rode were apparently perfectly used to this course, and they rushed through it with the ease of long habit, so that when Dunmore, flattened along the mare's back, came out into the more open forest, the stallion was twenty yards away.

She rode hard, still, as though confident that Gunfire had a limitless strength, and a red scarf she was wearing, coming loose at one end, streamed and snapped over her left shoulder. Once more she glanced back and he saw her shake her head as though in incredulous annoyance to find him so close.

That was a comfort to Dunmore, and as they plunged into thicker woods again, he was feeling secure of the race once more, when the ground began to dip, and they came to a narrow way where it seemed as though a tornado had fallen, for the trees lay tumbled, here and there, splintered stumps thrusting up, and the long trunks extending in a vast tangle upon the ground.

Gunfire flew through this dangerous ruin with perfect ease. Perhaps this was a familiar sport of the outlaws, to ride their horses through all the difficult ways on the mountainside. In case of pursuit by a strong posse, such places as these would prove an ideal trap for the men of the law to be led into.

For his own part, he studied the course of the stallion with care, and sent the mare exactly after him. She could jump, he knew, but he had not guessed that she was such a steeple-chaser, for she flew the obstacles lightly, and instead of losing ground, she cleared the last big barrier of a rugged trunk not a length from Gunfire's tail!

Beatrice Kirk looked back with a startled face, and Dunmore laughed and waved to her. He saw her lips tighten with angry resolve and then she straightened the stallion away through the woods again.

A roar of water began to roll out before them, and presently he saw the white flash of the fall through the trees, while the noise grew into a deep thundering and crashing, and he swept out behind Gunfire toward the brink of a deep and narrow chasm, filled with the flying spume of the cataract.

Gunfire did not hesitate, but with courageous head stretched straight out, he flew the long gap.

There was no chance to hesitate. Dunmore felt the hoofs of the mare slip on the brink of the wet rocks. Then she rose. He saw beneath him the white-faced cauldron of the stream as he hung in the middle air, and then they landed on the farther side not a half length behind the leader!

Beatrice looked about again, and he could see the white of terror in her face. Then the forest received them once more; a moment later the dust of the road flashed silver-bright, and they stormed out onto it.

She had given up the last of her maneuvering, apparently. And Dunmore grimly set his teeth and pursued. She had tried to distance him, to dodge him, finally to lose horse and man in the gap of the gorge, but now this murderous girl could do nothing but ride hard and trust to the strength of her horse.

There could not be half a mile remaining to the race!

Yes, now in the near distance, he saw the pair of stumps which marked the finish line, and he loosed the mare at it with a shout.

He had felt her going with undiminished strength beneath him, but he had not been prepared for this! Like a loosed bird she flew, and was instantly at the saddle girth of the stallion. But still she rushed onward strongly, and her nose was at his shoulder when Beatrice Kirk, with a wild cry, swung her quirt, as though for the flank of the stallion, and slashed Excuse Me across the face.

The mare swerved, reared, and when Dunmore had settled her to the running again, she was three or more lengths away to the rear. But it was as though she had been strongly spurred. If she had winced at the first pain, now she hurled herself valiantly into the contest. The road flowed beneath her like a silken white ribbon as she stretched to her work. And the stallion came back.

He had run valiantly, he had dodged and jumped well indeed, but in spite of the smaller weight that he was carrying, he was spent. A hundred yards from the end, Dunmore saw the head of the black begin to bob, and in another stride went easily, smoothly past.

The stumps jerked away on either hand, and then he spoke to the mare and brought her to a halt.

Beatrice Kirk already had pulled up and sat her horse as one stunned and sick.

So he went back to her with a cheerful word—no mention of her foxlike and desperate tricks during the race, but perfectly easy compliment.

"He's a grand horse," said Dunmore. "He's a cuttin' hoss, by the way he handles himself runnin' through the trees, and a mighty fine jockey you made, all right!"

This she did not answer but looked at him as though she heard his voice less than a voice which at that moment was sounding in her own mind.

"Perhaps you lacked the weight to steady him," said Dunmore soothingly. "You might have done better if you'd been heavier in the saddle."

She gave him a look filled with both fear and anger, and then turned the head of the stallion back toward the camp.

"I'll have the money ready for you this evening," she said.

"Thanks a lot," answered Dunmore. "You've got the ring ready now, though, I see?"

"The ring?" said she, starting a little in the saddle, as though from a blow which she was expecting and therefore dreaded the more.

"I see that it's on your finger now," said he.

"Why—the ring—yes," she stammered, and lost all voice.

"I could take that now," he said pointedly.

"I'll tell you what," she said, striving at heartiness and carelessness. "Of course, this ring is a sort of a personal thing that means something to me. But I'd give you its worth in hard cash."

"Would you?" said Dunmore, smiling so that his teeth flashed in the sun.

"Oh, yes," said she. "I don't think it's worth a hundred dollars. But you can have two hundred—if you'll take it!"

So saying, she smiled a little, with her head raised and a touch of contempt in her eyes, as though she wondered if there were a man in the world base enough to accept her offer. And Dunmore weakened under the strain of that steady regard.

His eyes half closed, he looked beyond her, wondering what he should say next, and it happened that at that moment he saw young Jimmy Larren leaning against a tree close by. Still as the very trunk by which he stood was the boy, but as the eye of Dunmore fell upon him, Jimmy winked prodigiously, and then grinned from ear to ear.

The indecision of Dunmore vanished at once.

"Two hundred more?" said he. "Well, that's a price, but I don't know much about the value of jewels, d'you see?"

"Make it more, then," she said, sneering openly. "Make it three hundred, even, if you like. I have that much money, besides what I lost on the race, I think!"

He looked calmly upon her.

After all, she was carrying off the thing very well. In her bearing there was no touch of shame for the trickery and the craft which she had used during the race; but when the mare tossed her head, Dunmore could see the long welt which streaked across her face, and his smile grew colder.

"Let me see," said he, and stretched out his hand.

She laid the hand with the ring lightly upon his own.

"It's only a small stone, you see," said she.

"I like the color, though," said he. "And it looks sort of lucky to me, d'you see?" Dexterously his thumb and forefinger closed over the ring. It fitted loosely, and away it came without tug or friction. "So I'll keep it, and you don't have to worry about the price," said he.

She reached impulsively for the jewel. For the image of Furneaux, his pride and his love, had flashed across her mind at that moment. Pale and shaken she faced Dunmore.

"It doesn't mean a thing to you!" she cried imperiously. "But—I've got to have it! I want it—I have to have it!"


## XXX

### • SPEAKING OF LUCK •


INCREDULITY that he could refuse her was in Beatrice's voice—amazement was in her eyes. Other words formed on her lips and remained unspoken. She stared at Dunmore as though he were more monster than man.

"Why, you could have it for nothing," said Dunmore gently. "I ain't the man to hang onto small things. But the fact is that I'm a superstitious sort of a gent. And I reckon that this here is luck for me."

He held the ring gravely in the palm of his hand and she looked as though she actually were on the point of snatching it.

"You're making a joke of it, Carrick Dunmore!" said she. "But it's not a joke. It was given to me by a very dear friend, and I never would dare to face that friend again without it on my hand!"

"Is this here friend a Westerner?" he asked.

"Yes. What of that?"

"I'll tell you," stid Dunmore, more soothingly than ever. "Every Westerner knows about luck. Your friend wouldn't mind at all if he knew that a man had got the ring that felt it was his luck. I could tell you a story about a gent that had an old mackinaw that he felt his luck was all wrapped up in and——"

"I don't want to hear it!" she cried at him. "Oh, Carrick Dunmore," she added, softening her voice with a wonderful suddenness, "you're only playing with me, but you won't really be cruel as this, I know!"

Dexterously she had swung the stallion closer, and

touching the arm of Dunmore, with parted lips and appealing eyes, she looked upon him like a child to its elder.

"Well, well," said Dunmore. "I can see how it is. This friend of yours is some old woman with a nacherally mean disposition. Some old aunt, likely, that'd clean go wild if she was to see that you wasn't wearin' the ring, eh?"

"It's worse even than that!" said she eagerly, feeling that he was softening a bit.

"Don't you worry none, though. You can tell her that you left it behind at the camp, and there ain't any danger of her seein' it on my hand. I never bother that sort of folk much! Why, I'd hate to think of grievin' you any, Beatrice."

"I know you would," she agreed heartily. "Such a fellow as you are, Carrick, couldn't be half a hero."

"Why, thanks," said he.

"I thought for a moment that you were angry because my quirt happened to strike poor Excuse Me on the face. I was dreadfully sorry about that. I wouldn't have claimed the race after that, even if I had won. You don't doubt that, Carrick, I'm sure?"

"Why," said Dunmore, "I wouldn't doubt you for anything in the world! Of course you wouldn't've claimed it."

"So you're not cross with me, Carrick?"

"Me? Not a mite!"

"Then you'll listen to reason, I know. You won't let me down in this way. You—I'll—we'll have a fair man, one that knows stones, put a value on it. We'll double that value. I'll pay you every penny, but, for Heaven's sake, don't keep the ring!"

"Now, there you are, all excited," said Dunmore gently. "All excited and worked up, and about nothin' at all. Why, I'd give you this here in a minute, if it wouldn't be that that would keep you from learnin' that mountains can be made out of molehills! But that's the fact. Doggone me if it don't cut me up to hear the way that you carry on over this, Beatrice. That's the only reason in the world that I'd keep it from you. Just for your own good."

She struck her hands desperately together and her eyes wandered as though in search of another thought.

Then she stared back at Dunmore.

"Are you serious?" she asked him. "Do you think that

it's only a joke? I tell you, if you take that ring back to the camp, and if you show it on your hand, there'll be a murder!"

"Tush! Really?" said Dunmore.

"Oh, for pity's sake, believe me!" said the girl. "If you won't give it back to me, keep it safe in your wallet! Never tell a soul that you have it. Swear that you'll do that!"

"Would it comfort you?" he asked her.

"Yes, yes! Will you promise that?"

"Reminds me," said he, "of that story about the gent that had the mackinaw with his luck all wrapped up in it. This here gent was by name of Jim Loyd. Likely you've heard of him?"

"No—I never heard of him—I don't care, but I don't want to be rude—only, will you promise?"

"You'll see that this is right to the point. This here fellow Loyd, he was bein' chased for a matter of liftin' a couple hundred cows, now and then, and finally for borrowing a hoss. He got chased all the way across eleven hundred mile of mountain-desert. Well, sir, all that way he wore an old plaid mackinaw. It was winter, and it served him pretty good to turn the edge of the wind. Got to feelin' that his luck was all wrapped up in it. Never left it off, day or night, and while he had it on, nobody ever could put a bullet into him. Well, sir, he was ridin' south and south, and pretty soon he come to a warm night, and the stars all out, and a south wind a-fannin' at him. So he peeled off his coat and rolled it into a blanket with a mackinaw bunched under his head for a pillow. You listen, now, to what happened."

She bit her lip, but instantly forced herself to nod and smile.

"Right there that same night, a voice hollered to him: 'Jim Loyd, stand up an' fill your hand!' He jumped up with a pair of guns, and missed his mark, and got shot right through the heart! And all because he left off his luck!"

"That's a wonderful story," she said. "I don't know how you could have heard it, but——"

"Why, I was the gent that had follered him the eleven hundred miles, because of him liftin' an old hoss of mine. A cuttin' hoss, at that! He lived about three seconds after

I'd shot him. And he spoke to say it was the mackinaw that had killed him, for leavin' of it off!"

"Carrick," said the girl, "it's a very strange story. But—I don't see what it has to do with this case!"

"Don't you, now?" said his smooth and genial voice. "Now, I'll show you. Here's this here ring that just fits right into my eye. I can see that it's my luck. Yes, sir, if that ring wasn't meant for me, I never would've chanced to win the race, with Gunfire goin' so strong, and such a handy rider on his back. Now, suppose that after gettin' that ring, I was to just drop it into my pocket. Suppose I wasn't to wear it where a ring's supposed to be worn, why, there'd be a mess of trouble, wouldn't there? The ring would go back on me and change all of my luck. Which I guess you wouldn't wish on me, Beatrice, would you?"

Her eyes flared at him as though she would have wished him reduced to a heap of ashes at that moment, but again she controlled herself.

"I don't want to think that you're joking with me!" said she. "You aren't, Carrick, are you? You won't refuse me when I beg you, with all my heart, to please give it back to me? Don't you see that I'm not being foolish? Oh, as sure as there's a heaven over us, there will be bloodshed if you wear that ring into the camp!"

"It plumb cuts me up to see you all so excited," he told her.

"I'm not being foolish and hysterical," she vowed to him. "I—I——"

Self-pity choked her suddenly, and the tears rushed into her eyes.

"There, there," said Dunmore. "Poor girl, I can see the way that it is. You been prizin' this here ring for a long time. Now you look at here. Here's my quirt that I got down in Mexico City——"

"Yes?" she said, making a desperate effort to control herself and to show further interest in this rambling talker.

"Got it from a special fine and high gentleman down there that was mighty rich and went in for fine fixin's on his hoss, and self. Except that his way of usin' his guns was a mite old-fashioned, he was a mighty bright gent, I can tell you! And from him I got this quirt. You see that it's got a fine big sapphire in the handle of it? Now, I'll tell you. You can have this quirt to make up for the ring. If you were to wallop a hoss with this, it'd cut him right to the bone, supposing that the cut came across his face say, in the middle of a race!"

Suddenly she understood. She jerked back Gunfire so strongly that he reared with a snort, and landed prancing.

"You—you contemptible—you bully!" she panted at Dunmore.

And she whirled her horse onto the back trail for the camp.

So it happened that for the first time she caught sight of young Jimmy Larren, upon whose face the smile was still lingering. She rushed Gunfire to him as though she would trample him into the ground; and Jimmy dodged behind the tree.

"You mischief-making rascal!" cried the girl. "You're behind this, in some way. If you ever dare to show your face in the camp again, I'll have you stripped and whipped! Do you hear?"

And off she shot down the road on the stallion, cutting him again and again with the quirt, until he bounded high in the air with the pain of the whipstrokes.

Jimmy, issuing from behind the tree, rubbed his chin as he looked after her. The mustang, coming out behind him, took his hat by the crown and playfully lifted it, but the boy paid no heed to this. His mind was intent on the vanishing form down the road.

"Look what kind of luck that I've got!" said he to Dunmore. "I've lost my friend that got me into the camp, and now I'm kicked back into Cousin Bill's butcher shop. I can sure feel the ache of the bones that I'll have after he gets through whangin' me for the first month."

"You'd have to go back to him, eh?"

"I dunno where else. Bill'll be glad to see me. Why, his mouth'll fair water as I come prancin' through the door. I can fair see the tears in his eyes as he kicks the door shut and reaches for my neck. Cousin Bill, he must be kind of fat and all out of exercise, since I left him in the lurch, chief!"

Dunmore nodded.

"You'll stay here," said he.

The boy looked wistfully at him.

"No," said he. "She's gunna make you trouble enough, account of the ring, without her having to have another excuse like me."

"You'll stay with me," said Dunmore quietly. "Why, Jimmy, I wouldn't know how to get on without you."

He dropped his hand on the lad's shoulder as he spoke, and the eyes of Jimmy, as he looked up, suddenly widened, grew bright.

"Jiminy!" said he. "Jiminy Christmas!"

# XXXI

## • ONE WHO CARRIES A BURDEN •

STRAIGHT and slender, desperate of eye, Beatrice stood before Tankerton in her own cabin, her back against the door, her hand grasping the knob of it, as though to make sure that he would not leave until she had spoken her mind to him.

"And I hate him!" she ended her story.

"Well, Beatrice, I don't love him particularly, for my part," said Tankerton.

"The smiling, sneaking, oily, smooth, detestable hypocrite and liar!" she cried. "I loathe him! If he stays in this camp, I leave it! I won't stay another minute if he's here!"

"Tut, tut," said he. "You're being desperate about things that are not so very important."

"Not important!" she cried. "But poor young Furneaux! Suppose he sees the ring on Carrick Dunmore's finger? He——"

"Well?"

"He'll fight, of course."

"It's unlucky," said Tankerton. "I've explained to you that Furneaux is a man I want to have with me. But—in that case he'll simply die young!"

"He won't!" said the girl fiercely. "He'll—he'll—he'll kill that smiling villain, that soft-voiced sneak! He'll kill him, James! He'll kill him, I know! Fate wouldn't let such a scoundrel kill a fine fellow like Rod!"

He did not answer, but remained gravely watching her, and her excitement.

The effect of that steady gaze was enough in itself, without the use of words. For suddenly she threw out both her hands.

"What will you do, James? You're not going to stand by and let Rodman Furneaux be murdered?"

His eyebrows lifted curiously. "Do you care a great deal for that boy?" he asked.

"Care for him? Of course I care for him! He's as clean and straight as a whistle, and there never was such a boy in the camp before. Are you going to let him be wiped out by that juggler, that worthless, useless Dunmore?"

Tankerton's lips pinched. What he had feared long before was that someone in the camp, this sharp-eyed girl above all the rest, would be able to guess, before the end, that Dunmore was not there on Tankerton's invitation, but had forced himself into the band. If that were known, Tankerton's own authority would be shattered to the ground. There was only one reply that he could make.

He said: "Beatrice, you know that I like to please you."

"Ah, I know what you're going to say!" she cried. "You'll give me good clothes, you'll be gay and cheerful, and all that, you'll give me nice horses, too—but when it comes to anything important, I'm not to be counted. What I want makes no difference!"

Tankerton drew a quick breath.

"Dunmore," said he, "is the most valuable man who ever came to these mountains! He's the straightest shot, the steadiest nerve, and the strongest hand! Do you think I can drive him away for the sake of a youngster like Furneaux? If Furneaux is going to make a scene, then Furneaux will die."

She wrung her hands in excess of despair and grief.

"Jim, Jim, you don't see! I don't want to think that you're cold-blooded, but if Furneaux is killed, his blood is on my hands—and on yours, on yours! You told me to do what I did!"

Tankerton paused before answering. He could see the perfect logic of what she had said, and finally he nodded.

"I'm going to do something," he said. "I don't yet know quite what. But I'll do something———"

His hand slipped inside his coat, in his moment of absentmindedness. She knew that it had touched the handle of a gun before it appeared again. And a blur of misery crossed her mind. She saw, as it were, the flashing of revolvers, and the roar of the guns.

"I can't stand it!" said the girl. "I'm going to choke—I can't breathe!"

And she fled from the house suddenly into the open air.

There, straight across the clearing before her eyes, she saw Jimmy Larren sauntering, carrying a bucket, and whistling as he went along.

That sight kindled the rage.

She had been speaking of men, strong and dangerous men, but that a snip of a boy should have dared to disobey her in this camp was too much for endurance.

"Harry!" she called to one of the three men who sat beneath an adjoining tree, playing stud poker. "Harry, will you catch that little demon for me? I'm going to give him a lesson!"

Harry, young, lithe, graceful as a panther, leaped to his feet and dashed at Larren with a laugh, glad to please Tankerton's princess.

But Jimmy did not run. He merely turned with his usual complacent swagger and held out the bucket.

"All right, Harry," said he. "You runnin' to help carry this here barn mash to Dunmore's hoss?"

Harry, hand outstretched for the boy's collar, checked himself in mid-rush.

"Dunmore's hoss?" he asked rather breathlessly. "You his errand boy, Jimmy?"

"That's the job that he's give me," said Jimmy carelessly. "But maybe he could use two, if you wanta help?"

"Run along, kid," said Harry. "I didn't know you was workin' for Dunmore."

He turned, scowling at the ground, refusing to look into the white and scornful face of the girl.

"Kid b'longs to Dunmore," he said slowly. "You better get Dunmore to take charge of him, then!"

She did not answer. She did not even appeal to any of the others beneath that tree, because she could see by the intentness with which they looked at their cards and refused to glance at her, that they would have answered in the same manner. Every man in that camp, she could guess, dreaded Carrick Dunmore little less than he feared the actual cold of death.

And she felt stripped of power, empty of hand, for the first time since she had stepped into a sort of mountain throne with these young desperadoes for subjects.

She was baffled. She could not understand. And yet as she looked into her mind, she could see that there was an actual difference between Dunmore and all the others who made up the membership of Tankerton's men.

And, even because she recognized that difference, she hated him the more!

At the side, as she moved slowly away, conscious of the grim and guilty looks of the men behind her, she saw Tankerton come out of the shack and start walking across the clearing.

She glanced in the direction he was taking, and there she saw Carrick Dunmore in a group of laughing and admiring men. He was juggling half a dozen brilliant red apples which had just been brought to the camp that day, and they flowed up from his hands and hung winking and spinning in the sun. They seemed to form different designs in the air; they seemed to drop of their own volition into the hands of the magician.

Dunmore began to whistle, and as he whistled, he danced.

She stopped short and watched him with wonder. She knew that he was a heavy man, solid as lead; otherwise that mighty strength which amazed and disheartened other men could not have been lodged in his limbs; but when he danced, he seemed to float lightly, easily. It was almost as though the unseen beat of wings supported him. His dancing kept the time of his whistle, and the apples flowed up and down in rhythm with both.

The cowpunchers around the performer began to laugh and cheer. They picked up the tune; they shouted and whistled it in unison; they beat their hands together to give a stronger pulse to the rhythm; they swirled here and there———

Like moths around a flame, Beatrice could not help

thinking, a flame that might singe and shrivel them to the heart, if it ever so much as touched them!

Then something moved near by.

It was Tankerton, who had remained rooted to the spot for a moment, watching the juggling and its effect upon his band; now he went forward with a set jaw, and she knew what it meant. He was going to try conclusions with his new gang man upon the spot.

She called to him softly: "James!"

He wavered, then stopped and came back to her.

"What is it, Beatrice?" he asked, his eyes absently wandering beyond her.

"I know what you've got in mind," she said.

"Well?"

"You're going to start for Dunmore now. You're going to fight him, James!"

He drew his glance down from the distance and centered it upon her. She saw that he was pale, though his eyes were as chilled steel.

"I can't have any man bullying you," said he. "You've practically asked me to get rid of him!"

"With a gun?"

"Well, how else?"

She went closer to him.

"I'd like to know what happened in Harper's hotel! What happened when you met him there!"

"I got in the first shot, if that's what you mean," said he.

"And then what happened?"

"No matter, Beatrice. We became fast friends. At any rate, we shook hands. Nobody had received a scratch."

"You missed? At close range like that?"

"It's a thing that I can't tell you about. I've said that before. You'll have to believe me, and besides, that has nothing to do with this!"

"Oh, but it has!" said she. "If it weren't for that, I'd be glad to see you go at him!."

"Do you think that he's my master?" he asked her.

"I think that he's not a man but all a fiend," she said, answering him indirectly.

Then she added: "Look me straight in the eye, Jim. You know that you'd rather meet any three others at once than that single man. Come back with me. We'll take a walk. Don't jump over a cliff—don't run against a strong wall. There's no use in that."

He hesitated: but then he turned obediently back with her. His head had fallen a little and he walked with short steps, like one who carries a burden.


# XXXII

# • A MESSAGE FROM A LADY •


A DEEP and mellow baying of dogs swelled out from the woods, immediately after, and Dunmore checked his whistle and his dance. The apples flowing down into his hands dropped gently into the pockets of his coat, except one, which he kept to munch, while he laughed and panted in acknowledgment of the congratulations of the men. They watched him with shining eyes. Such a fellow was a treasure, a guarantee that winter nights would not be dull, that long marches would have their lively moments, that the camp would not have to depend upon twice-told tales and poker to get through the idle hours.

"What's the hollering in the woods?" he asked of one.

"It's Furneaux. He's got the dogs," said the other.

"What dogs?"

"Why, didn't the chief tell you? Ban Petersen's spent about a couple o' thousand bucks to get together a pack of bloodhounds. Listen to 'em comin'!"

Out of the trees they broke—three big, full-bodied bloodhounds, with trailing ears and noses that brushed close to the ground. Coming into the presence of the men in the clearing, they halted as one of accord, and while Furneaux unwound the leashes which were fastened to his saddlebow, the dogs stood close together, and with raised heads began to howl. Their loose lips almost covered their mouths, and perhaps that was the reason that the sound seemed to be floating mellowly from a distance, from one direction and then from another, but not at all associated with the drawn-up bellies of the dogs. It was a doleful and yet a musical sound that made one of the men cry out suddenly: "For Pete's sake, stop them hounds!"

"Joe don't like 'em," interpreted another. "You had 'em after you down Louisiana way, didn't you?"

"I had," said Joe, with a shudder. "Three days and nights I was out there in a swamp, and the yelling of the dogs was never out of my ears. Three dreary days, and three dreary nights. I'd ruther've died than go through it, if I'd known how long it'd take!"

Furneaux gave the leashes into the hands of Doctor Legges, and went off to put up his horse.

"Watch that big fellow with the brindled mustache," he told the doctor. "He wants to take off the leg of the young dog on the left, there!"

"Well, well, my pets," said the doctor. "And here you are at last, just where the sheriff wanted you to be! What a pity that Ban Petersen can't see them here, eh?"

The gangsters laughed. They surrounded the dogs and patted their heads. "They got enough jaw and jaw muscles," said one of them. "They could choke you, quick enough!"

"That's what good ol' Ban wanted 'em to do, all right! How did we get 'em, doctor?"

Said the doctor: "Why, when Petersen had collected these dogs, he came in on a trail that he knew—Dunmore's trail, I mean"—here he paused and waved a hand courteously at Dunmore—"and he started working through the hills with a big party. Forty men, some say! The men got along pretty well, but the dogs didn't seem to have any luck. They'd find bits of raw meat lying in their way in the grass, and they'd gobble up the meat and be taken sick almost immediately. There were eleven dogs in that high-priced pack; but before one day was over, there were only three!"

"Who handled the game?" asked one man curiously.

"Oh, some of Tankerton's good friends. I sent them down a little recipe last year for just such a case as this, and our friends remembered how to use it! When we heard how affairs were going, it occurred to Jim that we might sometime need those dogs ourselves, so we sent down a message on the heliograph and, as a result, some of the boys down there slipped in and pinched the last three of the dogs. They brought them up, and it's said that poor Ban is a little discouraged and thinks he may as well give up this latest expedition of his! Can you blame the poor man?"

The others whopped with laughter.

"That's organization," remarked one scar-faced puncher. "That's what I call efficiency."

"It is," admitted the doctor modestly. "We try to take care of you boys. We try to block the punches that are started for you before they get close to your heads. I'm glad to see that you can appreciate it when you have the proofs under your eyes, now and then."

A hand twitched at the sleeve of Dunmore, and he looked down into the eyes of Jimmy Larren. Those eyes were dancing with excitement.

"Chief," said the boy, "she wants to see you. She's mighty worked up, and she wants to see you."

"Hello," said Dunmore. "Who's this that wants to see me? You kind of surprise me, Jimmy!"

"Sure," said the boy. "I reckoned that you wouldn't be able to guess her name."

"Is she young or old?" asked Dunmore.

"Tolerable young," said the boy, "but she knows the north side of a tree."

"Whacha mean by that, Jimmy?"

"I mean that she can find her way in the dark."

"Like a cat, Jimmy?"

"Well, I'd say that she's got claws, anyway."

"I'm wearing high boots," said Dunmore.

"But you ain't got on glasses."

"Well," said he, "I'll try to take care of my eyes, too. Where am I to find her?"

"Back yonder near the spring."

"Is the woods empty around her, Jimmy?"

"Why, tolerable empty, I'd say."

"No Tankertons floatin' around?"

Jimmy grinned, and his eyes snapped.

"I seen Tankerton go into his cabin, lookin' sort of serious and chewing one corner of his mouth like it was the butt of a cigar."

Dunmore nodded.

"I don't know why he should be so thoughtful, Jimmy," said he. "Maybe the same thing that's making her think, too?"

"Maybe the same thing," agreed the boy.

"Shall I go back and see her?"

"I dunno," said Jimmy. "If you can stand it, maybe you'd better go."

"Stand what?" said Dunmore. "I can usually stand anything that a girl has to say, Jimmy."

"Aw, sure. Who couldn't?" asked Jimmy Larren. "What I mean to say is: Can you stand it when they turn loose and cry?"

"Cry?" said Dunmore.

"Yep," answered Jimmy. "Her eyes is lookin' sort of starry. What I mean is, she's got a tremblin' lip, too. And she's got a handkerchief in her hand. And she takes a pass at her lips with it, now and then, like she'd just swallered something that was burning all the way down."

"Well," said Dunmore, "Maybe she has."

"Yep," said the boy, "she's on fire, all right, and she's ready to go *zip,* like a skyrocket. She'll bust up, and then she'll begin to cry. It's gunna be a pretty wet conversation, chief."

"I'm wearin' a thick coat," said Dunmore, "if she wants to cry on my shoulder."

"Humph," said Jimmy Larren. "I guess you know your own business but I wouldn't be takin' chances as close as that."

"What do you mean by close chances, Jimmy?"

"Why, it's like this. It ain't so hard to thumb your nose at the other kid when you got a fence between you an' him. But it makes a lot of difference when they ain't no fence at all between. Makes you feel kind of weak in the stummick."

"I understand," said Dunmore, "but I ain't going to thumb my nose at her."

"What I mean to say is," said Jimmy Larren, "that I've mostly noticed a gent can be pretty strong and straight-standin' and sashay along and pay no attention to the women, but when they come close enough for him to get a whiff of the perfumes that they dab onto their hair, the man, he ain't got a chance. It's like he's been hit on the button. He gets on a fool look and leans his elbow on the air and starts staggerin', and sometimes, I guess, he don't never fetch up agin' nothin' solid to steady himself, until he finds himself all married and guaranteed to give her oats and stable room for as long as she wants to wear a feed bag. It seems sort of like that to me."

Dunmore smiled appreciatively at the youngster.

"D'you think that I'm going to get giddy around her, Jimmy?" he asked.

"Aw, you can handle yourself fine, chief," said the boy. "But I've noticed you look pretty dizzy a couple of times when she went sailin' by, handin' out a smile to the clouds in the sky and turnin' up her nose at all the dogs and the men that she seen litterin' the ground around her feet!"

"Tell me, Jimmy. Don't you like her at all?"

He strolled away with Larren, listening eagerly, anxiously, in spite of the careless smile which he maintained.

"She brought me up here," said Jimmy. "I wouldn't never've knowed you, if it hadn't been for her."

"That ain't a whole answer, Jimmy."

"Sure, I know that it ain't. But I'd like to ask you, what good was Excuse Me, before she was broke and rode? What good was that there mare, chief?"

"Not much. She only busted necks. You mean that this here girl is like Excuse Me?"

"Well," said Jimmy Larren, "I dunno. All I gotta say is that you don't have to have a lantern to see her by. But all the same, she sort of scares me, like when the snow begins to slip, and you wanderin' along a thousand feet above nothin' at all!"

"Well," said Dunmore, "you tell her that I'll come an' see her when I can, but I'm pretty busy, just now."

Jimmy nodded with satisfaction.

"Busy at what?" he asked.

"Why—eatin' apples, maybe," said Dunmore.

At this, the boy burst into rippling laughter, and went off at a run, his shoulders still shaking. But Dunmore looked after him with a grave face.

# XXXIII

## • A BUSINESSMAN •

HE found her on the bank of the brook, just below the point where it bubbled up from the ground—where the music of its rising continually hung in the air. A pair of big pines dappled the place with shadow; great banks of ferns grew near to the water's edge; and a little brown water dog lay on a stone in midstream, and enjoyed a patch of yellow sunlight.

When the girl saw him, she threw up her head a little and waved to him joyfully.

And he crossed the shallow water, stepping from stone to stone, wondering in what spot crafty Jimmy Larren was hidden to see and to hear everything.

She sat down on the top of a broad boulder and indicated that there was room beside her. Dunmore gravely took his place.

"I wanted to talk," said she. "And I thought that there wasn't apt to be any better place for quiet than this."

"Nope," answered Dunmore. "It's a mighty quiet place, all right."

"And I've always like to watch the water here!" she suggested, and she turned and smiled at him sympathetically.

A dizzy sweetness mounted the brain of Dunmore, and the words of Jimmy Larren rang suddenly like a bell in his brain. He forced himself to look away at the water.

"Aye," he said at last, "this here water looks pretty peaceful. You wouldn't think that it ever got to ragin' and roarin' the way it does down yonder in the gorge. I mean, the one that we jumped this mornin'!"

He did not look at her, but he could feel her start beside him.

"I'm afraid that you're going to hold that race against

me," she said finally. "Of course you are! I was wrong ever to start it. I was wrong to risk so much on it. I don't mind the money—here it is!"

She held it out, and Dunmore looked at it with a sudden distaste.

"Why, ma'am," said he, "the fact is that I ain't so much interested in the hard cash!"

She insisted with warmth: "I tried every trick. I tried to lose you in the woods, get you brushed off under the trees, tangle you up in the fallen logs, and—perhaps see you slip and drop at the gorge——"

She paused. Her breath caught.

And he, suspecting a trick and clever acting, ventured a side glance but saw her hand gripped hard, and her eyes fixed straight before her.

"Then—I slashed Excuse Me across the face. I lied when I said that it was a chance. It was meant. It was planned. I—I couldn't dare to lose!"

Dunmore said genially: "Why, that was nothin'. A gent'll get carried away. In the middle of a race the best thing to think about is winnin'—no matter how short a cut you gotta take. Don't let that bother you, none."

She made a brief gesture.

"I didn't dream that there was a horse in the world that could be faster than Gunfire. I didn't dream that I could lose. I knew the way. I knew the tricks of it. But she won —you won with her!"

"She's all made of steel and strung with piano wire and piled full of works like an eight-day clock," said he. "It ain't any disgrace for any horse to be beat by Excuse Me!"

She nodded. "I see that now. But you see how I started the race, and therefore I want you to take this money. I want you to take it!"

She said it almost desperately.

And he knew, with certainty, that she was not shamming now. All was utterly sincere in her voice, in her eyes, in the tenseness of her body. He began to remember that she was very young indeed; very spoiled; proud with the pride of one to whom all men have given way.

That might explain her faults; and wondered to what end she was carrying this confession of hers.

She had held out the sheaf of bills before him, once

more. He actually reached for it, and then his hand re-coiled.

"I couldn't take it," said Dunmore. "I'd a lot rather take poison than to take that."

"Do you mean it?" she said.

"Why should that cut you up so much?" he asked.

"Because I know that if you won't take this, you'll never pay any attention to what else I have to say."

"Hold on," murmured Dunmore. "I dunno about that."

"You never will listen. But I'm trying to confess the whole truth. I didn't realize, at first, how serious it all was. I mean, when I bet the ring, besides the money. I didn't re-alize that you might want the ring for any deep reason—that I never could redeem it from you!"

"Well ma'am," said Dunmore, "the way that a gent sticks to what he figgers is his luck is sure a mighty surpris-in' thing to——"

"Don't," she said, and held up a hand.

"Don't what?"

"Don't laugh at me—don't make a joke of me! Luck? You know that your luck is in your own right hand."

"Now, there's an idea," said Dunmore. "In my own right hand! Matter of fact, that's where I've got the ring, just now, so you're right about it."

She drew a quick breath. In passion, she seemed about to burst out at him, but then controlled herself strongly.

"I want to be steady," she said, in hardly more than a whisper, "and I don't want to be put off as you put every one off. Carrick Dunmore, Carrick Dunmore, will you try to listen seriously to me?"

She laid a hand on his, a light-brown hand, exquisitely slender and small, made with a tapering delicacy that sur-passed all he had seen in his days.

From that hand he looked hurriedly away, and saw the tall ranks of the mountains swelling beyond the trees, and the blue gorges that crossed them, the bluish clouds beyond.

This was his kingdom, and in it he must act as a strong king. But, king or not, he was very glad that the talk of Jimmy Larren had somewhat prepared him for this en-counter.

"I'll sure be serious if I can," said he.

"Did I tell you that Rodman Furneaux gave me that ring?" she said.

"Why, he's a fine, upstandin' boy!" said Dunmore.

"He is, he is! And when he sees it on your hand, do you know what he'll do?"

"You figger that he might make trouble?"

"Oh, let me tell you everything! We were afraid that he'd—that he'd go away. I was to try to hold him; I talked to him. He seemed very excited—he said that he wanted to marry me—somehow, I let him give me this ring——"

"And a promise?" said Dunmore.

She pressed her hands against her breast, and he could see it rise and fall.

"Now, how much do you despise me?"

"Why," said Dunmore, "the way that things is pretty nigh always lined up, it appears to me that a gent has gotta cut a lot of corners to get anywheres, as maybe I've said before!"

He added: "But you had an idea that maybe he would leave you?"

"He said that he was going away and——"

"Him? Away?" Dunmore laughed.

There was in this peculiar irony which struck something in him and made a sudden vibration through his heart.

"What do you mean?" she asked.

"They ain't a dog in the world," said Dunmore, "that don't howl and holler when it hears the wolves bayin'. But mostly they stay home. They got the smell and the savor of the bacon in their throats, and they can't leave it. And you're home to Furneaux. Leave you? He could leave his own skin a lot quicker! The thought of you would pull him across the ocean faster'n a flyin' bird. Yep, he'd fly to you like a bird flies south when the autumn gets cold. You had to take his ring to keep him here with you?"

He laughed, and at that laughter, she began to tremble, as though the vibration touched her very soul.

"You mean that it wasn't necessary?" she asked.

"To do that? To keep him? My dear child," said Carrick Dunmore, "there was no more need of it than there would be to ask the tides to follow the moon, or the blown sand to rise in the wind, or the bird's wing to beat in the air, or the stone to roll down the mountainside!"

He paused. She was looking rather wildly at him.

"That's all a farce, too?" she asked. "The rough talk and the bad grammar?"

"Hello!" said Dunmore. "Why, I never thought of that! But the fact is that the school days, they come back over me when I'm least thinkin' of it."

She looked away.

"I never can do anything with you," she said in a dead voice. "I know that you're beyond me. You're up here for some purpose that I can't fathom. Why should I try? It would be like trying to reach my hand to the bottom of a well! I could talk—I could spread out my heart in my hand, and you wouldn't care to even look at it. I—I—and yet, to whom can I talk now except to you? Oh I wish I were never born!"

Dunmore stood up.

She rose before him. She was crying, as Jimmy Larren had said that she would cry, but there was no hysteria. Only, out of sheer anguish, the tears forced themselves into her eyes, and then down her cheeks.

She spoke softly, as though she were sufficiently ashamed of the tears, and did not wish to allow her voice to shake.

"I think you're right," she said. "He would have stayed. He never would have left. And it all was useless! It all was useless! And now he's no better than dead!"

"Oh, come, come," said Dunmore. "You're makin' a lot of fuss about this young chap. Are you cryin' because you got engaged to him, or why?"

She shrank away from him.

"You are cruel," she said. "Cold, and iron-hearted, and cruel, and you'll murder him without a second thought!"

"Not a bit," said Dunmore. "I'm a businessman, Beatrice. I'm for sale! What can you offer by way of a good price?"

# XXXIV

## • A STRANGE PROPOSITION •

So greatly was she surprised, that she almost forgot the emotion which had been tormenting her just the moment before, and with parted lips she stared at him.

"What have I?" she asked him. "What do you mean?"

He looked suddenly away from her. Edging between two slender tree trunks he saw the mischievous face of Jimmy Larren, but he almost forgot the child the next instant. For he was glancing into the very heart of his problem and it seemed to him clearer than ever that he never could take young Furneaux away without using the girl as the lure.

"Why, I mean what I say," said he. "I'm a merchant. I go where I can get what I want."

"And so you've come to me for what? For compliments?" she asked him suspiciously.

"What else would've brought me up here into the mountains?" asked Dunmore, in turn.

Again she looked full at him, and again she winced.

"Of course, this is another way of laughing at me," she suggested.

Dunmore picked a leaf from a shrub and puffed it off the palm of his hand. It spun and floated in the air, then winked down into the water.

"I can't be too serious," said Dunmore. "You're free to laugh and I'm free to laugh if I can. But what else could have brought me up here, except you?"

She said instantly: "The hope of getting into power here —of becoming the king up in the edge of the sky, here!"

This was so close to the truth, and so fitted in with what that other Carrick Dunmore, that first of the race, had said, that he could not help staring.

169

"I knew it was the truth," said the girl. "You'd really try to shoulder Tankerton off his throne!"

"I wouldn't mind the job, perhaps," agreed Dunmore. "But there comes along a time when a man gets to the marrying age, eh? So that age came along and found me!"

She laughed outright.

"So you went up into the mountains to find a girl, and there you found her. Lucky, lucky Carrick!"

She added: "You never had seen her. But that didn't make any difference!"

"You ever hear of the Red Pacer?"

"You mean the mustang?"

"Yes."

"He was captured by somebody, I think."

"Yep. He wore a halter for five years. That was a friend of mine that caught him, and he had never seen the Red Pacer, either. But he went out and worked for eight months to get him, and get him he did. Spent thousands of dollars on hired men; used up hosses like water, to capture the Pacer."

"And that's the way with you and me?" said the girl ironically. "You hear about me, and you just can't keep away, eh?"

"Well?" said Dunmore.

"Stuff!" said she. "I've heard men say such things before, and every one of them said it a lot better than you've done! Why, Carrick, there's no more love in you than there is blood in a carrot! D'you think I'm only about five years old?"

"No, no," answered Dunmore, "I'd say that you're as old—as the blue in the bottom of that canyon, over yonder. Do you want me to rant like a fool, Beatrice? Because I can, if you'd rather have it!"

He turned closer to her as he spoke.

He could see in her face doubt, bewilderment, and amusement. And at this moment a breath of wind furled the collar of her blouse about her brown throat and gathered her whole body into gentle arms. And something leaped in Dunmore, and rushed out strongly toward her.

"Ah!" said she, and caught her breath.

Then she struck her hands together and laughed again.

"You're simply the grandest actor in the whole world," she said. "I see that you could even do a love scene!"

He smiled at her. It was plain that she would recoil from a display of emotion, and that only an intellectual interest, as it were, would keep her amused by him. So he thrust back the tumult of feeling that had risen in him, and kept his smile impersonal.

"You won't believe that I'm wildly in love with you, Beatrice?"

"Oh, tush," said she. "We'll let it go at that. But what under the heavens do you want of me?"

"Are you interested?"

"Interested? Would you be interested if a mountain lion came and stretched himself up the trunk of a tree in which you were sitting?"

"Hello," answered Dunmore. "That's pretty hard on me!"

"I don't know whether you're more ghost than panther," said she, "but I'll bet that you know how to ride on the wind and how to walk through walls, all right! And now you're coming after me, d'you wonder that I'm all chills and fever?"

"It's good to be noticed," said Dunmore. "It's the first step to any business deal."

"This is to be a business deal, is it?"

"Certainly!"

"Very well, then. What do you offer me?"

"Furneaux's life," he said shortly.

She shrank, then faced him again.

"You'll not kill Furneaux—I wish to Heaven that I knew what makes you hate him so!"

"Because," said Dunmore, "I'm jealous of him. You've shown so much interest in Furneaux that I'd like him a lot better with his head off, or a hole in it!"

He smiled at her again, with a white flash of teeth, and she actually turned pale.

"You make me dizzy," said she, more than half seriously.

"You can stand and smile and laugh, here, but all the while, you're as ready for murder as a cat is for mice!"

"Not murder, Beatrice. I never take an advantage."

"Because other men have no chance against you! No,

no, I suppose you'd go hunting trouble for the sake of the danger in it? I think you would!"

"You look as if you were in a haunted house," said he. "Am I as bad as all that?"

"That's how I feel," said she. "As though the house were haunted and—ghosts were behind me."

She tried to smile as she said this, but her eyes remained very round and still.

"You'll not hurt Rodman," she summed up, "who you say you hate because you're envious—jealous, I mean to say."

"Of course that's it," said he.

"It isn't it at all," she retorted. "But let's go ahead. You'll let Furneaux alone if I'll give you what?"

"Your company for ten days," said Dunmore.

"My company—for ten days?" she cried.

"That's it."

"To do what?" she demanded.

"To ride down out of the mountains with me."

"Where?"

"That's my business."

"You won't say?"

"No, I won't say."

"You're not serious."

"I'm as serious as I ever was in my life."

"To go with you—out of the mountains—for ten days? To travel alone with you all that time, do you mean?"

"Aye. That's what I mean."

"Then," said the girl, "you're absolutely a madman!"

He shrugged his shoulders.

"Will you tell me," she said, "what you could gain by having me with you for ten days? Except the pleasure of making me talked about?"

He frowned. "I've thought of all that," said he. "We can get married in the plains, if you want——"

"I won't want!" she said, and her lips curled with distaste.

He could not speak on smoothly, but for a moment he had to look away from her disdain, across the bright surface of the pool, and at the glittering white pebbles, with translucent shadows rippling over them.

Then he could face her again with his customary half-smile that so puzzled and intrigued her.

"Otherwise," said he, "I don't think that most folks will talk very much about a friend of mine, woman or man."

He hesitated.

"If somebody started scandal floatin'," he said at last, "I'd promise you to pay him a call, if that would make you feel any better."

She stared straight through him.

"I travel with you for ten days—through the woods?"

"Aye. That's the plan."

"Suppose I tell that plan to Jim Tankerton?"

"He'd get his gang together to kill me, I suppose. That would make him fight! If the gang would follow him!"

"Do you think they wouldn't?"

"I dunno," said he. "It's a mighty good gang, but then they's some things that you can't noways expect a gang to like to do."

"Such as fighting a Dunmore?"

"They hate to make trouble for a good-natured man like me," said he.

"What could you gain by such a trick," said the girl, "except to cover me with scandal, and to make the whole gang chase you? What else?"

Dunmore shrugged his shoulders.

"I've talked it out as simple as a child sayin' a lesson," he assured her. "Will you let it go at that?"

"Do you think that I'll do such a crazy thing?"

"You don't like to think of Furneaux dying," he told her.

"Whatever you have in mind, it's something deep as the roots of the world. Whatever you're aiming at, I'm to be taken along and see the shot fired. But did any woman ever do such a thing?"

She came a little closer, curious and trembling with excitement.

"Will you give me one hint of why you want me to make that ride?"

"Love, Beatrice," said he. "I'm wild with love of you, d'you see?"

"And you smile in my face as you talk? What shall I do? What shall I do?"

"Make up your mind by dinnertime," said Dunmore, "or Furneaux will be dead before the meal's over!"

## XXXV

## • THE LAST OF CHUCK HARPER •

SHE went from him at once, stepping lightly over the rocks that cropped from the surface of the water; on the farther side, she paused and half turned, as though there was still some word she wished to speak but she went on again at once, with lowered head, and the brush closed about her.

"She kinda thought that you were jokin'," said a voice at the shoulder of Dunmore.

He turned and looked down into the face of Larren.

"Was she wrong?" said Dunmore.

"Aw, I'll tell a man that she was wrong," said Jimmy, "and if she'd had half an eye, she'd 'a' seen it!"

"Her eyes weren't closed, Jimmy."

"She was thinkin' too much, and thinkin' is always hard on the eyes," said Jimmy. "When Chuck Barnard come to town, I was pretty bad scared. His dad had been in the ring and knew all the slick ways of sneakin' a punch home. Well, I had to fight him——"

"Why did you have to?"

"Why, what else would I do?" asked Jimmy, amazed. "Was I gunna back up and give up the game of bein' boss before I'd had my chance at him? We had it out behind the Schuyler barn. He began boxing high and fine. He kept stickin' a straight left in my face and clubbin' me over my shoulder with his right. But pretty soon I noticed that he always was lookin' thoughtful, like he was tryin' to remember something. So I begun tryin' fancy stuff, myself. I began to feint for the stomach and then hit for the stomach. He could tell there was a feint, but he'd think that th next punch would be for the face. After he'd made a couple of mistakes like that he was no good, and pretty soon he was all upset and remembered that he had to go home and chop the kindlin' up!"

Jimmy paused, with happy eyes, and ran the tip of his red tongue over his lips.

"Chuck was thinkin' too much to really watch where my hands were goin'! And Beatrice, here, she was thinkin' too much about what you said to keep watchin' your face."

"Well, Jimmy, what will she do?"

"Go and set and think, of course," said Jimmy.

"And what'll come of that?"

"Why, what always happens when a woman goes and sets and thinks?"

"You tell me, Jimmy?"

"Sure, I can tell, and so can you. I seen my aunt once set and have a long think about would she go buy a new hat that day; she set so long that the bread burned in the oven. And that afternoon, she did get the hat."

Dunmore chuckled.

"Are all women like that, Jimmy?"

"Sure. When a man sets and thinks, mostly it means that he ain't made up his mind, yet; but you take with a woman, it's just the opposite. She don't really set and think; she's just makin' up excuses!"

"Then you think that Beatrice has made up her mind already?"

Jimmy thrust his bare toes into the verge of the stream and wriggled them thoughtfully in the cool mud.

"I dunno, just," said he. "I dunno. She ain't like common folks. You take a fast hoss and you see more of his speed than you do of his points. I reckon that she's that way. She could change too. But just now, I guess that she's aimin' to go away with you."

"I think she is," agreed Dunmore.

Jimmy sighed. "I'd be missin' you a good deal up around here, chief," said he.

"You're coming down with us," said Dunmore.

"Coming down where, chief?"

"Wherever I take you."

"You and me and her?"

"Yes, the three of us."

"I'd like that," said Jimmy, "I'd like that more'n a mountain of gold!"

"All right, Jim. We'll probably start to-night. You'd better get your mustang in order."

"Tonight?"

"I hope so."

"You ain't rushin' things, chief?"

"No, Jimmy. If I stay here more than another day, I'll never leave the camp alive!"

It was Jimmy's turn to express greatest wonder.

"Anybody been sneakin' around you, chief?"

"Nobody. You can smell wood smoke before you see it."

"A mighty lot!" agreed the boy. "Well, are we comin' back up here?"

"Except on a stretcher, no, I guess."

"Then I won't need the mustang."

"What will you do?"

"They's a piebald hoss in the barn that I been talkin' to considerable. He don't mind me and I don't mind him. So maybe we could get along together, pretty well."

Dunmore grinned. "Who owns him?" he asked.

"That Lynn Tucker, and nobody else!"

"Take him if you can. Get the horses out of the stable while the rest of us are finishing supper. Get 'em out and saddled. It won't be long after that before we're movin', three of us, or only two!"

They crossed the creek, the boy skipping across first, and Dunmore following more slowly; but as he reached the farther bank, Jimmy Larren turned with a squeal:

"Duck!"

And he flung himself straight at Dunmore's knees. That hard impact, so totally unexpected, dropped Dunmore flat.

"Harper!" the boy had ejaculated, as he struck home against the knees of his friend.

And as Dunmore fell, he actually felt the wind of a bullet beside his head. Falling, he drew his Colt, and fired at a vague outline behind the brush. Distinctly, like the thud of a fist against a soft body, he heard that bullet strike home.

Then the head and shoulders of Chuck Harper appeared above the brush, with both his arms flung high. It looked as though he were striving to leap out at the man he hated; for there were both malice and agony in his squinting eyes and grinning lips.

Instead, he crashed face downward through the brush, and rolled over on his back in the open.

He was in his shirt sleeves, and red already stained the breast of his shirt. He began to bite at the air, like a dog in a fit.

"Chuck," said Dunmore, "tell me if this was your own idea, or if somebody put it into your head. Tell me that, and I'll help you. Otherwise, you can lie here and bleed to death, you murderin' Injun!"

Harper beckoned twice with his right hand, so that Dunmore leaned over him. For that opportunity, Chuck had saved the last of his strength. He snatched from his belt a knife that jerked upward at the breast of Dunmore. But the barrel of the ready Colt dropped across the clutching fingers, battering the weapon from their grip.

One final oath bubbled red upon the lips of Chuck Harper; his death agony rolled him upon his face; the pebbles rattled under his clawing feet and hands; then he lay still.

Dunmore looked across at the white, strained face of his companion.

"Thanks, Jim," said he. "That was close!"

Jimmy laughed to cover a shudder.

"Did you have your gun up your sleeve?" he asked.

"Inside my coat. I'll show you the trick of it, one of these days. I'd like to know his secret, Jimmy."

"What secret?"

"Whether he was sent by someone else, or came by himself."

"Maybe he's got the answer in his pocket."

"Aye. Look and see!"

So Jimmy knelt by the big man. Presently he rose, a wallet in his hand, which when opened showed a thin, clean sheaf of bills.

"Five—hundred—iron—men," said Jimmy with awe, as he counted. "Think of havin' that much! That's about half the price that hired him, I bet on that, chief."

Dunmore nodded.

"A thousand dollars was high pay for Harper," he brooded.

"Sure. He hated you already a million dollars' worth," suggested Jimmy Larren. "But maybe he didn't hate you just enough to make him take this here chance. Besides, if the money was showed him, fresh and clean, he couldn't keep his paws off of it."

"You look a little sick, Jim."

"Do I? It's kind of a new game with me, chief!"

A shade passed over the face of Dunmore.

"This here gent was more hog than man, Jimmy," said he. "But death takes away something, and adds something." He sighed, and then added: "I never seen a man dead that I didn't wish alive again."

"It scares me, sort of," whispered Jimmy. "Him lyin' on his face—seein' what?"

"Seein' all the good of his life, and all the bad; and likely none of the things that he dreamed and wished. Go back to the clearin', Jim, and tell Tankerton that Harper went crazy and tried to kill me. I'll wait here."

Jimmy look around at the tall, darkening trees, in awe.

"Alone?" said he. "You gunna wait here alone, chief?"

"Aye," said Dunmore, "alone. Wait a minute, Jim. That five hundred is yours, if you want!"

The face of Jimmy brightened; then his lips curled with disgust. From his opening hand the bright new money fluttered down to the earth.

"It's not the kind of money that I like," said Jimmy. "It's a hoss, and a Winchester, and a saddle, and shop boots, and spurs, and a knife, and a beaver hat, and silver conchos, and everything. But I'd sort of itch under anything that money bought for me, I reckon!"

He hesitated for one last glance at the fallen greenbacks. Then he fled away through the trees as though to escape violently from temptation.

Dunmore listened to the last crackling of the twigs underfoot; then he began to pace up and down the bank like a sentinel.

# XXXVI

## • THE DOCTOR INTERFERES •

Down to Harpersville, the heliograph winked in the golden light of the later afternoon sun: "Harper is dead killed by Dunmore tell Mrs. Harper."

And in ten minutes back came the answer: "Bury him Mrs. Harper too busy smoking bacon to come"!

This message caused grim laughter in the camp; however, they prepared at once for the burial.

"He sure likes to sit in the sun," said Lynn Tucker.

So they dug his grave on the south front of the mountain where the shadows of the trees never could fall. All was rose and blue and gold when the company stood about the hole into which the bulk of Harper had just been lowered.

Tankerton then asked if any one wished to say anything before the grave was filled in, and this caused rather an awkward and depressing silence, as each man looked to his fellow, and all faces remained blank. There never had been in the band a more unpopular member than Chuck Harper.

At last, Doctor Legges stepped forward.

"I can see how it is," said he. "Every heart is too full for utterance; because Chuck Harper was big enough to fill any heart. Therefore, I'll say a few words about this remarkable man.

"He was the biggest man in the mountains, and the strongest man, until our new brother, Dunmore, came to join us. Now all that strength of his only serves to fill his grave more fully from side to side and thereby reminds us of the vanity of all human possessions, brothers, even thick necks and big biceps.

"But if the great body of Chuck Harper is now gone from us, we have many causes to remember him, and when I come to consider his moral excellencies, I hardly know where I am to begin.

"However, you all remember how Chuck loved the sun. He could not have enough of it and, as we all know, could sit happily in it from morning to night.

"He loved his land, also, so much that he forgot that it came to him from his wife; he loved his house, as well. I have heard him say that it was the finest house in the mountains, and that he would knock down any man who dared to doubt it! However, Chuck was not a man to paint a thing in order to give it a prettier face. He let his house go unpainted for that reason, beyond a doubt!

"Hypocrites we despise, and Chuck was no hypocrite. He loved saying what was in his mind, and rather than flatter a man, he was almost sure to go in the opposite direction.

"We also despise and scorn spendthrifts, and Chuck was none of these. Whatever money came into his hands he held with an iron grasp. Money was safer with Chuck Harper than in a steel safe.

"I must end by pointing out that Chuck was no destroyer of morals and I defy any one of you to say that Chuck ever stood treat in all his days.

"Finally, let us remember that Chuck's death was in perfect harmony with all his acts. As he lived, so he died. For myself, I am glad that I have known the biggest man who ever strained the back of a mountain horse. I wish him the best luck that can come his way, wherever he now may be."

The doctor ended and stepped back. At a signal from Tankerton the earth began to be shoveled back into the grave, but it was not yet half filled when a long halloo came wavering up the hillside, and then the familiar wail of the cook was distinguished: "Hey! Come and get it! Come and get it!"

Shovels were dropped at once and the whole crew streamed back toward the camp.

Dunmore went with the rest. He had told clearly and simply how the shooting took place, and Jimmy Larren was a vivid witness for the defense; afterward, he furnished a new blanket in which the body of the dead man was wrapped, in lieu of a coffin, before it was lowered into the ground. In this manner, it was considered that he had fulfilled his duties, and that the review of the case had ended when Tankerton had said: "We know how Chuck Harper was killed. If any man questions the story, now is the time to speak up."

No voices were raised.

"Then," said Tankerton, "this is forgotten; we'll bury every grievance in the same grave that holds Harper!"

However, that was not accurately the case.

Chelton stepped beside Dunmore on the way down the hill from the interrupted burial.

He said softly, aside: "Partner, are you satisfied with the layout around these parts?"

"Why not?" asked Dunmore.

"The boys don't look happy," said Chelton. "They're agin' you, Dunmore."

"Why?"

"Because they's been talk passed around. I think that Legges and Tucker have had their share of it. Don't talk to me, because, of course, they know that I'm for you. But the other boys seem to figger that you're different from the rest of 'em. That's the way that trouble starts, Dunmore, as I reckon that you know."

"I know," agreed he.

"All right," remarked Chelton. "If you got the cards to play this game, go ahead. You can count me in as part of your hand, of course!"

As they approached the cookhouse, another form stepped beside Dunmore. It was Beatrice Kirk, saying swiftly: "Will you give me more time, Carrick? He hasn't heard about the ring yet, I think; but if you wear it at the table, he'll be sure to see!"

Dunmore hesitated. "How long will you take?" he asked.

"Only till after dinner is over. I'll tell you then, I promise, if no harm has happened to Furneaux!"

"Very well," said Dunmore.

He slipped the ring from his finger and dropped it into a vest pocket.

"It's the last chance, Beatrice," said he.

He could see her make a gesture of despair, as she turned away from him; but he, staring after her, could not help wondering. She had seemed callous enough about other matters; she did not love Furneaux, he was sure; and he was amazed that she would face such sacrifices for the youngster. It showed her with new depths, and a new gentleness.

He went thoughtfully on to the noise and the confusion of the washing basins, where the men were lathering hands and faces with a great spluttering, then dashing water about liberally, and brandishing towels which left them with hair wet about the edges.

Into the dining room they stamped, laughing and chatting, and not a sign on any face to indicate that an old member of the band had been killed and buried that same evening!

Dunmore, with that reflection, entered. And as he looked about the wild crew, he realized that though the first Carrick Dunmore might have established a kingdom of the blue horizon, a kingdom above and outside of the laws, such a realm was not for him!

They were Tankerton's liegemen, his pledged vassals. And he, no matter what he had done to thwart the three leaders, or how he had distinguished himself in rescuing Chelton, was not really one of the gang.

He felt it still more as he sat down.

There were only two pairs of eyes that ever really met his and rest steadily. Those were the eyes of Chelton, whose life he had saved, and of Jimmy Larren, to whom he was a god.

But the others, in talking, spoke to one another, laughed and chatted across the table, but never gave to their new leader more than a flashing side glance, as though they included him more by force of circumstance than by wish.

The main business of eating took up the first few moments of every meal, with anxious reaching after the great platters, lest the choicest bits should be taken by a neighbor, but Dunmore paid little heed to this. He kept his attention fixed upon three people—Tankerton, young Furneaux, and Beatrice.

Furneax had no power to keep his glances from the girl,

and though she disregarded him frequently, once, at least, Dunmore saw her smile deliberately, tenderly on the youngster, and saw Furneaux color to the eyes with a sudden joy.

But all was going well for a peaceful termination of that meal, when suddenly the genial voice of Doctor Legges broke in: "Well, Dunmore, you got Furneaux's ruby out of him, I see?"

## XXXVII

### • GET READY TO RIDE •

WITH the shock of that speech, it seemed to Dunmore that the lights were a great dazzle above his head, but through the dazzle he strained his eyes at the grinning malice of the doctor, and then toward the girl and Furneaux.

Beatrice had been struck white! All her assurance, all her poise, was not enough, now. And she looked blankly before her.

Tankerton was as alert as a cat, instantly. It seemed as though he had known beforehand of this plan! Only Furneaux did not understand the speech, as it appeared.

"My ruby, doctor?" said he. "Beatrice is keeping it safe for me. I was tired of chipping it!"

And he laughed, rather foolishly, as though he expected every man to guess, at once, the heart of his mystery.

"Where's she keeping it for you, Rodman?" asked the doctor. "Not on her finger, I see?"

Furneaux glanced at the girl's hand and frowned a little. Then he looked up at her face. She was making a desperate effort to keep control of herself, but that effort was a failure, totally.

Jimmy Larren slipped unnoticed from his place and left the house at once; even Dunmore hardly noted what the boy had done.

Furneaux had no power to keep his plan

Dunmore would have liked to take the doctor by the throat, but that worthy now laughed and rubbed his hands.

"Ah, these girls!" said he. "We never know when we have them. The rascal wheedles a pretty ring out of you, Furneaux, and hands it on to this famous fellow, Dunmore."

The doctor laughed again, and still rubbed his hands; while Furneaux looked actually agape on Beatrice.

"To Dunmore?" he asked huskily.

And not a word came from Beatrice.

Then Furneaux, convinced, whiter than the girl herself, leaned back in his chair a little.

"Well," said he, "some men have a way of getting what they can—out of girls!"

He sneered at Dunmore, and a red haze passed over the eyes of the latter.

He saw every man at the table grow tense; he saw hands ready to thrust back out of harm's course, when the guns were drawn; he saw the eyes of Beatrice like staring wells of darkness, and Tankerton faintly smiling, an acid smile.

Then Dunmore understood. It was all arranged beforehand between Tankerton and the doctor. They were to make Furneaux badger him into a fight. Furneaux was a quick hand with a gun and a straight shot; who could tell but that he might drop even a more formidable fighter than Dunmore? Besides, in the confusion of the shots, might not someone fire from the side—the doctor, say; or Lynn Tucker, pale with malice?

But he, for his own part, was for the first time in his life digesting an insult without striking back!

He bent his attention to his plate, and went on with his eating.

He heard a little murmur, made by the indrawn breath of many men. They were struck with wonder to see him "take water"—he who had stood up to Harper, to the doctor, to Lynn Tucker, to Tankerton himself.

Furneaux raised his voice. "Did you hear me, Dunmore?" said he.

Dunmore shrugged his shoulders, and still did not look up. Both hands trembled with eagerness to get at his guns, yet he restrained himself.

"I said," went on Furneaux, "that there are some men in the world who are curs enough to hunt for what they can get—from women!"

Slowly, Dunmore looked up.

He saw, in his agony, the blood-red heap of apples which graced the center of the table. He saw, beyond them, the desperate and appealing face of the girl; and that sight gave him a sudden courage.

Furneaux was stiff and tensely alert in his chair. His left hand was on the edge of the table. His right hand was out of sight—gripping the handle of a Colt, no doubt!

"Doctor," said Dunmore, "you're handy to the apples, there. Will you throw me one?"

The doctor hesitated, frowning a little. He could not understand this request, at such a time; but eventually he reached out and picked up an apple.

"It's bigger," said the doctor, "but it ain't a ruby to set in a ring!" and he tossed the apple toward Dunmore.

There had to be some outlet for the pent-up fury which was working in the heart of Dunmore, and now he snatched a revolver out of the empty air, as it seemed to those astonished eyes that watched him; it flashed and exploded at the same instant and the apple, torn in two, fell back upon the table. One half struck a tin cup and raised a great rattling. The other half rolled off upon the floor.

Furneax, at the same instant, had made a move with his own weapon, but only the muzzle of it had appeared above the edge of the table before Dunmore drew and fired.

The inference was clear enough. The face of Rodman Furneax grew patched with purple, he bit his lower lip, and slowly put up the revolver.

"That apple was no good, doctor," said Dunmore cheerfully. "You can see by the inside of it that the worms were already at it. Pass me another, will you?"

Again the doctor threw and apple, but this time, Dunmore caught it with his left hand and started eating it.

"Try one, Furneaux," urged he. "You know what they say—an apple a day keeps the doctor away!"

He glanced at the doctor, as he spoke, and the worthy doctor lost control of himself so completely that he scowled broadly, for all to see.

Tankerton, too, sat with pinched lips, and Lynn Tucker was breathing hard.

One would have said that the least matter in the world —the mere falling of a leaf—would have made all three leap into immediate action. But the leaf did not fall!

Furneaux, brave as a lion and willing to fight, still hesitated a little, for he had seen his own death, as it were, rehearsed before his eyes, and the picture was something to remember. Besides, there still was the acrid taint of powder smoke in the air!

Yet the atmosphere was still charged with danger, when Beatrice Kirk pushed back her chair and rose.

No one spoke to her; she herself did not utter a word, but looked at Dunmore as though at the end of the world. Then she left the room, hesitating for an instant at the door, with one hand against the jamb of it, as though she were dizzy.

The long silence at the table continued. It began to grow breathless; Dunmore could see the brow of Furneaux shining with moisture beneath the lamp. He had turned paler than before, and his eyes looked hollow, but he was brave as any hero could be.

Finally, he thrust back his chair. The scrape of it on the floor was like the scream of a human being in that tense stillness, and every man at the table started.

"Dunmore," said the other, "I'm going to be waiting for you outside the door of the bunkhouse where I sleep. I'll have some things to say to you; you can talk to me. And it won't be an apple that answers you back!"

He turned on his heel and strode out into the darkness. However, Dunmore could see that he did not turn in the direction which the girl had taken, and that eased his heart.

Tankerton spoke for the first time.

"Dunmore," said he, "that was a fine thing to do. You kept Furneaux from joining Harper, and that would have been a crowded berth for him; besides, he wasn't ready to make the trip, I think."

"Thank the doctor, too," said Dunmore. "There's a fellow that's got my good at heart, and Furneaux's too. However, I got an idea that he wouldn't been standin' by doin' nothin'. Not him! Doctor, I drink to you!"

He raised a cup of coffee and drained off the steaming contents. Never had he wanted a stimulant more.

"When I finish with Furneaux," said he then, "I'll come back and have a little chat with you. Where'll I find you?"

The doctor turned gray-green around the eyes. The greater part of his face was covered by his beard. Yet he answered stoutly:

"I sit on the steps of the bunkhouse after dinner, always. You can come and talk to me there, Dunmore!"

"All right," said the latter. "We're going to be a chummy lot of friends, I can see."

He stood up, stretching himself, and as he did so, he felt all eyes dwell upon him critically. Dunmore smiled upon them, and then walked slowly out of the room.

At the door, as Beatrice had done, so did he do, pausing with his back turned full upon them, and waiting, as it were, in defiance of them all, but no hand was raised, and no voice spoke against him.

Then he descended quietly to the ground, and went out into the dark. There he paused for a moment, took note of the glimmering lights which showed through the windows and through the open doors of the bunkhouses, took heed of the gentle and irregular circle of shadows which embraced the clearing, and of the big bonfire in the center, now burning down, but with the great embers of the logs glowing rich and red.

There were fragrances, too, in this place—the scent of the fresh wood smoke, beyond all things appealing to lovers of the open, and there were the perfumes of the pines, and of flowers, mysteriously mingled with the other odors.

Dunmore, looking upon these things, inhaling the breath of the wilderness, watching the red-hot glow of the great logs rotting away in their own heat, sighed a little.

And he looked back, above all, to the brightest light, which was the illumination that streamed out of the door of the dining room. Looking at that maze of golden light, he could see in his fancy the faces of the men around the table. He could hear, also, the excited murmur of their voices, every moment growing louder.

He knew of what they talked, and he smiled grimly within himself as he thought of it. They were counting the ways and the manner in which he could be disposed of.

It seemed as though a shadow rose out of the ground beside him.

"Everything's ready, chief," said the voice of Jimmy Larren.

He reached out and gathered the skinny shoulders of Jimmy within his arm.

"Jim, old partner," said he, "the fact is that we're going on Old Nick's own ride, tonight. We've got about one chance in twenty of pulling clear, and on the way to it, they'll shoot down every man of us as if we were no better than dogs. They'd shoot you down, Jimmy, and forget that you're only a boy."

"Why," said Jimmy, "that's about all that I could ask, ain't it? I mean, to be mistook for a man, so's I could die a man's death! I wouldn't aim to die no better than alongside of you, chief, and it seems to me that a gent has gotta die some time. Ain't that right?"

Dunmore grew thoughtful.

"We have a few minutes, I suppose," said he. "They'll be talkin' for a while in the dining room."

"More'n a while," said Jimmy. "They'll be talkin' till the cows come home, if you wanta ask my idea of it. They never run up agin' anything like you before, and they'll never run up agin' such a thing agin'. So they got reason to talk, darn 'em all!"

"You don't like them, Jim?"

"I thought that they was free," said Jimmy Larren, "and that was the only reason that I ever liked their kind of a life."

"Well, Jimmy, they're free enough."

"Free to make fools of themselves," said Jimmy bitterly. "Is that bein' really free? I should say not! They ain't no freer than a hoss in a pasture; sooner or later, he's gunna feel the rope around his neck, I reckon."

Dunmore chuckled softly.

"Jimmy, where's the girl?"

"She ain't come out of her house."

"I'll go try to get her, then. Everything's lost unless I take her along."

# XXXVIII

## • THROUGH THE BRUSH •

AT the door of the girl's cabin, he paused for a moment, listening, and heard a throb of dull, soft sound within, almost like the pulse of his own heart.

He tapped at the door and heard a frightened gasp in response.

He pushed the door open, and saw Beatrice lying on the couch, in the very act of raising herself from it. She, at the sight of him, sprang erect.

"I'm ready," she stammered. "I'll go, Carrick."

He took heed of her carefully, as one who had no time to spare, because he could see that his ship was ready to sink, and yet he said to her: "Have you thought it out, Beatrice? If you go with me now, you never can come back! You leave this. You've been a sort of queen, up here, but you never will be a queen again. Have you figured on that?"

She nodded to him, dumb with sorrow.

"Only if you could say what I'm to be," said she. "Where I'm to go, what I'm to do."

"Go where I go," said Carrick Dunmore. "Ride as I ride, and ask no questions. I could say one thing more—but there's hardly any use of it."

"I want to know."

He looked at her tear-stained face and took a half step toward her.

"I mean you no harm, Beatrice. I hope it'll be for you as much as for myself."

It seemed to Dunmore that he never had seen her so beautiful, for the only light that was in the room, at that time, was the flame on the open hearth, which rose and fell, and flickered wildly, and gave to her body and to her face a strange life. Her weeping had not disfigured her. but it seemed only to have made her more feminine, with a helpless softness that went to his heart.

"I'm ready," said Dunmore.

She looked wildly around the room. "I'm ready," said she.

"Mind you," repeated Dunmore, "once you leave, it's forever."

She drew a quick breath, and then nodded. "What am I to do?" she asked.

"Jimmy has the horses ready. Shall we start?"

Suddenly she threw out her hands to him.

"Don't you see?" said Beatrice. "It's all hopeless. You want to take me away from them, but you can't. They're sure to follow. They're sure to catch us. Everyone in the mountains is devoted to them. Everyone is ready to fight and to die for them. They have signals that would cut us off. They know how to work every corner of the country. We'll be running into a net every step that we take! Have you thought of all that, Carrick?"

"Aye," said he, "I've thought of all that!"

"But still you'll try?"

"Still I'll try."

She gave one glance more around her, as though she were taking into her mind all that she never would see again—the two big grizzly-bear rugs on the floor, the skins of the mountain sheep that covered the couch, and on the floor the heads of elk and of deer that had fallen to her own rifle.

Then, with a little gesture, she went to Dunmore and gently laid a hand on his arm.

"I'll go," said she. She looked up suddenly to his face. "It was a grand thing, tonight," said she. "I never saw a man do such a thing. I never hoped to see it!"

And she went out before him into the dark of the night.

Dunmore, following, quickly joined her and led the way around the house and back into the trees.

There, among the shadows, they saw the outlines of horses.

Jimmy Larren's voice greeted them.

"I've got Gunfire and Excuse Me," said he, "and the

piebald for myself. Start quick! Here's been that fox, Lynn Tucker, walkin' along through the trees, and I was sure he'd see us!"

Dunmore gave the girl a hand into the saddle. Then he swung up on Excuse Me, and headed away through the woods, with the girl behind him, and Jimmy Larren last of the lot. But, as he went, an odd joy and surety filled the breast of Dunmore that the girl would not leave them. She seemed as much a member of the party as Jimmy's loyal soul itself; so he did not look behind him, but went straight forward and heard the cautious crackling of the twigs beneath the hoofs of the horses which followed.

After a time, they had passed sufficiently far to warrant his going fast and with a glance behind him, he swung Excuse Me into a gallop.

Steadily he rode, following the road to Harpersville, which he had such good reason to know. The trees flowed steadily past them. The road rang like metal beneath the hoofs of the horses, and the wind cut at his face.

So they descended two thirds of the way to Harpersville and were cutting along at a good clip when Jimmy Larren cried out. At that, Dunmore looked back, and he saw a light flaring on the forehead of the mountain behind them. It winked rapidly, and Dunmore drew Excuse Me to a halt.

"Do you know how to read that signaling?" he asked of the girl.

She already was spelling it out aloud.

"Ten — thousand — dollars — for — Dunmore — alive — or — dead."

" 'Ten thousand dollars for Dunmore, alive or dead'!" she said, putting the letters together. "I know they'd send out some message like that. But—ten thousand dollars!"

"It ain't possible!" said Jimmy Larren. "Why, every man in the mountains will be oilin' up his rifle and startin' for us. I pretty nigh wish that I was on the other side, chief. You ain't going straight on through Harpersville, are you?"

"We're going to skirt around it. Jimmy, you'll be able to show us a way where we're not apt to run into any one?"

"But the whole town is turned out by this time, blockin'

the trails. I dunno that I can do the job, but I'll try! You'll get scratched up a mite, though."

"How fast are Tankerton's messages relayed through the mountains?"

"Fast as you can think! There it goes ahead of us!"

He pointed, and from the tallest hill before them, they saw a light begin to blink, repeating the message.

"They's hardly a house but what's got somebody in it that can read the signaling. And every house on a high place is fixed with a strong light for the signal-makin'."

Dunmore nodded. Then, tersely: "Lead on, Jimmy. Beatrice, go next. I'll wind up the procession."

They started on obediently, winding off into a thick growth of trees and shrubs which constantly whipped them with projecting branches. Now and then, they could jog their horses at a slow trot, but most of the time, they had to go at a walk, and even at a walk, they had to pause occasionally.

Dunmore found himself straining his eyes into the thick darkness on either hand, though all was so black beneath the big trees that the most he could do was to make out the dim forms of the brush and the stalwart trunks when he was an arm's length from them.

They were constantly choked by the dust which had settled on the foliage and which now was brushed off into the air in clouds. Thorns tore at their clothes with many a sound or ripping, and now and then a horse would clear its nostrils with a snort that sounded to their frightened ears like the blowing of an alarm trumpet.

However, they sifted in this manner down the hillside, and across it, until finally they were able to see through a gap in the trees the scattered lights of Harpersville above them, and finally the tall, blocky outline of the hotel itself.

Jimmy suddenly halted; the girl pushed behind him; and Dunmore, bringing up his horse in turn, heard her gasp with fear.

Straight before them came murmuring voices.

After a moment Dunmore heard a gruff man's voice exclaim: "I tore off half my face on their brier! I ain't gunna go no farther along here. The kid's crazy!"

"I ain't crazy," answered a boy's voice. "When we was

playin' Injun, Jimmy always used to fool us by gettin' onto this old trail."

"Trail? It ain't no more trail than a cactus patch!"

"It got choked up a good deal, but you see that you can get through. Jimmy's with them, and he might show 'em this way. We better go along, Dad!"

"It's a fool business," said another man. "We're wastin' our time down here, with a kid to lead us, and somebody else is gunna rake in that ten thousand. My stars, ten thousand dollars!"

He said it reverently, and with an almost religious emotion.

"And something more for the girl and the kid!" exclaimed another voice.

"Hey, I wouldn't mind plugging that Dunmore, but I'd hate to try to handle that wild cat of a girl without thick gloves on, I'm gunna tell you!"

"Go on, boys. We'll keep along the trail, now that we're started on it. Keep your guns ready."

"I ain't gunna go another step. My face is all tore already. Besides, how could even Dunmore get the girl to ride along this here trail?"

"She's in love with him, ain't she? And a girl'll do anything for a man she's in love with. Love thickens up the hide of a girl till it's like the skin of a mule!"

"All right. Keep ahead. I'm gunna go back. So long, boys!"

"Don't you leave us, Jack! We need you, if we should run onto him!"

"Brave, ain't you? Three of you, at that!"

"If Jack goes back, I'm goin' back too."

"Then we'll all have to go. Dash the luck!"

With much swearing, they turned back, crashing through the thorny brush.

And the last thing that Dunmore heard was: "This here Dunmore, they say that he didn't come to the mountains for nothin' but the girl."

"Him? Nobody knows what he wants. Most likely he don't know himself. Ask a bull terrier why it loves to fight. As much sense in that as to ask what's in Dunmore's brain. Trouble raisin' is all that he's interested in!"

"A lazy loafer, they say."

"Sure, and a drunk."

"And a crooked gambler."

"Well, he held a hand that Tankerton couldn't beat!"

The voices faded away.

# XXXIX

## • IN THE MIDDLE OF THE NIGHT •

THEY waited without a whisper, until after all noise had died away, and a few minutes had passed, Dunmore said that they might go on. Therefore, they started again, with Jimmy again in the lead, and the very horses, as it seemed, stepping more lightly after their fright of the moment before.

Presently the trail widened a little.

That scene was printed forever upon the memory of Dunmore. On the left there was a run of water, beginning to sparkle under the pale-silver light of the moon, which was just floating up like a cloud above the branches of the eastern trees. Second-growth forest and shrubbery banked the hill to the right, and there was a nest of glistening rocks in the center of this little natural clearing. No sooner had they come well within the range of it than half a dozen rifles suddenly clanged in their faces. Voices yelled, but of them all, he could remember only one childish screech: "I told you! I told you they'd come this way!"

He put spurs to Excuse Me and rushed straight at the rock nest.

"It's Dunmore!" someone yelled.

A figure rose from among the stone. Guns blared in his face. And as he fired his revolver, he saw the lanky form of the first man topple backward.

Behind him, he sensed the sweep of the boy and of Beatrice riding for cover, and he swung off from the natural fort to get into refuge in his turn.

It seemed to be by miracle alone that he escaped being

hit. He felt the check and tug of bullets as they whistled through his clothes. His sombrero was knocked from his head. But he went on, unscathed, and the blessed darkness of the forest once more closed behind him.

He heard the yells of the marksmen—frantic yells of disappointment as ten thousand dollars in hard cash melted away from their grasp, but now the trail widened, and he was galloping over easy ground, with the girl and the boy a scant distance in front of him.

Joy rose in the heart of Dunmore. Let her ride with whom she would, how long would it be before she went with a man who dared what he had ventured on this day?

Then he saw her turn in the saddle.

"That was a glorious thing to do!" she cried at him.

"Nothin' at all," said Dunmore, with a chuckle, and brought Excuse Me up beside them.

He wondered at Jimmy Larren, who did not speak a word, but rode with his head turned straight forward. His wonder turned to anxiety when he saw Jimmy grip the pommel of the saddle.

"Jim! Jim!" he cried, swinging Excuse Me beside the lad.

The boy did not answer, did not so much as nod.

"Are you hurt, Jimmy?"

Larren shook his head.

"Jim! Jim! They've nicked you, darn 'em!"

Beatrice was cantering ahead, and Jimmy suddenly threw the head of his mustang over and galloped knee to knee with Dunmore.

"Get her out of it. I'll drop back. They got me, chief, but don't you let her know. She's got a funny, woman's way, and she'd be kind of apt to want to stay behind with me. Go on, chief. I'll pull through fine!"

Dunmore groaned.

"Where is it?" he asked.

"Why, nothin'. I'm only nicked. I ain't hurt."

But the lad rode bowed over the pommel.

"They got you through the body!" exclaimed Dunmore. "Oh, the skunks! They've killed you, Jimmy!"

And Jimmy gasped: "Don't make so much noise, or she'll hear you. Ride on, chief. Don't pay no attention. I had—to die, sometime."

He sagged heavily from the saddle as he spoke, and
Dunmore gathered him into his arms, and lifted him out of
the saddle. Limp as a half-filled sack lay the child against
his breast, a lean, bony frame, the head falling back and
bobbing over the arm of Dunmore. He had fainted completely away, and the pinto ran wildly on ahead, bolting
with the reins flying high above his head.

Beatrice reined sharply into them.

"Not Jimmy!" she cried. "They haven't hurt him!"

"I think he's done for," said Dunmore bitterly. "A better sort than you and me would ever be! Why should he've
been hit? Where'll we take him?"

"It's Jim! It had to be the boy!" said Beatrice. "There's
a light yonder. Take him there, for Heaven's sake!"

Dunmore asked no questions.

If they were followed even on foot, they might be locat-
ed in this house. The house itself might be a fortress and
strong-hold of their enemies. But he was more assured
when he saw it close at hand.

It stood in wide clearing. All around, in a great circle,
the trees had been cut away from a low mound on the top
of which stood a small shack, such as a hunter might use.

Here in this lower valley, the air was warm, the door of
the shack was opened to it, and from the open door shone
the lantern light, dimly. Whatever this house might be, it
was here that they must try to leave the boy.

So he rode on straight to it, and dismounted, holding
the senseless lad in the strong cup of one arm.

It was a trapper's cabin, and the trapper rose from the
work of making a stretcher on which to dry pelts. He was
an old man with a very long white beard that flowed down
from just beneath his eyes. Great overhanging brows, likewise heavily fringed with white, helped to give him a pro-
phetic look.

"Why, hullo," said this veteran. "What's matter?" Accident?"

Dunmore walked straight in and laid the boy on the
bunk. He waved a hand at the proprietor, and then, with
Beatrice hanging breathlessly at his shoulder, he bared the
breast of poor Jim Larren.

There was a great crimson slash over the heart. Beatrice
moaned at the sight of it, but Dunmore, teeth gripping

hard, put his finger into the wound. Straightway the tip of the finger struck the bone of a rib. That bone gave a little under pressure, with a grating sound, and Jimmy groaned in his sleep.

But the bone merely was cracked; it had not been cut through by the bullet which glanced on around the side of the lad, leaving a dreadful furrow from which the blood streamed.

"He'll be ridin' buckin' hosses inside of three weeks," said Dunmore, and the girl gasped with relief.

He ran out to his horse and brought in the saddlebag which contained materials for bandaging, and with lightning skill, Beatrice and the trapper helping, he soon had cleansed the wound and strapped a hard bandage around the body of the boy.

"Skinny little sparrow, ain't he?" remarked the trapper.

At that, Jimmy opened his eyes wide and looked straight up into the face of his impromptu host.

"Hullo," said Jimmy, "whose grandpa are you, mister?"

The trapper grinned. "You're gunna pull through, son," said he. "You been about as bad scared as you been hurt, I reckon."

The face of Jimmy puckered with anger.

"Chief," said he, "did I show the white feather?"

"Never a touch of it, Jim," said Dunmore.

"Go on, chief!" urged the boy. "You've gotta hurry! How much time you've wasted here on me might——"

"We have to ride on," said Dunmore. "If you'll take care of him for us, partner, I'll pay you."

The trapper raised his hand in protest.

"If I was a doctor or a hotel or some such," said he, "I'd sure be glad to get your money, but the way it is, I can't use it. The kid's gunna be all right with me. You run along and forget about him. I'll be glad to have him for company."

"Go on, chief, go on!" pleaded the lad.

Dunmore gripped both the hard, skinny hands in one of his and stared into Larren's eyes.

"You've been as straight as a gun barrel and as good as gold, kid," said he. "I'm comin' back for you later on. You and me belong together!"

Tears which his pain could not have brought to the eyes

of Jimmy Larren now misted his sight. He tried to speak, but there was only a twisting of his mouth. Beatrice kissed him; then she turned behind Dunmore toward the door.

He sprang out of it for the mare, but his hand did not get to her. Three rifles flashed from the brush on that side of the clearing as Dunmore appeared. One bullet nicked the hip of the mare and sent her off at a wild gallop; another slashed the cheek of Dunmore as he leaped back into the hut again.

He slammed the door, and looked savagely about him.

There was a small window at the back of the shack, but yet it was perhaps not too small for him to wedge his shoulders through and draw the girl after him.

He leaped to it and jerked up the sash. Instantly, half a dozen shots barked from the bottom of the hill and he heard the pellets of lead strike the logs with a soggy impact.

He whirled back again toward the door. Blind fighting instinct urged him to break out through that door again and charge the enemy, and he actually had taken a step toward it, scooping up his rifle as he went, when the thin, piping voice of Jimmy called out:

"Don't do it, chief! Don't do it, for Pete's sake! They got you cornered, but they ain't got you in hand, yet. Chief, take your time, will you?"

Beatrice ran to the door, shot home the bolt, and then put her shoulders against it. He, lurching forward still full of his first impulse, stopped to brush her aside. But she struck at his hand and shook her head.

"They're lying down, with beads all drawn," said she. "They can't miss you. Don't go, Carrick! Don't go!"

She was white. Her lips trembled with earnestness. And Dunmore stepped slowly back from her.

"You're right," said he. "I'll have to stay here. It's better that way, a lot!"

For though it might be that she had interfered as she would have done to keep any man from running out to death, still he felt that there was something more in the emotion with which she had spoken.

"Good for you!" called the boy. "Good for you, Beatrice. If that maverick had busted loose, they'd've turned him into beef in about two steps."

"Halloo!" called a voice on the outside. "Hey! Whitey Dodd!"

The old trapper went to the door and set it ajar a crack.

"Halloo!" he thundered back. "Is that, you Neighbor Parson, that's come here murderin' my guests in the middle of the night?"

# XL

## • THREE GO OUT •

"Guests, you old loon?" yelled Parson in answer. "It's Dunmore and Tankerton's girl!"

Whitey Dodd fairly reeled from the shock of this announcement, but he rallied instantly.

"Nobody from this here house is for sale, Parson!" he yelled. "And they can't raise the price high enough to get 'em!"

"You're cracked in the head," the other assured him.

There was a nest of rocks halfway between the house and the beginning of the woods, and from this vantage point the speaker called on behalf of the besiegers.

"I'd rather to be a cracked bell than a sold one," retorted Dodd hotly. "If you-all start for this house, I'm gunna be ready for you and I tell you that I don't miss my shots!"

"The old rattlehead," commented a voice from the rocks, perfectly audible in the breathless stillness of the night, "is gunna get romantic and bighearted. And he'll hold us up till the Tankertons get here and grab most of the reward for themselves. And here we are, ten of us, that had oughta be able to divide the profit among us! Whitey's beatin' us out of more'n a thousand dollars apiece!"

"I'd like to have his scalp!" said a companion. "Look sharp, old son. That Dunmore might bust loose any minute!"

"I'm watching, all right. I got that reward right inside

the hook of my trigger finger, in case he tries to bust out in this direction! Is that hosses?"

It was the wind, rattling with a sudden violence in the leaves of the trees, and then making the big boughs groan dismally. A film of cloud was instantly tarnishing the moonlight, and Dunmore, watching from the door which was still ajar, could thank his fortune that was sending a light less brilliant.

Even so, he could not see a possible solution of his problem. The house was solidly surrounded, and even the horses were gone. So that it must be a case of breaking out on foot, in which event there was hardly a chance in a million that they would be able to get clear. Besides, the Tankertons would soon be here!

Even as he thought of it, he heard a noise louder than the rattling of the leaves in the wind, and in a moment it had grown into the distinct beating of hoofs. They poured up to the verge of the clearing. Voices called; there was a triumphant Indian yell from many throats, the wild sound shrilling and thrilling the blood. And then all doubt ended, and all hope with it. The Tankertons were here!

"They've come," said Dunmore over his shoulder, without looking back.

"Let 'em stay till they rot!" said the trapper savagely. "They'll get no man out of my house."

"Won't they everlastin'ly lambaste us?" asked Jimmy Larren, laughing feebly. "Ain't they just gunna drill this here house from one end to the other, though?"

"These here logs will soak up lead like a blotter soaks up water," said Whitey Dodd. "Besides, will the Tankertons fire into the house as long as their woman is here?"

He turned toward Beatrice. She stood against the farthest wall of the cabin, staring steadfastly at Dunmore.

"In this here game of tag," said he, "it looks as though I've been caught. You're free to go whenever you feel like it. Just unbolt the door again for her, will you, Dodd?"

Beatrice shook her head.

"I've made my bargain. I'll stick to it," said she. "I'm not going to leave."

A loud voice called from the clearing at this moment: "Dunmore! Dunmore!"

He paused for another inquiring glance at the girl, but

she looked back at him as steadily as a soldier on parade. Then he went back to the door.

"Dunmore!" came the voice of Furneaux.

"I hear you, Furneaux."

"Dunmore, you're trapped and done for," said the boy. "But I'll give you a last chance to die like a man. Come out here and I'll stand up to you, man to man!"

Dunmore laughed. Rage and despair were in that laughter, but afterward he answered: "I know the way we would fight," said he. "You in the open, and twenty rifles among the trees. As Tucker, and Legges, and Tankerton fought, they'd fight again. One honest man don't make a square show."

"Is that final?" said Furneaux. "You won't come out?"

There was sufficient anger in Dunmore, considering his helpless position, to have made him leap at such a chance; but it seemed to him, as he leaned against the door and talked, that he could see again the dark old panel in the Furneaux house that showed his own features out of the old time dimly, like a face reflected in muddy water. But he was The Dunmore, and this was a member of his clan. That old pride of race which had sent him into the mountains to do the impossible now boiled up to him again, steadied him, and enabled him to answer almost gently:

"I won't come out against you, Furneaux."

"If you were any other man," called the boy, "I'd call you a coward and a sneak. Heaven knows what you are, Dunmore. But you've done worse than murder! You're going to die, Dunmore, and Heaven have pity on your soul. Where is she now?"

"She's with me in this cabin."

"Are you going to keep her there until the bullets have killed her?" shouted Furneaux.

"I'm going to send her out," answered Dunmore. "The rest of them go with her—Dodd and Jimmy Larren, I mean. Larren is wounded. What sort of care will he get with you?"

"I'll give you my word for that. I'll take care of the kid. Do you mean that you'll send them out freely?"

"Man," exclaimed Dunmore, "what sort of a low hound do you think I am?"

"It's finished, then," said Furneaux. "Tankerton has left

this job to me. I'll promise you one thing, and that is that there'll be no burning you out. You'll have as fair a chance as I can give you!"

"Why," said the prisoner, "that's more than any man could really ask you for. I'll send them out at once."

He turned to the other three.

"I dunno," said Whitey Dodd, "that I've ever been turned out of my house before by any gent that wanted to use it for a coffin. I claim it's big enough to hold two, and I'll stay!"

"That's your idea of it, Whitey," said Dunmore good-humoredly. "But step into my boots and you'll see the other side of it. Can I let you stay here and be butchered? Go out, Dodd, or I'll have to push you through the door myself."

Dodd was silent, but he nodded a little, looking off into the distance as though he were seeing and recognizing the truth there.

"You'll be able to carry Jimmy. He's light."

"Me?" shrilled Jimmy Larren. "Who's gunna carry me out?"

He worked himself up on one elbow. "Whacha mean, chief?"

"What good will it be to me to have you here?" asked Dunmore sternly.

"Can't I clean and load guns as good as the next one? You wouldn't turn me off, chief! What's the good of anything, if I can't make the last march with you? What's the good of belongin' to a friend, if you can't make the last stand with him, eh?"

Dunmore leaned over him.

"If the two of us are gone, Jimmy, who'll be alive to really look after her?"

Jimmy Larren opened great eyes. "You mean I'm to watch after her?"

"Aye," whispered Dunmore. "Even whether she knows it or not. I've tried to bring her down out of the mountains, Jimmy, and I've failed. You'll tackle it, one day, and win!"

Jimmy Larren looked at the ceiling with anguished eyes.

"Have I gotta leave you, chief?" said he.

"There ain't no other way, Jimmy. You can see for yourself. So long, old-timer."

They shook hands, and Dunmore, lifting him, placed him in the lean, strong arms of Whitey Dodd. One last glance Jammy cast at his hero. He tried to make a last speech, but his manhood, at that moment, deserted him. He buried his face on the shoulder of the old man and wept; fighting hard against the noise, so that it sounded only like a soft moaning.

Said Whitey Dodd in farewell:

"Possession is nine points in the law, young feller. You got your own life in your hand. Keep a-hopin', and you may learn how to keep it there! Nobody's dead till he's closed his eyes!"

He went out, bearing the boy, and Beatrice lingered an instant behind.

"Is there one big thing that you want done in the world?" she asked. "If there is, I'd try to do it for you!"

"You would? Then send Furneaux back to his own people."

"Send him back?"

"It's what I came up here to do, Beatrice. I thought that I could beat Tankerton and all his men. But I was foolish to think so!"

"Furneaux!" she gasped again. "But you taunted him, and worked up trouble with him!"

"One of the best ways of sending a man home is on a stretcher!"

"Then—I'll send him if I can. Is there anything else?"

"There's nothing else," he said, "except for yourself. Get out of Tankerton's hand, Beatrice."

"I shall! I shall!" said she. "I thought he was a lion, but after I saw——"

She checked herself, though the very heart of Dunmore yearned to hear more.

"Furneaux and myself—and nothing that is for you, Carrick?"

"Aye, one thing that's for me. Take Jimmy under your wing. He'll be worth the trouble, goodness knows, because I never seen the makings of a better man."

"I'll do it," said the girl. "Oh, Carrick, why did you make me hate you those other days? But I was blind. I should have known you were playing some deep game, unselfishly. I should have guessed from little Jimmy Larren, when he picked you out of all the band!"

"It's time to go," said he. "Furneaux and the rest will be wonderin' at you if——"

"Dunmore! Dunmore!" shouted Furneaux loudly. "Are you holding the girl back?"

He led her to the door. "She's comin' at once," he answered, and added softly to her: "There's one last thing you could do. Remember me on Sundays and on holidays, now and then; and think of me as a fellow who lived a lazy and a useless and pretty crooked life, but before the end he thanked Heaven that he tried to do one decent thing—and failed tryin' it. And he found one woman and loved her, and lost her; but died mightly glad of the findin'."

He saw that she would have spoken again. But, like Jimmy, she seemed choked.

"Good-by," said Dunmore, and helped her through the doorway, and closed the door after her.

# XLI

## • BY THE THROAT •

WHEN Dunmore was alone he looked around him and prepared to die.

From the edges of the clearing, he heard a sudden shouting and whooping, by which he knew that the girl had come to the hands of Tankertons again; the next moment, it seemed that a hundred rifles blazed. He distinctly heard the thudding of the bullets into the wood, and then a clank and a crashing from the pans that hung on the wall behind the stove.

That answered what Dodd had said of the impregnable walls of his house! In certain spots, at least, the lead would fly through like water through a sieve.

He tried the flooring. The boards were loose and came

away easily in his hand. He ripped up three of them. From a corner he took a shovel and started scooping up the earth beneath the flooring.

*Clang!* rang a bullet that glanced from the iron blade of the shovel. And another clipped close past his head.

But every swing of his arms drove the shovel deep into the soil and quickly he had entrenched himself.

As for the wound on his cheek, it was a trifle. Already the blood had stopped flowing. He laid himself down behind his barricade and waited.

Wasp sounds darted above his head. Again and again the pans crashed against the wall; a steady tattoo drummed upon the stove; they were searching the cabin through and through with rapid fire from repeating rifles and no doubt they would continue steadily.

No, now the firing died off. Only a single shot came now and again, as though, having vented their spleen in a first outburst, they were content to keep him disturbed with an occasional shot.

He chose that moment to slip across the floor to one of Dodd's loopholes, and when he looked out, he was glad that he had come in time.

For he saw a pair of shadows work out from the trees and slide rapidly along the ground toward the nest of rocks.

He drew up his rifle and fired. The leading shadow twisted into a knot, like a worm that has been stepped upon. The second bounded to its feet and fled. Dunmore fired low, aiming between hip and thigh, and saw the fellow topple. The speed of his running carried him along, and with a cry he rolled back into the shelter of the trees.

There was a wild burst of rifle fire, a chorus of fierce shouting that reminded him of the baying of a pack of hounds, and something stung the calf of his leg.

At the same instant the door of the cabin swung open with a loud creaking. There was only the deadly whistling of the bullets as they cut through the opening and lodged with sullen thuds against the rear wall of the house.

Then he knew what had happened. The rusty bolt had been cracked in two by the impact of bullets, and the weight of flying lead had driven the door wide open.

He was not really sorry. The door itself was too thin for

a shield, and with it open he had a wider view of what was happening outside. He could see, for instance, the wounded man rolling on the ground in agony.

At the first letdown in the fire, he raised his head above his trench and thundered: "Go get your sick man, Tankerton. I won't shoot you down!"

A bullet, as though in answer, struck the dirt before him and filled his mouth with a loose shower of soil.

He spat it out with a curse, and heard the clear, ringing voice of Tankerton calling:

"I'll take that offer, Dunmore! Two of you fellows go out and get Mike."

There was a pause. Dunmore even could hear the muttering of the distant voices, almost immediately drowned by a roar of the wind, which was rising rapidly.

Then, out from the shadows, appeared two men without guns in their hands. They skulked along uncertainly, as though they expected bullets at any moment, but Dunmore held his fire.

He saw them reach Mike, and pick up the hurt man between them; Mike groaned loudly, then was carried away, still groaning at the jolt of every step. He would remember this night, if he lived past it!

The bearers, when they were close to the trees, lurched forward in a run, like children fleeing from the dark, but still Dunmore did not fire. And, as a result, he got a rousing cheer from the Tankertons.

Yet he would not trust them as much as they had trusted him. He went instantly to the back of the cabin, as the firing recommenced, and from a loophole there he scanned that side of the battle.

The ground was empty, as well as he could see, but sight now was difficult. Rapid clouds had swept across the face of the moon and the woods were blurred masses of shadow. A moment later, the rain rattled against the thatched roof. The wind whistled it into the cabin, and the face of Dunmore was wet with water and with blood.

The firing instantly increased in volume. Across the threshold of the door and against the window, a steady succession of bullets plunged. That was to keep him from trying to break away in the dimness caused by the rainstorm.

He had other troubles within the shack, for with a sudden crashing, the stove, battered by many bullets, lurched to the floor. The room filled with smoke and steam. Scattered embers rolled everywhere, and he had to become a fire fighter.

With a blanket, he thrashed right and left, and stamped out the bigger fragments. He won, but a stifling mist had filled the room. He could hardly breathe in it, and through the mist the wasp sounds of bullets still were darting everywhere.

A knife thrust, it seemed, raked his left side—much such a wound as Jimmy had received.

Dunmore sat down with a sudden sense that he was lost indeed, that moment.

"The cabin's on fire!" he heard a voice yelling—the voice of Tankerton. "Charge him, boys!"

"Charge him yourself!" answered a bass roar. "Let the fire take care of him."

Dunmore tore off his coat. He did not wait to draw his shirt and undershirt over his head, but the tough cloth parted like paper under his mighty finger tips. He was naked to the waist, and fumbling through the confusion of the cabin, he found on the bunk the remnants of his roll of bandages.

Around his body he passed a thick, binding arm of cloth and tied it tight. He could have laughed as he performed that operation; but the strong grip of the cloth numbed the pain and left him more at ease. It would make him more fit for the final moment of his life, for he intended, when the weakness from his wounds increased upon him, to fling out of the door and rush the enemy. If he could get to them and die fighting hand to hand, that would be the vital comfort for his end.

The fierce thought of it warmed all his blood!

The darkness increased. It was one of those mountain storms during which the clouds seem to be built like the ranges over which they were floating—a league-thick belt of densest moisture! All starlight, all moonshine had disappeared. The night became blacker and blacker.

But still the rifle fire continued. They had spotted the window and the door, and such a steady flow of bullets swept at those vital points that it was impossible for any creature to pass through the stream unmaimed.

There was another possibility, however.

With the shovel, he enlarged the hole of his trench, found foundation logs, and in a few minutes, had mined beneath them. Once the hole was open, he thrust his head up into the open air, and ducked again as a rifle spat fire not ten strides away from the cover of a fallen log!

He heard the bullet hum over his head and felt sure that he was seen. But when he raised a broken section of board, it did not draw the enemy's fire.

No, the man had been blazing away blindly at the house!

Dunmore crawled back into the house to consider for a moment. He went for a last tour of the loopholes, peering anxiously into the mist on every side, until it seemed to him that something stirred to the south of the building.

Aye, three forms suddenly loomed, running hard toward him, not twenty feet away, as it seemed!

He fired point-blank. It was death, he knew, as he curled his fingers on the trigger. The middle man of the trio bounded into the air with arms and legs spread-eagled. His yell stabbed the brain of Dunmore like a blinding flash of light. That cry was cut off in the middle, and the body dropped heavily to the earth, while the two companions, shouting with terror, turned and bolted.

In half a second, the gray penciling of the rain had entirely covered them from view!

He went back to the trench and lay curled there, while the outburst of revengeful fire he had expected beat upon the shack; but in the meantime, his hands were not idle.

He was lashing a revolver to a piece of wood. To the trigger of the gun, he attached one end of a big ball of string. This ball he next passed through the mouth of a large loophole and let it fall on the outside. The gun itself he then fixed with the muzzle protruding from the loophole, securing it safely there by means of the board which already had been tied to the handles.

After that, he was ready for his great experiment.

He returned to his mine beneath the wall of the house and crawled out, secured the fallen ball of string, and began to wriggle forward toward the log near by.

He had hardly started when the rifleman fired again. Dunmore lay flat, then tugged the string. Behind him, the revolver banged. His plan had worked almost too well, for the bullet actually skimmed the hair of his head!

He went on. He pressed himself into the mud and worked as a snake would work, but holding now in his right hand a heavy Colt. Not for firing. It must serve him as a club, now!

Then, when he was hardly a half-arm's distance from the log, the pale gleam of the rifle and the dark outline of the sharpshooter's head appeared again.

Were there two men behind the log? If so, his plan was totally spoiled, but he had to take that chance, and as the rifleman's head was raised, Dunmore struck with the butt of the revolver.

It barely reached not the head but the face of the other. He pitched back, with a cry; but the blow had so stunned him that even his cry was faint. The next instant Dunmore was across the log like a wild cat and had the fellow by the throat!

# XLII

# • OLD HOUSE ABOVE THE TREES •

THERE was murderous force in the hands of Dunmore, for his own life depended upon his ability to dispose of the man without allowing him to make a sound, but as he grappled with him, he recognized, as he thought, something in the face of the other, in spite of the dimness of the light.

He jerked the man closer till his face was a scant inch away. And it was Chelton.

Already the outlaw had forgotten all gratitude to the man who had saved him from a death by hanging! He struggled furiously, tearing at the hands of Dunmore, and

beating at his wounded face. But in a moment that throt-
tling grasp had done its work. Chelton lay still!

He was not dead; he breathed with a faint, harsh rattle
in his throat, and Dunmore poised a revolver like a club to
strike a final blow; but he could not!

At least for some moments Chelton would lie here in
the rain incapable of speech or motion, and Dunmore decided to leave him where he lay, unharmed.

The hardest portion of his work lay before him, now.

Once more he found the twine, tugged at it, and instantly the gun at the loophole spat fire behind him. He took
note of that and crawled on.

Soon the rim of the trees was not far away.

Then twice he pulled on the twine and twice the gun far
behind him barked. He actually heard the bullets cut their
way through the branches before him.

Then came an oath, and half a dozen shots in rapid succession from a rifleman who fired from the cover of a tree
just before him. Dunmore stood up and ran forward.

The muzzle of a rifle struck his breast.

"Who's that?"

"Chelton, you simpleton!" said Dunmore. "It's too
close work, out there. Tankerton can have that place behind the log for himself, if he wants it!"

The rifle was removed, and the outlaw muttered:
"Looks like that Dunmore can see in the dark. But why's
he usin' a revolver at that distance?"

"If you wanta find out, go up and ask him," growled
Dunmore, and strode away.

He saw other shadowy forms couched behind the trees,
peering through the blindness of the rain, but he himself
was behind the lines! If only Chelton did not give the
alarm at once!

But, now that he was through the greatest peril, he
paused to slick off with his hands some of the mud that
covered him; and as he paused, he thought again of the
work which he had attempted and which apparently had
failed in his hands.

By miracle, he was safe for the moment. What if he
could strike one more blow?

A light flared farther back among the trees and toward
it he went. The rays were broken, passing through the

rain; they dazzled the eyes of Dunmore as he came closer, cautiously stealing from tree to tree, but at last he saw the sleek, glistening forms of horses; then he heard voices, and finally he was in secure cover between a bush and a tree looking out upon the main council of his enemies.

The doctor and Tankerton were there. At one side was Jimmy Larren, with Beatrice Kirk and old Dodd taking care of him. Gunfire was stamping impatiently, but Excuse Me, as though she cared not for the fate of her master, plucked at the green tips of some shrubbery contentedly. Furneaux was cinching a saddle upon the back of a fine bay gelding.

"What'll you do?" the doctor was asking.

"Rush the cabin," said Furneaux curtly.

"You'll use up half a dozen men, if you do," said the doctor. "Tucker's dead already; and Dunmore apparently can see clearly enough even in this light."

"If he's in there another half hour, the fox will find some way to get out," said Furneaux curtly. "He can't escape! He's got to die. You hear, Beatrice?"

He turned on the girl, brutally. But Dunmore could see that his face was pinched and wrung with anguish.

She was on her knees at that moment beside Jimmy. At Furneaux's words, she started up and turned on the speaker. She said nothing. No words were needed to reinforce the white contempt and scorn that shone in her face; and Furneaux turned away with a twisted mouth of pain.

"I'm on the rounds again. Will you walk 'em with me, doctor?"

"Glad to," said the doctor, and the two went off together.

"You see how it is, Beatrice," said Tankerton calmly.

"I know that he's as good as dead," she answered steadily. "But I hope that he makes some of you know him still better before he dies!"

"My dear," said Tankerton, "this interest you're taking in him doesn't worry me. It's a child's romantic interest, and you'll be laughing at the memory of it yourself, inside of another month."

She did not answer.

For out from the shadow of a tree she saw a dreadful form appear. It was Dunmore, naked to the hips, except for the red-stained bandages that girded his body, plastered with mud, and with the blood slowly rolling down from the wound on his face, which had been broken open again during his struggle with Chelton.

He came from behind Tankerton, and in the full light of the fire he paused, gun in hand.

"Tankerton!" he said quietly.

The outlaw gasped, and spun like a frightened cat, stooping low, and bringing out his gun as he swung about.

No man beneath the sky could have moved faster. His side leap made the first bullet fly wide of the mark; but Dunmore's second shot roared as Tankerton's own weapon spoke for the first time.

A whiplash mark of crimson sprang out on the naked side of Dunmore; but he saw Tankerton stagger, and held his fire.

The gun dropped from the chief's hand. He made a few staggering steps forward with an oddly blank face, then sank to one knee. He coughed, and red bubbled on his lips.

Beatrice instantly was beside him. It was into her arms that he tipped sidewise and then—fell prostrate.

He lived for a single second, muttering: "Marry him, Beatrice. He has the only hand that's strong enough to hold you!"

One convulsive shudder jerked his body, and then he lay still, smiling at the rain that streaked into his face.

"Hello!" called the voice of Furneaux from the distance.

Dunmore caught Beatrice from the ground, where she kneeled, weeping like a child.

With a sway of his strong arms, he lifted her into the saddle on Gunfire.

"Hello!" called Furneaux, coming closer, "Do you hear me, Tankerton?"

"Go it, go it, chief! I knowed they'd never beat you!" said Jimmy Larren.

Dunmore was already away through the trees, with the volleying rain crashing into his face, washing the mud from his body.

They dipped into a narrow gully; and they were in the midst of it when a ringing clamor of voices broke out behind them. It seemed to Dunmore that he could hear the shouting and the cursing of Furneaux above the rest. Then they lost all the sound of the Tankertons in a fresh roaring of the wind that ripped away the clouds from before the moon and let its light through.

Dunmore glanced up at it with a wild emotion, for it seemed as though that bright moon had been covered merely to screen him in his escape and that now it shone again to illumine his way.

The horses broke into a gallop on a level stretch. Through the trees they wound. Gusts of rain still rattled out of the sky, from time to time, and cut and hammered at Dunmore. But he knew that the miles were flowing rapidly behind him. He saw the girl rocked easily in the saddle on the stallion, always half a length before him, and the confidence of victory grew great in his heart!

His blood no sooner had warmed with that sensation than a shuddering chill of weakness passed through him. It was as though all the vital power had drained out of his heart. He could understand it. He had lost enough blood to have been the death of a normal man. Even his own frame could not endure it!

But he locked his teeth, and endured.

The forest spilled away behind them. They rode out onto lower ground in the open, with a sense of rushing into the brilliant heart of the moonlit sky. Then, beneath them, he saw the rolling of the foothills, and he saw the flat country of the range beyond like a mist.

A warmth fell over his shoulders. It was a blanket, thrown into place by the girl, and now she tied it securely.

He blinked to see her more plainly, for a mist troubled him, like the breath upon a windowpane.

However, he could see that she was looking at him coldly, critically.

"Are you very bad, Carrick?" she asked.

"I'm well enough," he told her.

She said no more. They went on, knee to knee, down the trail which sloped and flowed among the hills. Sometimes he raised his head and turned it, hearkening for the sound of hoofs behind them, but never once was there an alarm of that sort.

His head began to spin; moments of utter mental lapse

came. He roused from one of them to find that his knees
had been lashed up with the saddle straps, and that the girl
was riding close beside him. His weight had slumped heavily on her shoulder.

Shame thrilled him back to life.

"Seem to be mighty sleepy," he muttered to her, and his
lips were numb.

He had to peer with effort to make out her face. The
moon was gone. There was warmth in the air, a dazzle in
the sky.

It was the sun, and they had ridden out of the night into
the full of day!

The shock of this discovery made him take a brighter
note of the things around them, and he saw with joy that
they were actually on the road to the house of Elizabeth
Furneaux. He had kept enough of his wits during that dim
night to enable him to keep to the trail!

But here the landscape began to act in a strange fashion. The level ground heaved itself into soft swells and
these waves traveled around and around the horizon with
increasing speed. He could no longer find Beatrice Kirk.
She had disappeared! But her voice came sharp and
strained with fear, out of the distance.

"Old house on right—above the trees—white———"
said Dunmore, and then he bowed his head in the darkness and gripped the pommel with both hands.

# XLIII

## • JIMMY CONSENTS •

DUNMORE dreamed that he was a bubble, floating high in
the sky, with the sun shining through him.

He roused a little from the dream, drifted slowly back
to consciousness, and realized that it was not the warmth
of the sun that he felt but the comfort of a soft bed. He
heard the voices of two people in the distance, a man and

a woman. They seemed to be walking toward him, but suddenly the voices were just beside his bed—Elizabeth Furneaux, and her nephew, Rodman!

He would have opened his eyes, but they seemed weighted down with lead. Only his brain waked; the rest of his body was heavy with slumber!

"Aunt Elizabeth," said the boy, "I don't doubt what you've told me. But what could have made him tackle such a job as that? Certainly he didn't give a rap about me; and you hardly had enough money to hire him for such a job!

"I had no money. I hired him with a shameful trick, Rod. I would have loathed myself, if the thing hadn't worked out so well."

"A trick?"

"You know the old panel in the library?"

"Yes, of course. The old effigy, you mean?"

"Well, Rod, I planned this thing with a good deal of care. I want you to take a look at the face of that effigy, and you'll find that it looks like——"

"A donkey with a dead smile on its lips?" said the boy.

"Not a whit! The fact is that I painted out the face of the effigy and painted in a pretty fair likeness of Carrick Dunmore. Than I made up a little story for him, about that wild ancestor of ours, the one who went to Scotland from France in the days of Bruce. I simply switched the names around and put in ones that fitted the new case. Before I got through, Carrick here, was reasonably sure that he was the head of the family!"

"Great Scott!" said Rodman Furneaux. "What——"

"What will he do when he wakes up and finds out about the sham? I don't know. Perhaps we can keep him from learning, ever! I'll tell you what, Rodman, he wouldn't be a bad head for this family, I should say!"

There was a little pause, and then the youth replied: 'He's more man than I ever saw packed into one skin before. But he'll be furious when he learns how he's been tricked."

"Well, he has his reward, you know," said Elizabeth Furneaux. "Do you really feel as sick as you look, when I say that?"

"A little sick. But I'm learning to give up, pretty fast. Of course, she couldn't think much of me with such a man as that inside the horizon. How is she now?"

"She's sleeping. Worn out, poor child. What a beautiful girl, Rodman!"

"Don't rub it in," he grumbled.

"You'll forget her in a month," said his aunt.

"Aye," said he. "A month of hard work ought to rub out something. I'm going to pitch in."

"I think you will, Rodman!"

"I swear I will," said he. "Aunt Elizabeth, you can't imagine what shame I feel when I look at that fellow there on the bed and think what he's been through for you, and all for nothing except your benefit and mine. I feel as though I'm only a half-man!"

"Do you think that it's a permanent change, Rod? Won't the lure of the old, free life come back over you?"

"How could it? The Tankertons are split to pieces. Legges tried to hold them. They killed him an hour after the old rascal tried to handle the reins. The rest of 'em are scattering fast and the sheriff has gone up there. For the first time he's got inside the stamping grounds of the Tankertons, and they'll soon be pacified, I can tell you! We'll have Jimmy Larren down here in a few hours, and he'll be able to give us the latest news."

The voices passed slowly from the room, and Dunmore lay still and digested the news which he had heard.

At last, he laughed and opened his eyes.

He was lying on his side, and his glance passed straight through the window and far off to the mountains. He saw their white caps, their dark robes of trees, and above all the piled blue of the valleys and the canyons which checked them. There was his kingdom of the horizon, his blue kingdom which he had inherited, as he had thought, from Carrick Dunmore of the other century!

He smiled a little bitterly.

All this had been rubbed away to nothing. He had ridden up into that kingdom to follow a lie, as it were, and now nothing remained!

A sound of trotting horses on the road ended in the screech of a brake against iron tires.

Then, up the front path, he heard a familiar voice saying: "Aw, I can walk, all right! I don't have to be carried.

Hullo, Furneaux! Hullo, ma'am. Aw, I'm feelin' fine. Only —I'd like to know how's the chief?"

The voice of Jimmy rose sharp and high.

"How's Dunmore? Why—why don't somebody say?"

A reassuring murmur answered this demand; they passed indoors.

Other voices spoke distantly in the house.

Then, "Hey, Beatrice! I am mighty glad! How's the chief? Kin I see him?"

"Hush, hush!" said the girl. "Walk softly, Jimmy. He's sleeping sound. He's been delirious for days. You'll hardly know him. But now he's better. He's sleeping. Walk softly, Jimmy. I don't want to waken him!"

Dunmore closed his eyes.

He felt them come closer, and a sense of guilty joy rose in his heart. Yet there was also an odd weakness in him, so that he felt as though he hardly could endure looking upon them, face to face.

They stood beside his bed.

"Oh, my stars!" he heard Jimmy gasp, presently.

"He looks thin—and wild, Jimmy. But he's much, much better. He's going to get well. Do you hear, dear? He's going to get well!"

"Why," said Jimmy, with a choking gasp, "I kind of thought—he looked like—like he was dead, Beatrice!"

"Look at the pulse in his temple, Jimmy."

"Yeah! I see it now. Well, it wasn't much fun to stand here and see!"

"Oh, Jim, the hours that I've been through, hoping and praying! And Miss Furneaux and Rod. We've all worked! And now we've won!"

"Aye," said Jimmy Larren, "you look like you'd been workin' for about the first time in your life! Is he gunna marry you, Beatrice?"

"I really don't know, Jimmy," said the girl.

"Do you hope he will?" asked Jimmy roughly.

"What d'you think, Jim?"

"Why, I think you ain't a fool," said the boy.

"I hope I'm not," said the girl, and she laughed a little, in the softest of voices.

"You might try to put in a word for me, Jimmy," she added.

"Me?" said the boy. "Why, sure I will, Beatrice. I'll get the talk around to you, some way. Now you go along and have a rest. You look sort of tuckered out."

"Who'll take care of Carrick?"

"Why, who but me?" said the boy.

"Are you all right, yourself, Jimmy, dear?"

"Me? Why, sure I am. I'm gunna set here and rest, and take it easy, Beatrice. You go along."

"Very well, then. Good-by for a little while, Jimmy."

Her footfall whispered from the room. The door suddenly closed with a light click.

There was utter silence; then Dunmore felt that a face and breathing were close to him.

"You faker!" said the sudden voice of Jimmy.

Dunmore breathed deeply.

"You faker!" said Jimmy more loudly. "Open your eyes. You've been listenin' the whole time!"

Dunmore looked up.

He saw Jimmy, looking pale and thin, close beside him, scowling. The scowl disappeared in a vast grin.

"It's sure good to see you ag'in, chief," said he.

"It's good to have you here, kid. How's things?"

"Pretty good. The Tanks are busted to bits. You took the heart out of 'em, and then they fell to pieces."

"I'm not sorry, Jim."

"Naw, what should you be sorry about, chief?"

They paused and regarded each other thoughtfully, fondly, as brothers long tested might do.

"You figgered where you and me head for, from here?" asked Jimmy at last.

"No, I ain't. But, Jim——"

"Well?"

"Suppose there was three in the party, Jim? What would you think?"

"Her? Aw, I don't mind. I've got used to her!" said Jimmy Larren.